ERRATIC MAGIC

THE HIDDEN PROPHECY TRILOGY BOOK 2

LILY SKYY

Erratic Magic
Copyright © 2022 by Lily Skyy
www.LilySkyy.com

First Edition: March 2022

ISBN 978-1-956525-18-2 (ebook)
ISBN 978-1-956525-71-7 (paperback)

Published by Books to Hook Publishing, LLC.
www.BooksToHook.com

CONTENTS

CHAPTER 1

THROUGH THE RUINS

The smoke burned Kinza's eyes as she picked her way through the rubble. She kept the back of Zaid's shirt in her line of sight as best she could, but he was moving quickly, almost jogging through the alleys.

They had run through a short field of tall grass before reaching the edge of the slums that hugged the outskirts of this side of the city. As they got closer, Kinza could hear screams coming from inside the city walls and someone was crying to her left but she could not see them through the smoke. A few fires burned the remains of the houses nearby; barely more than huts this far out. Zaid looked around frantically as if trying to orient himself. After passing a few of the destroyed huts he seemed to know where he was as he took a sharp left and started moving faster. He was soon outside of Kinza's vision.

"Zaid, wait!" she called, coughing. She moved away from a still-burning shed—or maybe it had been someone's home—and came out into slightly clearer air. Right then a hand shot out and grabbed her wrist. Kinza yelped when Zaid started tugging her along.

"It's not far," he said.

"What's not far?" she asked. A shout was heard a few alleys over, startling them both. It sounded like a fight had broken out, but between who? What had happened to the city? Kinza could see the tops of long limestone buildings on the other side of the city wall, but could not make out how much damage was done. She assumed only marginally better than the slums they scurried through.

Something tickled the back of Kinza's mind. It was almost like she heard whispers, or maybe prayers, from several people. It was too faint to make out but she peered around her, looking for the people who were speaking. Nothing moved, though, and the whispers faded.

Zaid's attention was quickly focused again on the direction they were headed, ignoring the shouts. It only just now hit Kinza that this was his home and any of these people could be his family or friends. She had been so shocked to finally see the vast city stretch out before her after the wild events of the last few days.

Rhapta is real! she thought to herself. Between everything she had seen from Zaid, the assassins, and even herself, she shouldn't have been surprised. But physically seeing an entire city that the rest of the world didn't know about and could not get to....it was surreal.

And it had been destroyed.

"Who would have done this?" she asked aloud. "Who *could* have done this?"

"I don't know, maybe..." said Zaid, looking around the corner and dragging her along, "I just don't know."

They were getting closer to the city wall, the ramshackle homes slightly larger here, but still built with nothing more than plywood and grass. A portion of the wall had collapsed and Kinza could see a leg sticking out at an odd angle; it wasn't moving.

Bile rose in her throat and she took deep breaths trying to keep it down, but that just forced more smoke into her lungs. She coughed, loud enough that Zaid turned around in alarm; whether to snap at her for being loud or to see if she was okay, she didn't know. The more she looked, the more she saw bodies lying motionless on the ground. Horror panged through her but she could not look away. Despite the shouts they had heard and the occasional person crying, it was eerily quiet. Something felt off even within the destruction they walked through.

Her sandals were not the best footwear at the moment and she kept tripping over stone and debris, little cuts appearing and healing on her feet. The pain was a distant thought compared to the carnage. She still could not look away from the bodies, some were tiny; little hands covered in blood and ash. She swore she could hear whispers coming from somewhere nearby.

Kinza felt the bile start to rise again and was about to ask Zaid to stop, but he said, "There!" He let go of her hand and hurried to a building up ahead. It was slightly larger than the rest, maybe the size of a small gas station, with half of the roof collapsed inward. Zaid kept his head on a swivel, peering around them before trying to open the door. It was stuck. He rammed his shoulder into the side and it burst open with a loud bang. They both looked around, but no movement came from within the smoke.

Ignoring the whispers, Kinza followed him inside.

At first, she could not make out anything in the room. Only half of it was accessible, the other half covered with the fallen roof. Darkness shrouded the corners and as her eyes adjusted,

Kinza noticed bottles smashed on the floor by the far wall. All kinds of herbs lay scattered around and a few remained on the many shelves that lined two of the remaining walls. A workbench lay toppled opposite the room.

"Khalil?" Zaid whispered into the darkness.

Nothing at first, and then a small cough came from behind the table, near the far wall. Zaid leaped over and said, "Khalil!" louder this time. He threw the table aside and started frantically dragging back piles of debris near the collapsed roof. Kinza gasped when she saw what was under the pile.

A man lay on the floor, but Kinza could only see as far down as his stomach because the bottom half was crushed beneath the collapsed ceiling. Ash clung to his face and arms, making him look like a corpse. If he hadn't made a noise a moment ago Kinza would have thought he was dead. In fact, he still didn't open his eyes as Zaid started shaking his shoulder, trying to wake him.

"Khalil!" he said. "Khalil, c'mon, open your eyes. What happened?" Khalil's head rolled the other direction, but he didn't speak. Zaid groaned and looked up at the fallen ceiling. Like the rest of the building, it looked slightly larger than the thatched roofs of the other huts. This one at least was made of wood and a bit of stone that was unfortunately on top of the man. Zaid tried lifting the edge, but she could see he was straining and barely made it an inch. As he released it back down, a scream tore out of Khalil's mouth at the weight. For once, Zaid looked like he was worried.

"Could you use this?" Kinza asked, pointing to a long wooden plank that had fallen on the other side of the room. "To prop up the roof just high enough? I can try to pull him out."

Zaid nodded, having run out of other options. Kinza had no idea how long ago the destruction had happened, and subsequently how long Khalil had been like this. But based on the soot-stained buildings and dwindling fires, it had been at least a day. She didn't know how long someone could live like that.

This was not the situation she imagined being in after all she had heard about Rhapta over the past few days. She thought she would be taken to a grand palace where a judge or a king would inspect her and, hopefully, deem her *not* one of the blood-crazed ubir maniacs that escaped into the cities. The assassins who had come to kill her had told her there was an ancient prophecy that an outsider would come to Rhapta one day and either save the city or destroy it. The latter had obviously come to pass but it didn't have anything to do with her, did it?

Another sick feeling churned her stomach at the mere thought of causing this kind of pain to another person, let alone a whole population. Something had to have happened recently, but who was strong enough to attack Rhapta other than the Anunnaki themselves?

Zaid wedged the plank under the edge of the ceiling. "Pull him out quickly, but be *careful*, Kinza."

"I will," she said, positioning herself by Khalil's head. Up close she could see he was handsome in a gentle sort of way. His dark hair looked soft and curly, despite the ash that coated it. And long, dark lashes rested on high cheekbones.

"Okay, on three," Zaid said. "One, two, three!" He shoved the plank down and the ceiling raised much higher this time.

Kinza grabbed Khalil under the shoulders and pulled as hard as she could. He was heavier than he looked and she was worried for a moment that she would not be able to move him, but he started to slide out. She almost dropped him when he ground out another scream from between his teeth. Kinza got him out just far enough that she could see his long legs were mangled before setting him down gingerly. It did not look good.

Zaid set the plank, and the ceiling, back down gently and hurried over to the door to listen. When he stiffened, Kinza froze in response, kneeling by Khalil. Khalil was panting now and starting to moan. Zaid waived a hand at her, eyes widening. He must have heard someone outside.

Not knowing what to do, Kinza grabbed Khalil's hand and whispered, "Hey, hi, my name is Kinza. You're Khalil, right?" She felt like a moron. "Um, well, I know you don't know me but, there might be some bad guys outside and I really don't want to die right now. Could you just be as quiet as possible for a minute? Please?"

Miraculously, Khalil's moaning stopped, but he was still breathing hard and fast. Kinza squeezed his hand gently, hoping he knew he wasn't alone. Zaid had taken out one of his obsidian daggers and crouched a little lower. Kinza's heart beat a little faster knowing Zaid heard things she could not. A moment later she heard shouts coming from far off; it sounded like a group, and they were getting closer.

Heart pounding, she slowed her breathing as much as she could, hoping whoever was out there could not hear her. It would be just her luck if they were found not because of the moaning guy with the crushed legs, but because of the mouth-breather trying to shush him. Zaid didn't even glance in her direction and that gave her hope that she wasn't as loud as she thought she was.

The shouting got closer and it sounded like a small group of men, maybe five or six of them. They were speaking in the same language that Zaid had spoken only yesterday, back in Moshi, the waypoint just outside of Mount Kilimanjaro. It sounded like they were going through buildings, and by the sound of the occasional screams, they were part of whoever had attacked the city.

They could not have been more than two huts down and Kinza was starting to panic, blood rushing in her ears. Zaid stayed tensed and Khalil stayed semi-unconscious. The men were so close now she could hear their laughter, it sounded like they were mocking someone they had found. She jumped when she heard a heavy thud just outside the door. She tried to bury the thought somebody having been murdered mere feet from her.

Kinza hadn't realized until now, but the familiar prickling feeling at the back of her neck was at an all-time high, sending a tingling sensation down through her limbs and molten heat pooled in her abdomen, just behind her tattoo.

Oh no... she thought. Three times before, her tattoo had erupted into a blinding white light of telekinetic force, each time more explosive than the last. While she appreciated her body trying to defend her from her near death experiences, the explosion would most likely cause more harm than good at this point. It was a wonder that Zaid hadn't been obliterated in the two times he got caught in it.

She focused instead on Khalil and holding his hand, letting Zaid worry about the group that was now coming up to the door. The heat in her abdomen settled, marginally. The voices were right outside and brought her attention immediately back to them. Zaid raised his dagger a little higher, preparing to strike.

A loud yelp came from further up the street followed immediately by someone sobbing. Kinza could not take it anymore and moved to get up, but Zaid threw a hand in her direction, motioning for her to stay where she was. The voices were moving away toward the direction of the sobbing. Tears rolled down Kinza's cheeks as they listened to what could only be a woman being beaten.

Eventually the sobbing stopped and Kinza could not contain her own tears.

Shh, Kinza. It'll be okay, it's nothing, Zaid said inside her head, almost startling her. They both knew it was a lie, but the voices retreated further down the street. She had forgotten about this new mental connection they had developed just the day before. Zaid said that all Anunnaki could speak telepathically, at least those who didn't live on the outskirts of the city. Anunnaki who spent too much time outside the city walls started to lose their telepathic abilities. She, of course, was an anomaly.

They waited, frozen, Kinza's tears and Khalil's quick breaths the only movement in the room for several minutes. Eventually Zaid relaxed and she released a breath she didn't realize she had been holding.

Zaid stalked across the room and knelt at Khalil's side. He heard Kinza's galloping heartbeat start to slow, but Khalil's heartbeat was slowing faster and for a much more worrisome reason.

"Khalil, can you hear me?" he asked his friend. They had met when they were children, Khalil was just a few years older than Zaid and had been his best friend for most of his life. He had been born to a poor family out here on the outskirts, earning him disdain from many people in a way not unlike Zaid had.

This area of the city was still inside the psionic barrier that surrounded Rhapta, but outside the walls. In truth, the walls had never been built to protect from invaders since no one knew the city was even here. It was built to separate the wealthy and the powerful from the poor and disgraceful. Poor families, and those with no or useless abilities were slowly forced out. The Elders claimed that they tried to help everyone equally, but the better resources were always given to those inside the walls.

Along with losing their telepathic abilities, people in the outskirts had other diminished or stunted abilities. All Anunnaki healed insanely fast, but those out here healed slower and sometimes even sicknesses spread; it was almost like living in the slums of a human city. Very few Rhaptan healers deigned to come out here and heal those who truly needed it, but Khalil was different.

Khalil's family was both poor and had almost no or menial abilities in over three generations. When he was ten, Khalil's ability came, astounding many in the city. A healer, from the outskirts? He had been offered a home near the central plaza, a luxury very few people would ever receive. But Khalil had declined, choosing to stay in the outskirts and help those who actually needed his ability. A relatively quiet man, you could still see the disdain on his face anytime a messenger came asking him to come to the warriors' quarter and heal a pupil who was too impatient to wait for his injuries to heal. All the while, he was curing diseases and viruses that spread like wildfire through the ramshackle huts out here.

When Zaid had been tapped to become a *venari,* one of the bounty hunters that hunted the ubir and brought them back to Rhapta, Khalil continued to be his friend when the rest of the city shunned him. *Venari* seldom had many friends, but Khalil never treated Zaid any differently after he found out. A friend that loyal didn't deserve to die like *this.*

Khalil's breathing was starting to slow, in time with the

slowing heartbeat Zaid could hear in his chest. He had to do something, but Khalil was the healer, not him. He reached out with his own Aura, searching for Khalil's.

Tell me what to do! he shouted to Khalil. But he could not find the man's Aura. This was bad.

Kinza, who was silently crying next to him, suddenly gasped.

"What?" Zaid asked. Kinza was staring at Khalil, eyebrows knitted together.

"I think," she said, "I think he's in my head or something. Is that an Anunnaki thing?"

"You mean like telepathy?"

"Well, yes, no, kind of. He's not speaking, but it almost feels like a...tugging?"

"I just looked for his Aura and could not find it. Without the Aura there is no telepathy, and regardless, Khalil has lived at the edges of the city for a long time now. His telepathic ability is mostly gone anyway. There is no way you would be connected to him."

That was more words than Zaid had spoken in a long time and he realized how hoarse his voice was from breathing in the smoke. It reminded him that the city was still burning and those men were still out there. He did not know what had happened. Was it the ubir? Or one of the rebel groups? There were a few that lived on the fringes and operated in the city's shadows, but he had just been here less than a week ago. His mother, was she....dead? He shoved the swirling thoughts down into the dark place he had created in his mind to hold these types of things. What remained was cold clarity as he looked back at Kinza.

"Tell me what he's saying."

"I think I'm supposed to..." she trailed off, looking over Khalil's body in confusion. Her head snapped up and looked around the room for something. In a moment she was across the room digging through the bottles that were shattered around the floor, the glass making little cuts at her feet and ankles and healing almost immediately. She didn't even wince as she was so focused on digging through the vials.

"Ah, yes," she said, holding up a small sprig with tiny leaves running along its edge. It was covered in more of the ash that coated the room and she wiped it on her shirt.

"What is that?" he asked. Medicinal herbs were not his specialty and he hadn't realized Kinza knew anything about them either.

"I have no idea," she said, easing open Khalil's mouth and placing it inside. *Ah.*

"Now what? Are you sure it's him talking to you? I can't find his Aura at all and I never showed you how to look for one. Do you see a dark green light anywhere? That's what his looks like."

"Shush for a second, I can't concentrate on both of you," she snapped. Her eyes remained focused on Khalil, the tears having stopped. She hesitated and placed one hand on his forehead and the other on his left bicep, where one would find his tribal tattoo under his sleeve. After a slow exhale she closed her eyes.

At first nothing happened for several seconds and Zaid was losing his patience. Khalil was dying and there wasn't a lot of time left. On a good day he would have had a hard time speaking telepathically with his friend, but now? How was Kinza able to connect with him? Nothing made sense today.

Kinza gasped again, softly this time, and a faint, dark green light started pulsing under her hands. At first it was slow and sluggish, then erratic and frantic, and finally evened out; steady as a heartbeat. Zaid listened for Khalil's heartbeat and realized his heart was actually beating in time with his Aura.

It wasn't common for Anunnaki to need extensive healing such as this, so he had only seen this kind of work once or twice in his life. It was usually done to speed up their natural healing ability for more fatal wounds. Despite healing quickly, Anunnaki were not indestructible. If the wound did damage faster than the healing could keep up, they would die. As he watched Kinza, it looked almost like she was drawing Khalil's own Aura to the surface, coaxing it to heal faster.

Zaid sat still as a statue for several minutes before Khalil's legs started shifting. The bones *popped* back into place and the man moaned in pain, still with his eyes shut. The cuts on his legs, from what Zaid could see between the tears in his pants, started healing much faster as well. Khalil groaned much louder this time and his eyes opened.

"I am fine, I am fine," he mumbled, spitting out the leaves.

Kinza's eyes popped back open as well and stared at him incredulously. "Oh, so that actually worked?" she asked. Zaid wanted to roll his eyes.

"Yes," Khalil said, struggling to sit up. "I should hope my own methods would have some measure of effectiveness."

"Khalil," Zaid said, relieved his friend was okay, "what *happened?*" He shoved some broken bits of stone and bottles aside so Khalil could lean back against the wall behind him. His normally neat hair was in a wild disarray and he looked more haggard than ever, but he was whole. It gave Zaid the tiniest bit of peace and he would take whatever he could get.

Khalil coughed and said, "Are they still outside?" He eyed the door across the room.

"No, there was a group that crossed by a few minutes ago, but they kept moving. Khalil, I need to know if my mother is even alive. *What happened?*" Zaid asked.

"The Unfettered, I'm pretty sure at least. Two nights ago, I was here working when I heard screaming coming from outside. I have no idea how it happened but I went out and the city was on fire, Zaid. Rhapta was on fire." He coughed again. "Within minutes fighting broke out, people were scared and running, and these men started going through the streets attacking people. I recognized a few as being part of the Unfettered. I had a boy in here I was healing, Tashiq, I hurried him home to his parents and ran back. I was almost caught by one of the groups but they got distracted. They were going through the outskirts and setting fire, home by home. I came back inside and shut the door, but another group came through and sealed the door somehow and set fire to my roof. I was in here when it collapsed and have been basically in and out of consciousness since."

He took a deep breath.

"I'm pretty sure the only reason I'm alive is because it rained yesterday, putting out most of the fires. That, and due to the fact that both of you arrived." He turned to Kinza who was still staring at him, clearly befuddled at what she had done to help him. "It seems I have you to thank," he said to her with a tired smile.

"Um, hi, I'm Kinza," she said.

"I know, I heard you," Khalil replied.

"Oh, ah, right." She cleared her throat.

Zaid sighed. "It's a long story, but yes, this is Kinza, she was my target but apparently she's Anunnaki...and most likely the origin of the prophecy. You know which one I'm talking about." That was a whole other mess that needed to be dealt with.

Kinza's head snapped up to him. *It's fine,* he said in her mind. *I trust no one more than him.* She relaxed slightly at that.

Khalil grunted and sat up a little higher. "Fascinating." Zaid truly hadn't expected much more from him, little could shock him. One of the many reasons they got along so well.

"How exactly did you manage to connect with her though? I could not find your Aura at all and we haven't spoken telepathically in years." Zaid kept one ear toward the door, listening for both voices and heartbeats nearby. He could detect a few in the distance, they might have been moving closer.

"I'll explain later, right now we need to get somewhere safe. I suspect the Unfettered are still looking for survivors and I don't want to be here when they get back." He struggled to his feet, Kinza immediately helping him.

"The Grand Hall?" Zaid asked. "I'm not sure what is considered safe if the whole city was sacked." Zaid looked toward the door, there were definitely voices coming closer, and not those of frightened people.

Kahlil looked toward the door as well, hearing the voices, too. "I don't know but I think we need to just go. I'm sure you could take a few on your way down, Zaid, but I really don't want to attempt it. I think we should go deeper into the city. Maybe some of the abandoned sectors are still standing."

The voices were right down the street now.

"I second this motion," Kinza said, "I don't want to die here. No offence," she said the last part to Khalil.

He sighed, "None taken."

CHAPTER 2
THE ART OF MANIPULATION

Tahir strode through the camp, a perfect image of a capable leader. The other Elders that had come with them were back in the main tent in the center of camp, squabbling over what they should do next. They didn't know yet, but Tahir would help them make a decision.

The camp sat in the plains north of Mount Kilimanjaro, behind a psionic barrier he had created himself. He was quite proud of it really. It had taken years of research inspecting the stones that were mined in the quarries. They were in his jurisdiction naturally. But he had made sure of that when he took the position of Elder.

It was already a general belief that the source of the Anunnaki's power and that of the psionic barrier was due to Aurastone. Previous attempts of moving bits of stone out of the city caused it to crack and become Deathstone. So no one had ever thought moving massive slabs of stone out instead would prove any different. The idea was his own, noting that the larger quantities of Aurastone in one area, the stronger the barrier that surrounded Rhapta.

A few years ago, he started having slabs of stone moved out here secretly, just in case. One never knew if they needed to flee the city. And he had never planned on bringing over half the city with him either. People clustered together in groups now, many of them reaching out to him as he passed by. Everything was going exactly as it was supposed to.

By now, Zaid and the girl, Kinza Solace, would have arrived. It was unfortunate that his assassins had failed. He had figured as much when they didn't check in at the designated time. Was it Zaid who killed them, or Kinza? He hoped it was the latter. In fact it was more likely. He probably knew more about her own abilities than she did.

He smiled at that. Tahir loved knowing things others did not.

That knowledge could be used against her of course. If the people knew how destructive and unpredictable her abilities were, they would be more likely to distrust her. It would all work out.

Tahir made his way aimlessly through the people. Despite the sorrowful occasion, the sun was shining down on the plain making everything bright and warm. He wanted the people to see him standing strong and tall; unafraid. It seemed to be working as Rhaptans came up to him, some wanting to touch his hand or bow their heads in respect. He was their savior after all. He was the one who got them out of the city as it was ransacked.

Elder Tahir, a younger man said, approaching him. *Please, do you know anything about what happened? Who attacked us?* The man had honest, trusting eyes. He believed Tahir would have the answers.

Tahir adopted a sorrowful expression, placing his hand on the man's arm. *What is your name, son?*

Barwani, the man replied. People had stopped to listen,

hoping to get a shred of news. Anything that would reassure them their loved ones were safe and that those behind the attack were held responsible.

Barwani, I am sure you are as confused and angered as I am. The great city of Rhapta has been attacked, and for the first time in history, its inhabitants forced out. Tahir made sure he was just loud enough that others could hear, but quiet enough that they needed to draw closer. *I am on my way to see Grand Elder Hakim and I hope to learn more through him and his visions. Did anyone see the attackers as we left the city? Any information that would help us?* He addressed the crowd at the last part.

A short woman stepped forward. *I saw several of them with black bands tied around their arms.* Several others nodded in unison.

A boy spoke up, *They set everything on fire!* Others nodded along with the boy's anger.

Tahir nodded, acknowledging what they had learned on their own. *That is in line with the vision Hakim had before the attack. As many of you know, the only reason I had time to warn you, to get you and your loved ones out was because of Grand Elder Hakim. His vision of destruction, mere minutes before the attack, is what saved us. We must trust in him now!*

A larger crowd had started to gather. People nodded along and shouted in agreement.

Hakim's vision was of a group of dissenters already known within the city for being chaotic and destructive. He too saw the black armbands and fire in our homes. I believe it is the Unfettered who are behind the attack.

The people roared in anger, crying for justice and retribution.

Quieter, Tahir said, *But someone must be leading them. The Unfettered have never had a unified agenda in the past and I find it *hard to believe that they do now. Someone had to unite them in this common cause of pandemonium and fear.*

He paused for effect.

Who could have done it? someone asked. Others piped in with suggestions and whispers started through the increasing crowd.

Was it the Apostles of Truth?

Could humans have found us?

An ubir?

People talked amongst themselves until someone spoke a little louder. *Elder Tahir, could this be related to the prophecy? The old one?* The whispers died out as people shot furtive glances between each other before looking to Tahir. He allowed that thought to plant a seed in their minds, and he would water it.

As I said, Hakim's visions are never wrong. I go to him now to inquire whether he has been given another and we will know who has done this to our home. I don't want to believe it, but if it's the outsider from the prophecy, then we have our enemy.

People erupted into cries of rage and demand for atonement as Tahir walked away. The whispers would spread throughout that camp that it was a very real possibility that the outsider had attacked them. He had given them an outlet for their anger and he would let it fester.

As Tahir slowly made his way to Hakim's tent, a figure diverged from the crowds and fell into step with him.

Do you truly believe that? the young man asked.

Yes, Mikah, I do think it's at least a possibility. Tahir looked at his apprentice, a charming young man who paid close attention to Tahir's words, as was his job. Mikah had been his apprentice for many years now, Tahir knew the boy's family paid a great deal of money, and allegiance, to get him that position. It was distasteful in Tahir's opinion, but he had proved to be attentive, if not open-minded. He could not be faulted for that, and maybe with time, Tahir could mold him into having a bit of initiative.

Do the other Elders know this? If we have an enemy on our doorstep, the council will need to act fast, Mikah said. He walked straight-backed with a relaxed smile across his face. It was something Tahir had taught him; you never want the public to know what you are thinking, especially when you are nervous.

Patience, Mikah, Tahir said. *I do not want to bring this to the Elders if it is not concrete knowledge yet. As you know, some of them are flighty and make quick decisions. We must first find the truth from Elder Hakim.*

Is there anything you would like me to do? Mikah asked.

Yes, seek out Commander Kartik. I will need a detailed report of how many warriors we have in our number. There is a chance we may enter into battle soon. Tahir knew very well how many warriors there were, but Mikah didn't know that.

Isn't Elder Yuvaan representative of the warriors? Mikah asked.

Yes, but Yuvaan is occupied at the moment and I would not disturb him. Go, I'll receive your report in a few hours.

Mikah gave a short nod and went to find Commander Kartik. Tahir needed to be careful, the boy asked questions where others tended not to. Regardless, he was obedient.

Tahir arrived at the second largest tent in the camp, not far from the center. The warriors at the entrance nodded to him as they pushed the flaps aside. The room was stifling and Tahir could see it was due to the low brazier that sat to one side of the tent, sending perfumed smoke throughout the room. Hakim was cold these days, his body was slowing down, conserving his energy for the visions. The elderly man now lay on a small bed at the back of the room, surrounded by blankets and furs, his attendants close by.

Two others were within the room. Hakim's apprentice, a

quiet young woman whose name Tahir usually forgot. She sat cross-legged on the ground with her eyes closed. At one point, Tahir had hoped to use her visions as well, but they proved to be lackluster and devoid of the magnitude that was Hakim's Sight. The other was Elder Ekbal, Hakim's own nephew and representative of agriculture in Rhapta. Ekbal had, unfortunately, never taken to Tahir's charm and frequently questioned his motives.

Just now, Ekbal's small eyes narrowed even further as Tahir swept in. *Tahir, what are you doing here?* Ekbal asked.

To check on Hakim of course. I know the journey here was not long, but for one so frail...I wanted to make sure he was well, Tahir replied.

He is. But I know you have ulterior motives, Tahir. My uncle's mind may be failing, but mine is not.

Tahir adopted an expression of guilt. *You are right, Ekbal. I have just spoken with the people and they clamor for answers. They want to know who leads the Unfettered. Hakim's visions,* Tahir said, gesturing to the man within the mound of furs, *could provide that.*

He is rarely lucid anymore, Ekbal said looking to his uncle forlornly. *What makes you think you will coax a vision from him?*

Hakim and I have known each other longer than you have been alive. You cannot deny that my encouragement of him has brought out more visions. Did he not just have one a few days ago that saved all of our lives? And was I not by his side when we received it? I believe it is memories of the past that help Hakim see forward.

The look Ekbal gave him was that he wasn't buying it.

Please, Tahir said graciously, *let me have a few moments with him?*

Ekbal just looked at him under lowered brows and said, *Come, Eta. We will leave my uncle with Tahir.* The young woman finally opened her eyes and got up without looking at Tahir, like a dormouse avoiding eye contact with a snake. Tahir nodded to the attendants and they filed out as well.

He took a deep breath now that he was alone. Hakim was, of course, still there, but the man slumbered in his furs, occasionally whispering incomprehensible futures. Tahir walked up and knelt next to him, placing a hand over Hakim's own.

My dear friend, Hakim, he said. *The people need your visions. They need your guidance. Look for them, look and tell us who is behind the attack.*

Nothing happened and Hakim still slumbered. Tahir didn't have much patience for this. Ice crept out from his palm and ran over the elder man's hand, up his arm to wrap around his torso. It was just a thin layer of ice, the beautiful fractals looking almost like white tattoos over the leathery skin.

Hakim started to shiver, eyes cracking open to look at him. They were surprisingly clear, as if the cold had shocked him into lucidity. Tahir knew it would pass, though. He let the ice spread further and the old man started shivering violently before he whimpered.

Who was behind this Hakim? Tahir prompted.

Hakim's eyes took on a glassy look and Tahir knew he was entering a vision.

You, Hakim croaked out, eyes focusing again.

Tahir rolled his eyes and moved to leave, withdrawing the ice. There was no point in trying to force a false vision. Hakim's eyes took on the glassy look again and Tahir paused, crouching back down. This one lasted much longer, Hakim's eyes roaming back and forth frantically.

Prince Malik, Hakim gasped out. Tahir froze at the name of the last heir to Rhapta. A monarchy that died with the death of the king and the disappearance almost two hundred years ago. *Crowns of light. Glowing Aurastone,* Hakim started speaking gibberish next and Tahir could not make out the words. He let a little of the ice creep back out and the shivering started again.

Kinza Solace, Hakim whispered before his eyes came back into focus. They slid to Tahir for a single moment of defiance before his fell back into a deep slumber.

Tahir sighed, that was definitely not the guidance the people needed, Kinza would only lead them to ruin. Not more than a child who had never set foot in Rhapta, he could not allow his people to put their faith in false idols.

He stood and exited the tent. Only Ekbal and the attendants remained, Hakim's apprentice had left.

Well? Ekbal said.

Tahir lowered his eyes to the ground. *We have our answer,* he said reluctantly.

Ekbal's eyes focused in momentary disbelief and one of the attendants gasped. *Who is it then? Who led the Unfettered to attack Rhapta?* Ekbal asked. The warriors that stood outside the tent remained stoic, but Tahir knew they would be listening as well. They would go back to their bedrolls tonight and whisper to their brothers and relatives of who had attacked them; of who was responsible.

It was Kinza Solace, the outsider from the prophecy.

Tahir sipped on his wine, it was made from *guakal,* the fruit native only to Rhapta. The liquid was almost sickly sweet but coated the inside of his mouth. It was surely an acquired taste, but he was glad of the few bottles that had been brought during the escape. He would need to thank the attendant that thought to bring wine while fleeing a burning city.

His own tent was further from the center, nearer the

people and away from the Elders. He had claimed to be a man of the people, that he was no different from them, regardless of the title of Elder. Truthfully, he wanted to listen. He could hear the chatter that moved like a wave through the camp as rumor spread that Hakim had confirmed the prophecy was here, it was happening now. The outsider had come and turned their people on each other, causing mayhem and destruction.

Scuffles had broken out here and there as the day wore on. Tensions were high and people longed to go home as much as they longed for the head of their enemy. Walid, the overseer in the quarries had assured him there was enough Aurastone out here now that the psionic barrier they had created would hold, but the small size of the camp forced several thousand people together in cramped quarters. It would be enough for an escape, but they could not stay here, they needed to go back to Rhapta, and soon.

The flap in the tent was pushed aside and Mikah strode inside, giving a slight bow in greeting. Tahir found it a bit obsequious but let it slide.

Elder Tahir, I have your report, Mikah said.

Tahir had almost forgotten the useless errand he had sent the boy on. He nodded and gestured to one of the low seats next to him. Instead of sitting upright, Mikah reclined as if he had been invited into Tahir's most trusted confidants.

What do our numbers look like? Tahir prompted.

I spoke with Commander Wash and we have about two thousand warriors available, if you include the pupils. It actually looked like that majority of the warriors had escaped with us and only a few didn't make it out, Mikah said.

Good, Tahir nodded. *We may need them.*

Mikah hesitated. *Is it true then? Did Hakim have another vision?*

Yes, Tahir said, taking a small sip of his wine. *Unfortunately the prophecy is upon us and it has turned out not to be in our favor.*

Mikah didn't say anything but looked worried.

It won't matter, Tahir continued. *Our forces are still strong and we will retake the city. She does not know us. Do not forget that she has never set foot in Rhapta before now, she is in unfamiliar territory.*

Her name is Kinza, then?

Tahir nodded. *I want you to stay in touch with the people, stay visible. If a leader is not present, if they are hidden, then the people soon forget them. Find out what their fears and their needs are.*

The flap to the tent was pushed aside again and one of the guards poked his head in. *Excuse me Elder, there is a man here. Says you wanted to speak to him? Looks like a farmer to me.*

Ah, yes. Thank you, Tariq. Send him in. Tahir turned to Mikah. *That will be all for now, Mikah.*

The boy stood and gave a short bow again. *I will return with news.* On the way out he crossed paths with the farmer. He wore only a light cloth wrapped around his waist and through his legs to form something like trousers. Thick calluses coated his palms and his eyes darted around and settled on Tahir. He shifted back and forth on his feet and waited until Mikah was gone.

You made it back into the camp all right, I see, Tahir said to the man.

Yes, I came last night in the dark. Tahir knew the man could go unnoticed if he needed to. His ability was to thank for that.

What news do you have from your captains? Any sign of her in the city?

No, not yet. We haven't seen anyone with the abilities you mentioned, nor have any venari come back recently, the man said.

Tahir nodded, thinking. *And what of you and yours? Are you still doing as I asked?*

Yes, we are going door to door where we can, burning down buildings, but staying more to the outskirts. There are a lot of people still in the city though, and they holed up together in large groups. I think they might be planning on pushing back.

Don't worry, Tahir said. *She will come before that happens and all will change. What of the remaining Elders?*

Still in their castle, the man snorted, but quickly composed himself at Tahir's scathing glare. *We are mainly camped in the central plaza. Sir...*the man trailed off.

What is it? Tahir asked.

A few of my captains wanted me to ask, he licked his lips, *they want to make sure you can deliver what you promised. We want to be able to leave.*

The faintest wisp of a smile graced Tahir's features and he stood. Pulling his robes to the side he revealed his tribal tattoo that was on his lower chest. The other man's eyes widened when he saw it. Tahir didn't need to look to know his tattoo was much larger than anyone else's, even the *venari's*. It also looked clearer and more intricate, like beadwork.

Tahir pulled his robes back into place. *It's not something that we have the capacity to provide to all Anunnaki, but those who aid me will be first in line to receive it. You may tell your captains you have seen proof that it is real.*

The man nodded, looking dazed.

Return to the city tonight, help further the cause in any way you can, Tahir said. The man nodded vigorously and left.

Tahir sat back down and poured himself another cup of wine.

CHAPTER 3

SURVIVORS

Kinza looked around in wonder as she followed Zaid and Khalil through Rhapta. They had left Khalil's workshop and sneaked back through the outskirts to the collapsed portion of the city wall she had seen earlier. Zaid cautioned them to stay in the shadows as much as possible, but so far she hadn't seen a single soul. Despite the evident destruction, the inner portion of the city was, so far, quieter than the outskirts.

Even through the soot and ash, Kinza could see that Rhapta was magnificent. It wasn't anything like the glass and metal skyscrapers that she was used to seeing in downtown Chicago, with its grit and chaotic streets. The long, limestone buildings of Rhapta were regal. Wide boulevards of white stone lined with miniature baobab trees crisscrossed through strategically placed plazas. Pools of water or marble statues sat at the center of these plazas and along the main thoroughfares were the occasional lamppost. Or that is what she assumed they were. They were alabaster pillars with azure stones—about the size of watermelons—that sat on top and glowed faintly in the daylight.

"Are those Aurastones?" she asked. Zaid and his friend Haris had told her about them.

The city sat on the world's only minable deposit of a mineral called Magalkan'a, or just commonly called Aurastone. It was surmised that it was the stone that gave the city's inhabitants their otherworldly abilities and long life. Smaller deposits sat around the world, but those were deep down in the tectonic plates where no human could reach. Those usually opened up the portals like the one Kinza and Zaid had taken to get here.

"Yes, hopefully none of them are broken," Zaid said. They had told her about Reykalkan'o, or Deathstone, before as well.

When the Aurastones were taken out of the city, or defiled in some way, they turned a murky white and cracked. The resounding noise that emanated from them was enough to send an Anunnaki to their knees. Contrarily, Deathstone had no effect on humans.

"How would they break? Just throw them on the ground and *bam*, Deathstone?" she asked. They crept through a small plaza with a shallow pool of water in the middle.

It was filled with ash and blood, and the rest of the plaza looked like the surrounding homes had vomited their contents onto the street. The area they were in looked like a neighborhood of smaller buildings, almost like apartments. Homes were stacked on top of each other, only three at most, with several open air doorways, balconies, and terraces.

Stairs wound throughout the buildings and led to the uppermost floors. Here and there rope crossed over the smaller streets, connecting balconies of neighbors where bright bolts of cloth, beads, and feathers hung.

"No, you would need to..." Zaid looked around, distracted

again. She wondered if he was looking for his family. She knew he at least had a mother, but not much else about who was close to him here.

Thankfully, Khalil finished explaining. "Just smashing Aurastone would not do anything otherwise we would have a big problem over in the mines on the south side of the city. Aurastone is considered pure as it was given to us by the Creator, so when an act of defilement is done upon the stone, only then would it lose its color and crack. Usually it's something like if the blood of someone recently murdered fell upon the stone, or something like that." Kinza noticed Khalil spoke in the same accent that Zaid did, but his voice was smoother, more fluid. She didn't want to ask how he knew English so well if he never left the city. Did all the inhabitants know other languages?

"Ah, that does sound bad. Where are we going, Zaid?" They had moved on to another plaza similar to the one before. His steps were purposeful, he definitely knew where he was going.

"My mother's home, I just need to see..." he trailed off.

Kinza wanted to reach out to him, but hesitated. She could not imagine what he was going through right now. This was his *home*, and people had destroyed it and possibly those who he loved. Even though she knew the soul-cracking despair of coming home to dead parents, she never wanted anyone else to go through the same thing, even the man she had all but hated just a few days before.

Kinza was pretty sure she and Zaid were in a much better place than they had been. She supposed saving each other's lives several times over would do that, but there was so much she didn't know about him, and she realized she was curious.

Zaid rounded a corner, looking both ways, and started jogging. Khalil and Kinza followed behind, keeping both eyes and ears open. Many of the fires she had seen were small and it did look like it had rained yesterday by the occasional bolt of wet fabric on the stone. She had only seen a few bodies after walking through the inner portion of the city, but not nearly enough to be the entire population. Where was everyone?

Zaid jogged up to a narrow staircase set into one of the buildings of stacked homes. Intricate pottery, clothing, and books lay scattered on the steps. He just jumped over them and climbed the twisting staircase to the topmost home, Khalil and Kinza right behind him.

As they had walked through the neighborhoods, she could see Khalil's strides getting steadier by the moment, whatever he had told her to do had worked and he seemed almost in perfect health despite the weariness on his face. Was this another ability of hers? Or was it like a surgeon telling you the exact steps to take to perform heart surgery? More technical skill than special ability. She would ask later.

They came to a small, but cozy home at the top of the building. The front door had been ripped from its hinges and household items lay destroyed on the walkway.

Mother? Zaid's voice came. It sounded different then when he spoke in her mind directly, that was sharp and clear. This was like listening in on a conversation across the room. The sound was slightly further away, but trailed off like smoke on the wind.

Kinza followed the two men inside. There was a front room that looked like it doubled as a dining, and sitting room all at once. Silk pillows were scattered around. A short bookcase sat toppled by the back corner. Papers that looked more like soft papyrus were crumpled as well. Zaid had gone down a short hallway at the back of the room. She assumed that's where the bedrooms and bathrooms were. He came out a moment later, face as stoic as usual.

"She's not here," he said flatly.

"That's a good thing, right?" Kinza said. "That means she could have escaped and hidden somewhere."

Khalil nodded in agreement. "My own family would have gone into hiding as well, I'm just not sure where."

"Is it just me, or are there no people here?" Kinza asked. "I know you said the Anunnaki population was dwindling, but I haven't even seen ten people yet. There are not enough....bodies," she cringed as she said it.

"I noticed the same thing," Zaid said, pushing aside a curtain that hung skewed across the front window and peered outside. "It looks like the city was destroyed, but either many of the people escaped, or they are all in one area of the city. Khalil, have you heard anything over the past few days? I haven't been gone that long."

Khalil had sat down against one wall and absently leafed through a few pages on the floor next to him. "I haven't. Everything has been the same. The same rumors about both the Unfettered and the Apostles of Truth." He eyed Zaid as he said it and Kinza wondered what it meant. "But there were no warnings that I heard. That being said, I was on the outskirts so those on the inside could have been warned, but I don't really know." He wiped a hand through his soot-stained face.

"Who are these people, the Unfettered, that you keep talking about?" Kinza asked.

Zaid replied, "They are people who reject the rule of the Elders and think they, and anyone who wants to, should be able to leave the city; even if that means becoming ubir."

"Anarchists," Khalil said bitterly.

"Yeah, basically. The group has been around for hundreds of years, living in the shadows of the city, staying hidden and out of sight. They don't like being controlled."

"Well I would not entirely blame them on that account, who would want to be told they can never leave the city they were born in. I mean, I'm not one to talk, but I do have the right to leave Chicago whenever I want. I could not imagine being confined to one small area of the world forever."

Zaid looked at her through lowered brows. "Even if that means luring people in with the promise of freedom and brainwashing them into believing human sacrifice will set them free?"

"Er, well, no," she said awkwardly. She sighed. "Well, what do we do now?"

"I say we head over to the south quarter. That section of the city was the most abandoned to begin with and there are a lot of fortified buildings that people could have hidden in," Khalil said standing up.

"How far is that?" Kinza asked.

"We are in the lower east quarter now, so maybe twenty minutes if we hurry?" Khalil said.

"All right, but stay close. If there are people there then it's more likely the Unfettered are patrolling the area," Zaid said. He looked at her, "Try not to blow anything up."

Khalil's eyebrow quirked up. Kinza just curled her lip in response.

ZAID KEPT his anxiety and fear locked away. His skin crawled looking at the destroyed buildings, the baobab trees on fire, and the severe lack of people. Where was everyone? He didn't know if this was better or worse than finding people dead. He just didn't know.

They left his mother's neighborhood and made their way back out to one of the large boulevards, but kept to the edges. He hadn't felt any heartbeats the entire time they had been in the city walls. Whether that was a good sign or not was another thing he didn't know. He prayed to the Creator, something he rarely did anymore, that his mother was okay. He didn't think he could handle losing the last person he had left in his family.

He turned another corner and almost immediately went to his knees, Kinza and Khalil gasping in pain behind him. The high-pitched ringing of a Deathstone assaulted his brain, making him shove his hands over his ears hard enough to cause more pain. He gasped through his teeth and pried his burning eyes open. There, just ahead was a Deathstone that looked like it had fallen from one of the lampposts. Blood was dried on its side and he could see why. A man lay not far from it, motionless. Zaid could see the blood that had pooled around him and eventually ran a few feet down the street to the fallen stone.

Zaid groaned as his muscles started to seize, but through the pain he reached back and snagged one of his obsidian daggers. Another wave of near-debilitating pain wracked him as he stood and sprinted over to it. His vision swam and he knew that if he didn't hurry, he would be unconscious soon. He slammed the dagger down into the stone repeatedly. It took several attempts as the spams in his muscles were getting stronger but eventually he got it and the stone split and the high-pitched ringing stopped.

The three of them sagged to the ground in relief. He could hear Kinza gulping in air like she had been drowning. "Stab rock, sound stops," she gasped out. "Got it."

"Only with obsidian," Zaid choked out and got to his feet. "Let's keep moving."

"Sure, no need to rest," Kinza mumbled behind him. He didn't know how she could still be so sarcastic in a time like this. Did she ever stop joking? It must be some sort of ridiculous human coping mechanism she had acquired from living in Chicago.

Within twenty minutes they were at the edge of the south quarter. This area held more of the long, limestone buildings, but many of these were already in some state of ruin prior to the attack. In fact, nature had started to reclaim much of it. In between cracked and crumbled walls, flowering vines, ferns, and trees had started to grow in the space provided. The pools of water at the center of the plazas were no longer clear, but filled with mossy green water, flowers growing along the edge, frogs leaping into the rainwater pools as they walked by. His mother always thought this area was beautiful as it was nature taking back what belonged to it.

Several heartbeats came into his awareness not far away so he stopped listening.

"What is it?" Kinza asked behind him, loud as a chattering chimpanzee. Was she trying to get them caught? He sighed, knowing the stress was getting the better of him, but still.

"Shh," was all he said. They were definitely getting closer and were coming fast. Within moments he could hear shouts of men. The three were standing in the middle of a small boulevard, in plain sight. He motioned for the others to follow him into the nearest street. The group of men would be on them in seconds, they needed to hide.

Unfortunately he had led them into a dead end. What he had thought was a street, was actually another small plaza with walls on three sides. It looked like beneath the vines coating the edges, there had been stone seating here one facing a large fountain in the middle. The fountain itself was dried up and the statue in the middle had long ago crumbled. In its place were ferns half as tall as he was.

He turned to back up but it was too late.

Five men came into view. They were in a random assortment of worn clothing, but each had a black armband tied on their right bicep. It was the Unfettered.

Both Khalil and Kinza's heartbeats started a frantic pitter-patter. One of the men spoke in Rhaptan, "Well look what we have here, trying to make a run for it are we?" He was tall and slender. It's not surprising that they spoke aloud. Most of the Unfettered were known to reside in the outskirts and would have lost their ability to communicate telepathically.

"Just back up and we'll be on our way," Zaid said, trying to buy time. He would need to distract them so Khalil and Kinza could run away, but that plan was quickly dwindling as the five men moved in a semicircle, boxing them in.

Another man with a shaved head was eyeing Kinza and said, "I would not mind a souvenir. Mbalo, let's be quick with this one." He drew a long obsidian sword. Kinza just glared at him, but it was tainted with confusion. Zaid remembered that she wouldn't know Rhaptan.

Two of the men were circling toward Kinza and Zaid attempted to honor the man's wishes and quickly whipped his dagger at him.

He dropped like a stone.

Two of the other men roared and everything moved quickly. The tall man came at Zaid and he narrowly avoided being mauled as the man's hands morphed into the paws of a bear, with the long, razor-sharp nails nearly gouging his eye out.

Zaid was faster though, as he always was. In the time it took for the man to swing his arm again, Zaid had dodged and spun around to the man's back where another long obsidian sword was strapped. This one was old and not well-kept, gouges along the edge. Zaid didn't think twice and drew it before plunging it into the man's back.

Zaid turned to go help Kinza and Khalil but a white-hot explosion tore through the plaza, sending him to the ground.

Dammit.

When his ears stopped ringing he got to his feet. One of the men was backing away from the plaza, wide-eyed. He had long hair braided down his back. Zaid stepped in his direction and he fled, running down the street. Zaid turned back toward Kinza.

She had already crawled to her feet and was running over to Khalil. There was a small crater in the ground where she had stood, and the two remaining men lay strewed around in a circle. Like trees flattened by a bomb. Khalil was several feet away on the ground with a gash in his forehead. He blinked his eyes open.

"What about 'don't blow anything up' did you not understand?" Zaid growled at Kinza. "You could have killed him."

"He was already down," she snapped at him and helped Khalil to his feet. "Are you all right?"

"Yes, I am well. I take it that was your ability?" Khalil asked, rubbing his head. The wound was already stitching itself back together.

"Yeah," Kinza said with a chagrined smile.

"The last one ran away," Zaid said. "I don't want to be here when he comes back with reinforcements, let's go." Seeing that both Kinza and Khalil were not, in fact, dead, he left the plaza and turned right, away from the fifth man.

Kinza followed Zaid and Khalil again, not feeling the slightest bit guilty. Why should she? She had taken down two people who had hurt Zaid's friend and were now trying to kill her, or worse. It hadn't been a particularly controlled explosion, and she wasn't sure she could have controlled it even if someone else had been close, but at least she wasn't dead. She shouldn't be sorry for saving herself and Khalil.

She glared at Zaid's back as they walked through the south quarter. The scenery did help distract her from the chaos around her. The flowers and vines were beautiful as they wove through the ruins. She imagined playing in the abandoned buildings had she grown up here.

Looking ahead, Khalil talked quietly with Zaid in Rhaptan and something tickled Kinza's brain. Before, when they had been hiding from the Unfettered, she had heard the words they were saying, and she could have sworn she understood what they had meant. But the feeling had left as soon as it came. Now she strained her ears to listen to what Zaid and Khalil were saying.

Individually, she couldn't make sense of the sounds, and when she thought about them, she knew she had never heard the words before, yet...every third or fourth word just made *sense*. She couldn't explain it, but she felt that Zaid was telling Khalil about a group of something. She tried to concentrate harder on the words and all she got was 'caution.'

Kinza was staring at them so intently, she was startled when Khalil glanced back at her. He gave her a polite smile and responded to Zaid's question. The man was just slightly shorter than Zaid, but willowy instead of muscular. She liked him so far. It was ironic that she could like both of Zaid's friends, but the man himself routinely set her teeth on edge.

Zaid turned back to her, "There is a large group of people up ahead, I'm pretty sure it's a group of survivors, but be cautious just in case."

She *had* been right! How was is possible that she was

understanding Rhaptan? It was spotty, like a bad connection, but she shouldn't understand it at all.

Zaid eyed her as if to say *don't blow anything else up*. She sighed. They had been just fine that morning in the car as they drove up to Mount Kilimanjaro. But that felt like a lifetime ago already. Smoke and clouds still hung about the city and it was hard to tell what time it was, but she guessed it was sometime in the afternoon.

A long building came into view. It was more intact than some of the others. It looked like the majority of the walls were standing even though vines and trees wound around the outside. They entered the plaza opposite the building and were immediately met by several men with obsidian-tipped spears and wary expressions.

At first it looked like nothing was happening and then Kinza started to hear the whispers again and she realized what she had been hearing was the telepathic thoughts of the people. They were speaking. Zaid spoke with them telepathically in in Rhaptan and Kinza had a harder time picking up the words, gleaning only that the conversation was not one of hostility. Her brain hurt from concentrating so hard.

Zaid's expression changed to one of relief and she knew she was right again. While they were talking, Kinza noticed men had filed in behind her as well, silent as the dead. After conferring with Zaid, they motioned the three of them to follow.

They were indeed taken into the long building that Zaid had pointed out. The doorway was crumbled, but several boards and large stones were placed over the opening. One of the men slid one of the boards aside and they all filed in. A small spark of relief washed through Kinza as she saw close to a hundred people camped inside the cavernous building. The whispers grew jumbled in her head and it was hard to focus through the garbled noise. Just like when Zaid was speaking, she could only pick up on the intent of the conversation, not the words themselves.

The room was mostly shrouded in twilight as the windows sat high up toward the ceiling. People gathered around fires spaced evenly throughout the room. Women and children huddled together, some still with soot and tears stained on their faces. But at least they were alive.

As Kinza walked through the room, the barrage of words in her head were, ever so slowly, becoming clearer, to the point where she started to understand the comments were less than friendly.

One of the spearmen led them to the other end of the building. Heads turned toward the three of them and started speaking. Some of them eyed Kinza's clothes, but most of them looked at Zaid or even shied away.

Kinza leaned over to Khalil. "Why are people eyeing us like that?" Didn't they know it was rude to stare?

"Zaid is *venari*, and they are not treated well within the Anunnaki. The job is considered distasteful due to the fact they are out in the human cities and are capturing their own. Even though the ubir had gone mad, they were all someone's father, daughter, sister, cousin. And usually when they are brought back by the *venari*, the ubir is killed. People associate that with the *venari* unfortunately."

"That's stupid."

Khalil looked at her and gave a small smile. "Yes, Kinza, it is."

A slender, graceful woman broke away from one of the groups and ran over to them. She was crying out in Rhaptan, and bright and clear, the meaning of the words came into Kinza's head: *My son.* It must have been Zaid's mother. At first she hit him on the shoulder and then immediately pulled him into her arms as she patted at his face and arms, tears in her eyes. Zaid hugged her back and spoke in hushed tones. After a moment her eyes flicked over to Kinza and widened marginally before becoming more reserved.

Zaid led his mother over to where they were standing and said out loud in English, "Kinza, this is my mother Ekaja, and Mother you know—" To Kinza's surprise, Ekaja had immediately pulled her into a hug and she felt an old ache at missing her own parents.

"Ahh, nice to meet you," Kinza said. A smell similar to jasmine enveloped her and she breathed in.

"It is so nice to know you, Kinza," Ekaja said smiling as she pulled back. She turned to Khalil, "And I have not seen you for some time now, Khalil. I hope you are well."

"I am, thank you," Khalil said, embracing her. "Have you seen my parents at all?"

"I have not, but I have heard there are other groups like this across the city," she said and placed a comforting hand on his arm.

"Mother, does anyone know who actually did this? Khalil thought it was the Unfettered, but why?" Zaid asked.

"Yes, it was them, but we are still looking into why. Me and a few neighbors ran to this quarter when the fighting broke out. Come, let's talk with Nazim," she said, ushering them further to the back of the room. Kinza noticed there was a ring of older men talking intently around one of the fires in the back.

"Nazim? The old trainer? He is here?" Zaid asked.

"Yes, he has taken on a role as a leader within our group. He has had a few warriors sent out as scouts to gather information. He might know more but progress has been slow today. Most of the fighting stopped by yesterday morning, but skirmishes still broke out. He thinks the Unfettered are patrolling the city and going building by building and attacking people," Ekaja said.

"Yes, we ran into a few of those," Khalil said drily.

Kinza saw a giant of a man standing to the side of the fire, talking to what could only be one of the warriors. The larger man had a shaved head, but his grey speckled beard made up for the missing hair. He was imposing as he stood with hands clasped behind his back, but the weathered face gave away his old age. The young warrior he spoke with nodded and turned and left the room.

"Ekaja," the man said with affection. His voice rumbled like thunder and they spoke for a moment in Rhaptan about the current situation they were in, Zaid speaking up as well. It was odd to see someone make Zaid look small, but regardless the man seemed to speak respectfully toward Zaid, if not a bit sorrowful.

The man's dark eyes came to rest on Kinza as he said, "Ah, if one of our guests does not speak Rhaptan, then we will converse in English."

Kinza smiled sheepishly. She didn't think it was the time to mention that she had understood almost half of what he had been saying. She would have to ask Zaid about it later. Maybe it was due to her tattoo. "Thank you. My name is Kinza Solace."

Nazim gave a slight nod of respect and said, "Welcome Kinza and welcome back Zaid. I understand Kinza that a few unusual events surrounded your trip to Rhapta?"

"You could say that," she replied.

"Well I'm sure you are hungry and need to rest. Please, have a seat and I will tell you what we know."

CHAPTER 4
THE DRUMS OF WAR

Tell him that my men are getting restless, Commander Kartik said, pointing his stubby finger at Mikah. *Pass that along to the other Elders as well. We need to know what we are doing, the people don't want to just sit here in fear another day.*

Commander Kartik wasn't an overly tall man, but he was tall enough to look Mikah directly in the eyes. And he was built like an ox. One would think that the warrior's commander had an ability of strength or tactics, but no. His was precision; every shot landed, every hit counted. It also seemed that his instructions were precise as well. The beads and feathers on his obsidian-tipped staff rattled with every jab of his finger.

We also need more space, there is no room to move and we have no shelter from the sun, he pointed up above like Mikah could just conjure a cloud. He wanted to roll his eyes but instead he reassured the man.

I hear you Commander Kartik, he said with a nod of his head. *I will report this directly back to my mentor and the other Elders. You can count on it. It will not be forgotten that our warriors were the ones who protected our backs as we fled the city. We need you to continue to be strong and capable.*

The older man's chest puffed out a little bit.

Mikah! a clipped voice shouted behind him. The two men turned to watch Elder Yuvaan striding through the grass toward them, his jowls shaking in irritation.

Elder Yuvaan, Mikah said with another slightly deeper bow, *it is nice to see you are well and made it out of the city. I was worried you got caught up in the fighting.*

Tahir has no business gathering reports from Commander Kartik, the warriors are not his jurisdiction, Yuvaan said. Mikah could see sweat stains under the arms of his white robes, and the black beads of the Elders were nowhere to be found around his neck. Disheveled would be a kind word to use to describe Elder Yuvaan.

Yes, of course, Elder Yuvaan. I am but the messenger, Mikah said.

And are you going to take charge, Yuvaan? Kartik asked. *Neither you nor your apprentice has come to us in the two days we've been here. At least Tahir has the decency to make sure all of us are taken care of!*

Now, Commander, Yuvaan was saying, *these are times of strife and we are all working as hard as we can. I have been meeting with the Elders all day and night, trying to get information on what is happening in the city. A meeting Tahir has not been a part of, need I remind you.*

And what have you accomplished? Nothing! We've been sitting here with nothing!

Mikah discreetly detached himself from the conversation and made his way back through the camp. Circles of shirtless warriors in red paint congregated everywhere on this side. Swords and spears scattered about. The chaos did not appeal to him. The warriors may have been the strength of Rhapta, but it was the Elders that controlled that strength. His father had impressed this upon him as a child and he found he agreed.

Past the groups of warriors was the small section dedicated to food. Anunnaki really only needed to eat once every few days, so they hadn't needed much, but people were being pushed to their mental limits and food was always a comfort. The air was scented with spices as he walked past into the areas dedicated to families.

Parents, children, brothers, and cousins alike had settled here. Some were lucky enough to receive tents, but most had only the clothes on their backs, having rushed from the city in the middle of the night. Some people wept and others prayed to the Creator. He heard others wondering at the marvel that this camp even existed. How long had it been here? How was it possible that they could leave the city and come here? They were slowly starting to learn it was Elder Tahir who had created it; a rumor that Mikah himself had started. Was it still a rumor if it was true?

Over everything else was the talk of the prophecy and the girl, Kinza Solace. The name crept up in whispers and the occasional shout of anger. Maybe the name would soon become a curse. Mikah didn't know but he was sure he would find out soon. He enjoyed his position as apprentice to Elder Tahir. People spoke his name with respect as he would most likely be an Elder one day himself. Apprentices studied under the mentor they hoped to replace one day, but it wasn't always certain.

When his father had first proposed the idea of tutoring under Elder Tahir, he had scorned the idea, thinking Tahir's position as representative of the quarries as useless. But he quickly learned the man was a true leader. He may officially represent the quarries, but he did so much more. He stepped up where other Elders fell behind, taking on responsibilities that were not his own. When the time came to inquire about the apprenticeship, he was the first one at Tahir's door.

A few people recognized him and gave half-hearted smiles or waved as he walked by. He nodded to all of them, looking each of them in the eyes, hoping they remembered him again. He adjusted the fall of the wrap that crossed over his chest, leaving it partially bare and held his chin a little higher. Eyes lingered a little longer as he passed.

Tahir's tent came into view but before he could reach the entrance a man entered before him. He looked rugged, his clothes were worn and Mikah could see spots of blood. The man's long braid fell to the side as he ducked into Tahir's tent.

Mikah would just have to wait then.

He stood for a few moments, hoping the man would come back out quickly, but they must have been in deep conversation. Mikah started to wander around the camp again, this time toward the back where supply carts were being kept. A few tents with valuables or personal items for the Elders were kept here. Mikah could see which was Tahir's based on his particular beadwork and feather combination hanging outside the door. Two warriors stood guard when none stood outside any of the other storage tents.

Pushing his shoulders back into an easy posture, Mikah strode over to the tent and made to enter. Twin spears clanged together in front of him.

No one is allowed to enter, one of the guards said.

Mikah gave one of his most charming smiles. *Don't worry, I'm here at the behest of Elder Tahir, I'm his apprentice, Mikah Sultan.* He gave one of his slight nods in respect.

The guard's eyes narrowed and the other shifted on his feet. *I'm sorry, but we were instructed not to let anyone in.*

I'm sure you were, and you are doing an exemplary job. I will let

Tahir know that even on a hot day such as this, and during times of such hardship, you two are standing here at attention, guarding an Elder's personal belongings.

The guards stood a little taller.

But I must remind you that Tahir instructed me to go inside and check on something for him. I don't think your exemplary status will continue if Tahir has to come here himself and deem you insubordinate. Especially when there is an enemy at our doorstep.

The two guards glanced at each other and the spears moved aside. Mikah gave them one last smile before entering. He was expecting boxes of books, precious artifacts, clothing, or food. The Elder's themselves generally led minimalist lives but some of them had trinkets or mementos of sentiment. He didn't expect that of Tahir though.

And he definitely didn't expect to find a prisoner.

Mikah looked down at the scruffy man on the floor. He sat with legs splayed out in front of him and arms bound back against the large chest he leaned against. The man's chin rested on his chest, giving Mikah a view of the top of his head, scraggly hair peppered with gray stuck out in a mussed halo.

Huh, Mikah said. *Well that's interesting.* He knelt down in front of the man and poked him in the chest.

He just grunted but was clearly asleep, or drugged.

Mikah poked him again. This time the man's head bobbed up slowly and he could see he wasn't as young as he had thought, maybe later thirties at best. The man's round face sagged as he tried to focus on Mikah's face.

Drugged it was, then.

What is your name? Mikah asked.

The man just groaned again and tried to mumble. Mikah sighed and looked around. There was a crate to the side that he pried open. It held a few glass bottles of *guakal* wine and a few of drinking water. He grabbed one of each and popped the top off the water. Holding it to the man's lips, half of it dribbled down to his robes, which he now noticed were a deep blue. The man was a scholar then. Why would Tahir have a scholar tied up?

He dribbled more water on the man's face, at least a few drops getting in his mouth. He sputtered and took a shuddering breath. Mikah sat down against the open crate, popped the top of the wine off and waited for the man to focus. He took a sip, it was sickly sweet and he hated it. He drank it anyway.

After several minutes of allowing the man to regain as much consciousness as he could muster, Mikah asked again. *What is your name?*

Hunar, he mumbled this time, coming to focus again on Mikah's face. *Have you come to kill me then?* he asked, becoming more lucid by the moment.

Mikah quirked an eyebrow. *Not exactly my area of expertise,* he said, flicking a piece of non-existent lint off his leg. *I would like to know why you are here though? Did you do something to anger Elder Tahir? I feel like that would be difficult to do.*

The man snorted. *You must not know Elder Tahir very well then.*

Ah, but I'm his apprentice. I know him better than anyone in the city. Or in camp. He took another pull at the wine.

Hunar took a long shuddering breath and huffed a laugh. *Clearly you do not. No one in Rhapta seems to know who he really is.* He said the last part quieter. Mikah was amused by the turn of this conversation and was starting to see where it was going. The Elders were generally loved and respected in Rhapta, but there were, of course, those who rejected the idea of leadership and order. The Unfettered and the Apostles of Truth were the foremost of those. The Apostles of Truth were known to be the least physically active. More of an underground group of scholars who tried to defame the Elders based on made up historical records, citing that they were the true rulers of Rhapta. But everyone already knew that.

Almost two hundred years ago that last Rhaptan king died and on the same night the heir disappeared, leaving the city in a power vacuum. The king's advisors then became the defunct leaders and created the council of Elders. No one disagreed with that, but the Apostles of Truth seemed to think it was cause for an uprising.

Mikah found the whole thing hilarious.

Oh, and you do? Please, tell me, oh wise Hunar, what you know of my mentor, Mikah said.

Hunar's head rolled in his direction. *Why? You would not believe me anyway.*

Humor me. He took another swig.

Tahir is the one behind the attack.

You are sure it was her? Tahir asked, rising from his seat.

The man had arrived a few moments ago, one of his men who had stayed with the Unfettered in Rhapta. He looked roughed up, but alive, with an odd glint in his eyes. To Tahir's dismay it resembled something like awe.

It is exactly as you described. A young woman, but wearing human clothes. Two of the Unfettered were approaching her and suddenly a white light exploded around her. It killed the two men, it did. And sent everyone else flying back. It was incredible! He barely maintained his composure.

And was there anyone with her or was she alone? Tahir started pacing, becoming exhilarated by the progressing events. Things were moving like clockwork, just as he had hoped. Hakim's visions of Kinza truly were a blessing to him. Knowing thy enemy gave one a distinct advantage.

Yes, two people. One looked like that healer on the outskirts? You know the good one. And the other looked venari to me, he said it with a sneer.

The venari, Tahir said, turning toward the man, *does he live?*

Yes, he was thrown back, but looked fine to me. Tahir nodded, pleased. Even though he had no limits on how far he would go for his people, he didn't want to see Zaid hurt. The boy was admirable in the least and absolutely singular at his best. Over the years he had come to care for Zaid in what he assumed was a fatherly manner. If he hadn't been tapped to become *venari* he would have insisted Zaid become his apprentice. And he would have done it, the boy accepted duty in a way many his age would never understand. Tahir would have to find a way to get to him and bring him into the fold again, slowly.

Good, good, this is excellent!

Sh—, should we kill her then sir? I can have the men find her again, the man asked.

No! Tahir said, then quieter, *No, for now continue as you have been. We need to alert the public though, they need to know she is in the city. Come,* he moved toward the doorway before turning back. *Let's go and gather our forces, I see a battle on the horizon.*

You really are a lunatic, Mikah said to the prisoner. *Tahir* saved *the city.*

Hunar settled back against the chest and closed his eyes.

I'm sure Tahir is spreading the rumor now that the prophecy is happening, the old one.

Yes, of course.

And that the outsider has come and they are the one who is behind the attack.

Yes, and it has been confirmed through Hakim's vision, Mikah replied.

Who was there to receive that vision?

Tahir of course, he is close with that old bat. Mikah didn't feel the need to play a part too much around a prisoner.

And who else? Hunar had a grim smile.

What? I have no idea, no one? Mikah wasn't sure what he was getting at.

So how do you know the prophecy Tahir spoke of was real?

Mikah barked a laugh. *That's your big reveal? You think Tahir created a false vision and told the people it was Hakim's?* He truly rolled his eyes now.

How was this camp built? Hunar asked instead.

Tahir made it, it was his design and he was the one who figured out how to create a psionic barrier.

Why?

What?

Why did he do it? Why did he create a camp away from the city and not tell anyone?

Mikah was starting to feel the effects of the wine, but just slightly *I don't know, foresight? Progress? The future? Is that it?*

Hunar opened his eyes again and looked at him, squinting a little. Mikah realized, based on the faint indent on the man's nose, that he wore glasses. It was extremely rare for Anunnaki to need things like that as their healing abilities were extensive, but sometimes people who lived on the outskirts picked up those genetics over generations.

How did Tahir know to get people out of the city right before the Unfettered attacked?

Mikah sighed, growing tired of this repetitive conversation. *Yes, Tahir was with Hakim when he had the vision, and no, no one else was in the room. But if Tahir had a vendetta against Rhapta, why would he get people out when the fighting started. If he wanted to hurt people, he could have just left and not said anything.*

Hunar coughed and gave a bitter smile. *Tahir doesn't want to hurt people. He wants power. And the prophecy is a threat to that.*

I think you are jealous and bitter that the Elders are loved, Mikah said, rising to his feet. The overall din of the camp had suddenly gotten loud enough to reach him.

You will see, Tahir keeps more secrets than anyone in Rhapta. He is a spider weaving a web and we are all caught in it like flies. He promised the Unfettered something big enough that they would start a war for him, Hunar was sitting alert now, having come fully awake.

Mikah just shook his head, he had lost interest in this game and the wine was really hitting him now. *And what could he possibly promise them? Money? Property?*

Hunar's eyes bored into his. *A way out.*

What? Mikah wasn't sure he heard him correctly, the sounds of the camp were getting louder.

The Elders, they know how we can leave the city and remain as we are. His eyes glinted. *They know how but they are keeping people locked up. In here they can control us, but out there,* he jerked his chin toward the edge of the camp and out to the human cities and lay beyond. *Out there they have no power.*

Uh-huh, Mikah said. *Well, this has been a fun chat but I'm going to have to cut it short.* He knelt down in front of Hunar, trying not to wobble too much. *This won't hurt much.* He placed his hands on either side of Hunar's head and closed his eyes, concentrating.

What are you—Hunar started to say but Mikah was already in his head, like a fish moving upstream he dug through the most recent memories, of the conversation they just had, of Mikah being here at all. Mentally he tied a thread around them and yanked. Hunar shuddered. They ripped free and floated away to wherever lost memories go.

Out of curiosity he swam up the river of memory a little more. It was mostly blackness with the occasional glimpse of a guard's back. Mikah tried to push a little more. The further he went upstream, into the past, the harder it was. Instead of moving against a gentle stream, he would soon find himself going headfirst into whitewater. He got as far as a few nights ago, during the attack. He was bound and being pushed through a tunnel. Then Tahir moved on ahead of him. Mikah could not go any further and pulled out.

Hunar slumped forward as far as he could go with the bindings. Within a few moments he was snoring and Mikah turned to exit the tent. People were hurrying by towards the other side of the camp and Mikah started moving in that direction, stumbling a little from the wine. His system would burn through it pretty quickly though, Anunnaki didn't tend to stay drunk too long, the healing was too fast.

Mikah grabbed a man passing by. *Where is everyone headed?*

The man shrugged him off but said, *To the center, Elder Tahir has news and requested the whole camp.*

Everyone?! Mikah said, but the man had already moved on. Mikah started to follow instead, weaving in and out of the crowd of people. Why hadn't he been told of an announcement? He was usually the first to know. Tahir knew that the people were aware of Hakim's most recent vision already, was he going to announce it as well? That seemed unnecessary unless they had new information.

As he got closer he saw the gathering crowd was huge.

There were probably close to five thousand people in the camp and they all pushed to get closer. Children cried as their parents towed them behind, men made way for their wives and elderly. He could see a small dais had been erected near the Elders' main tent. Several of them stood to the side looking anything but pleased. They must not know what Tahir was announcing. And frankly, Mikah felt the same.

They all stood for several minutes before anything happened. A pretty woman ascended the dais and strode to one side, placing her hand to her left, palm up. Mikah vaguely recognized her, she attended all public meetings when voices needed to be broadcast louder. Something to do with her ability.

Tahir ascended next, moving slower. *Always make them wait*, he would say. His white robes were immaculate and the black Elder beads that hung around his neck glinted in the sunlight. He placed his hand on the woman's and spoke, his voice echoing out through the crowd.

Welcome, I thank you all for gathering so quickly as I have urgent news. The remaining council of Elders has been working very hard to gather information on what is happening in the city, who attacked us, and why. I have sent one of my own scouts back into the city, undercover to unearth this information for us.

Mikah could see a man standing near the dais and recognized him as the man who had gone into Tahir's tent before him. He stood looking at the crowd as Tahir continued.

Many of you have already heard the news that Grand Elder Hakim recently had another vision, one of our attackers. It is true that he has confirmed we were attacked by the Unfettered, and that he also identified their leader: the outsider from the prophecy.

People gasped and started talking again.

Tahir spoke a little louder now. *The name of the outsider is Kinza Solace and Hakim has confirmed that she is behind the attack. We do not know what triggered her wrath against us, but we will not stand for it!*

The noise in the crowd rose, people became restless. Shaking fists, raised swords, calls for justice.

Unfortunately there is more! Tahir cried, and people quieted again, barely. *As I mentioned, my scout bravely went back into the city and returned with new information.*

Mikah knew he was pausing for effect now.

Kinza Solace has been spotted inside the city.

Screams of rage rose through the crowd, not a single face wanted peace. No, these people wanted blood, the blood of an outsider. They demanded war against Kinza's army that had destroyed their city and many of those they had loved. The bloodlust was starting to make Mikah nervous and he tried to back out of the crowd but kept getting jostled about. The wine had lost its effect, but the heat of bodies was making him dizzy.

Up on the dais, Tahir motioned for his scout to ascend the steps. The man did, looking uncomfortable standing in front of so many people. *I would recount the description my man has said to me, but I think it is better you hear it from his own lips,* Tahir said and stepped away.

The man timidly reached out and placed his hand on top of the woman's. *I—, I saw—,* he stuttered and paused to lick his lips. *I saw her,* he said this time. *I saw Kinza Solace and what she can do. Elder Tahir had told me she would have abilities unlike anything else, but I was not prepared for what I witnessed.*

The rage in the crowd focused on the man's every word.

I saw her fighting alongside the Unfettered, and she—, the man's eyes were feverish, in awe or in fear, Mikah could not tell. *Ten people tried to take her down at once. I tried to help, but before I got close a white light erupted, throwing me back. By the time I woke and the smoke had cleared, she was gone.*

. . .

THE SCREAMS in the crowd returned, begging for blood.

But the carnage she left behind....

The council of Elders looked to each other, frantic and fearful. Mikah tried to leave again, shoving people aside. He got an elbow to the face for his efforts. Something warm and wet dribbled down his chin.

There was a crater where an entire plaza used to be.

Calls for war. Death to Kinza's army. Death to Kinza.

Homes leveled and bodies ringed the crater. The bodies of families.

Mikah gasped for air as he stumbled away from the violent crowd, blood dripping down onto his clothes.

The screams from the crowd went on for hours.

CHAPTER 5

ACCUSATION

Kinza sat around one of the fires with a cup of some kind of vegetable soup. To be honest, she hadn't been hungry all day and was drinking it more for comfort than anything. People conversed around the fire in hushed tones. The whispers had started again but she could not see where they were coming from.

Kinza saw a young boy grab a large rock and to her amazement, the rock started floating in the air. The boy's father scolded him and the rock tumbled to the floor. Another woman's skin flickered through varying shades as she talked with the woman next to her. It looked like the changes were happening in time with her distress. Many of these people had lost or could not find those they loved. It was apparent in the tense conversations that people were afraid and confused. What was happening? And why?

Nazim, Zaid, and Ekaja came back to the fire and sat down on the other side of her, Khalil to her left. Nazim addressed the small group, but spoke again out loud and in English for Kinza's benefit.

"As you may have heard, we were attacked two nights ago by men inside the city. It has been confirmed that the Unfettered are the ones behind the attack, but they have never been organized like this, nor have they ever been united in a common goal. We have guessed that someone either convinced them, or paid them to attack the city. We just don't know who."

"Have you captured any yet?" Zaid asked. The other people around the fire listened intently.

"No, but I have a few warriors out right now attempting to. The problem is they move in packs, not unlike the ubir can," he said the last part to Zaid who nodded knowingly. "They don't seem to have a goal other than to cause destruction. Homes have been demolished but largely unlooted."

"What of the Elders?" Ekaja asked, worry in her eyes.

"From what we know the last we saw of them was in the Grand Hall, where they always are. But we can't get close. A large force of the Unfettered are camped in the central plaza. It seems they are just keeping the Elders penned up, but not harming them."

"If only we had the wisdom of Grand Elder Hakim's visions at this time," Ekaja said mournfully.

One of the women on the other side of the fire spoke up, but in their minds. She had startlingly blue eyes set in a long face. *Do you think this has anything to do with the prophecy? The old one I mean?*

Zaid's eyes snapped to Kinza before he said carefully, "Why would you think that?"

The prophecy said there would be someone who would come to the city and either save it or destroy it. From where I'm sitting, this looks like destruction. The woman's eyes narrowed and glanced toward Kinza who was clearly wearing clothes from outside of Rhapta. She was the outsider.

"We could easily be *saved* from this destruction by an outsider as well, Anjali," Ekaja chastised. "And how would an outsider have anything to do with the Unfettered?"

The woman was spared from answering when one of the warriors came to speak with Nazim. Kinza realized he looked like one of the many warriors she had seen in her nightmares. They all had red paint markings on their skin and stood tall and proud, as if their status was a mark of nobility. Each of them also carried various types of obsidian weapons, mostly spears and swords.

Kinza leaned toward Khalil, "People would not think I did this, right? Like there is literally no way."

"People are afraid," he said quietly. "And people do and believe in things that have no basis in logic when they are afraid." He looked at her reassuringly, "I'm sure once we find out who is actually behind this, the people will turn their attention to that person instead. For now, the only thing unfamiliar to them is someone who is from outside of Rhapta."

Nazim stood and said, "A skirmish had broken out, I'm sorry, I must speak with my men." He left toward the front of the room where a few warriors with torn clothing and broken weapons hurried in.

The young boy who had floated the rock came over and sat next to Kinza, eyeing her clothes. He could not have been more than ten or eleven.

Where are you from? he asked inside her head. Apparently others could hear that as well because a few people, including Zaid who was talking with his mother, looked up momentarily. Most of them turned away discreetly, but she knew people were listening.

Chicago, she said, hoping she did it right. *It's in the United States.*

Where is that? he asked, grabbing a pebble and floating it up in the air.

Kinda far from here, she said. *You can make things float?*

He looked up at her and grinned, clearly pleased with someone's interest in him. *Yes, but only rocks or dirt.*

That's still pretty cool, Kinza said. She was impressed that he could hold it so still. She supposed she could make rocks move too, but only as the result of a violent explosion.

Do you have an ability? the boy asked, he added another pebble to his palm and the two started orbiting each other.

Kinza hesitated and she could tell people around the fire held their breath. What was she going to do? Lie? She wasn't very good at lying and Grams probably would have scolded her for it.

Yeah, I guess I have a few, she said, hopefully being vague. That must have been the wrong answer because the whispering in her head turned to a cacophony again. Zaid closed his eyes and clenched his jaw. One of the very few signs he was stressed.

The boy's rocks dropped and he gasped and stared at her in wonder. *You have more than one?* he asked in amazement. Kinza realized her mistake.

Um, yeah, but nothing special. Just a few light tricks is all. Khalil coughed next to her. Her answer truthfully wasn't a lie, it was just a teeny, tiny portion of the whole truth. Her white-light explosion and the fire were both lights. And the teleportation you could not even see. She didn't count what she had done to help Khalil as she wasn't sure if that was her own ability yet or not.

The boy's father scolded him for asking questions of strangers. The boy skulked back to the other side of the fire and Kinza turned to Khalil.

"I was going to ask you," she whispered. "How exactly did I

heal you? I didn't think I had a healing ability, but I know it was you that told me what to do."

"I'm not entirely sure, Kinza. Truth be told, in theory I supposed I could teach anyone how I do certain healings, but the problem is the Aura. Yes, Anunnaki can speak telepathically, but we cannot share *understanding* because the connections between each other are not that strong." Khalil thought for a moment, brow wrinkled. "But somehow the connection with you was much stronger, so I was able to show you how. What is even more odd is that my telepathic ability is almost entirely gone. I can hear the occasional whisper here and there and when someone connects with me directly, but that's it. I shouldn't have been able to connect with you at all."

Kinza picked at her nails. "Is it possible that I could actually understand the Rhaptan language?" At Khalil's confused expression, she added, "I mean, without hearing or studying it."

Khalil eyed her from the side in a curious way. He spoke a few sentences that tickled Kinza's brain again, and then waited expectantly. Just like before, she had never heard the words before, but she just *knew* what they meant.

"No, I've never seen an eight-legged donkey with a purple coat before," she replied in English.

Khalil's eyebrows rose. "Now that's remarkable..."

"So it's not a normal Anunnaki thing?" she asked with a sigh.

Khalil shook his head, eyebrows still up. "No, it's definitely not. Try saying something in Rhaptan."

"I don't know how," she said with a shrug. How was she supposed to speak words she had never heard?

"Just try. Tell me what month you were born."

Kinza scrunched up her face, knowing she was going to

look like a fool, but tried anyway, saying words that sounded like gibberish to her.

Now Khalil had a wide smile to go with his elevated brows. "Well, that's something. I was born in April as well."

"*That made sense?!*" Kinda whispered furiously, earning a few glares from people on the other side of the fire.

"It did," Khalil said, looking at her like she was a puzzle to figure out. "How clear is your understanding?"

"Earlier I couldn't understand at all, but as I'm listening to it, Rhaptan is becoming clearer by the minute. Somethings are fuzzy, but I think I'm getting the general gist of it."

"Has this happened with other languages before?" he asked.

"Nope," Kinza replied with a shrug.

"Interesting..." Khalil said and rested his chin on his fist to ponder the next facet of her oddity.

Eventually Nazim came back to the fire and sat down. His mouth was set in a frown within his large beard. "We lost one of the men in the skirmish, but it sounds like they will be back within the hour. I need to go and gather as many people as I can to fight. Please excuse me."

Nazim got up again and this time Zaid followed. Kinza assumed to help in the defense. Honestly, he could have scared them all off with the scowl he had permanently glued to his face.

Kinza sat with Khalil and Ekaja and the others around one of the fires and waited. She tried to focus on the jumble of whispers and words she both understood and didn't in her brain but it was just giving her a headache.

"Are you well?" Ekaja said, looking at her in concern.

"Oh, yeah, just a headache. Up until a day or two ago I didn't have this whole telepathy thing. At first it was just Zaid, which wasn't a problem. But now..." She looked around the hundred or so people in the room conversing silently.

Ekaja nodded in understanding. "I can see that it must be an abrupt change for you. Try to stop focusing on one single voice and just let them happen. Trying to listen too intently to conversations that are not directed toward you can give anyone a pain in the head." She gave a wry smile.

Kinza tried doing what she said. She stopped trying to separate the different voices and threads of conversation that crossed over each other. For a moment it sounded just like buzzing or a dull crowd murmur, but changed slowly. Some of the conversations started becoming clearer and Kinza had to focus on trying *not to* listen too intently. But the conversations were not good.

"People are talking about me," she said to Ekaja. "They think I'm somehow to blame for this."

"Yes, I hear them," she replied. "We very rarely see anyone from outside the city, and very few of us leave. You are famous," she joked. Kinza almost chuckled, it was so bad. She was pretty sure the word "infamous" might be more in tune.

"I didn't do anything though. Just a few days ago I didn't even know Rhapta and the Anunnaki existed!" she said a little louder this time. Ekaja placed a hand on her knee. "I didn't have any of these abilities and I certainly could not hear other people's thoughts." Not to mention she could understand them.

"It must be very difficult for you to deal with so many changes at once." After a moment she said, "My son told me what happened with the assassins that were sent after you. I am very sorry to hear what happened to your parents."

Kinza just looked down at her hands and nodded, if she tried to speak, the frustration would turn to tears.

"But if it is true," Ekaja said, turning Kinza's face toward her, "then you need to know that there are many people in this city that will rejoice your arrival instead of fearing it. I do not understand the prophecies well, and I'm sure many of them are open to interpretations, but I do not believe the Creator would send someone to destroy us. She is the one who gifted us with the beautiful Aurastone and all of these wonderful people have lived happily because of it." She gestured around the room.

Kinza wondered again how they all spoke English so well when they never left and mustered the courage to ask. "Ekaja, I hope I'm not being rude or anything, but how do so many of you know other languages if you don't leave the city?"

Ekaja chuckled. "I'm not sure if Zaid mentioned it, but Anunnaki learn some things a lot faster than humans. Things like languages, math, and historical dates. As children we are all taught several languages so, as a people, we do not forget what is outside the walls. We don't want to entirely lose our ability to connect with humans if we truly needed to. So we are taught English, Mandarin, Swahili, Japanese, Punjabi and many more. My great-grandmother knew Akkadian very well, but we've stopped teaching that since the language is basically extinct now."

Kinza wondered if that had something to do with her understanding of Rhaptan. It also occurred to Kinza that Rhapta is probably the oldest standing city in the world. If their histories were correct and the Anunnaki existed without the psionic barrier between them and the humans in the times of Mesopotamia, then Rhapta was at least 4,000 years old, possibly more. These walls that surrounded them held people that walked the Earth before the pharaohs of Egypt, before

Rome existed, long before America was discovered. She wondered what messages and remains from older times lay in the hidden cracks of Rhapta. She almost itched to walk the streets again. But no, that would be dangerous.

"Ekaja," Kinza said, "when we were on our way here, we saw almost no one, as if the city had been abandoned. I'm sure that there are other people hiding in groups like this one, but is there anywhere else that Anunnaki could go?"

Ekaja thought for a moment. Talking with her was proving a distraction from the distrustful whispers at her expense that were spreading slowly throughout the room.

"Not that I know of. As far as I am aware, the barrier surrounds the city, with about a quarter-mile to a half-mile of space between the barrier and the city wall depending on the exact spot. If someone were to leave, we would slowly lose our abilities and memory of the Anunnaki."

"Then what happened to everyone? Did they all just choose to become human?"

Ekaja sighed. "I'm not sure, but with the threat of death, even humanity would not seem that bad." It was not the answer Kinza had hoped for. She wasn't watching the extinction of an entire race, was she?

An hour or so went by, Zaid had gone with a group of other men and a few women. Apparently there was fighting a few streets away and they were trying to keep the Unfettered from getting any closer. Zaid was capable, but she knew he was used to dealing with only a few ubir at a time at most. It wasn't the same as defending a hundred people from bands of Anunnaki hell-bent on destruction.

Kinza sat and watched the flames and tried not to listen to the conversations around her. Ekaja's advice had helped immensely with filtering through the whispers, but that just meant she had a better idea of what people were saying. People were calling her "the outsider," or the "one from the prophecy," or a smaller few implied that she was the one who did all of this. Kinza tried not to let it affect her but heat rose to her cheeks. She wanted to scream and shout at them that she hadn't even known they existed and even if she had she certainly would not do this. They knew nothing about her. Grams would tell her not to worry about the opinions of sheep, but what if their opinions put you in danger? Was she supposed to sit by and let them talk?

The sun had started on its downward arc and the shadows grew long within the building when Zaid and the others finally came back. Nazim was apparently too old to fight any longer but had waited for them out in the plaza. He walked with Zaid in deep conversations. Zaid's shirt had a slash near one shoulder, but he looked otherwise unharmed to her relief. Their faces were tight though, and when Zaid looked to Kinza, she could not read his expression, but it wasn't good.

Nazim came over to Kinza, a few of his warriors trailing her. She thought they stood a little too close to her. "Kinza, come, let us speak alone," Nazim said. That really didn't sound good, but she got up and followed him to a far corner where flowers clung to vines that hung down from a hole, high in the ceiling. Somehow Nazim's face was both cautious and full of pity. Zaid stood silently to the side, leaning inconspicuously against the wall.

"Is everything okay? Did someone get hurt?" she asked, looking back and forth between them. The warriors that had trailed Nazim were less conspicuous than Zaid and stood in a semi-circle behind Nazim.

"We did, sadly, have a few casualties, but that is not why I needed to speak with you. As I mentioned before, we have been trying to find out who was truly behind the attack, or who at least hired the Unfettered."

"Okay, did you find them?"

"We aren't sure. Some of the Unfettered agreed to speak to a few of our men from afar. Our men asked who was leading them and they provided a name."

"All right, so what does that have to do with me?"

"The name they gave us was yours."

Zaid watched Kinza's face go slack.

"What?!" she said incredulously, looking up at the mountain that was Nazim. He didn't entirely blame her. When he had heard what the Unfettered were saying he thought he had heard wrong.

Zaid had gone with several people and a few warriors back to the location of the fight earlier. It was on one of the larger boulevards towards the northern edge of the southern quarter of the city. The people who knew he was *venari* gave him a wide berth and scathing eyes. Some of them even muttered things about him "bringing" the outsider into the city. All of that stopped the moment it started and everyone focused on the Unfettered. A group of twenty of them had collided with Nazim's small forces. Very few of the Unfettered were trained though, most of them had lived in terrible conditions on the outskirts and could not match up to the inner-city Rhaptans. Toward the end, a few of them held a spot across the street, one of them throwing projectiles with deadly accuracy causing Nazim's force to keep a wide berth. They had gotten to shouting back and forth and a warrior asked who their leader was. The men across the street had paused and then shouted back, "Kinza Solace!"

Zaid had thought he had been hit in the head. "What?" he yelled back.

"WE FOLLOW THE ORDERS OF KINZA SOLACE!" one of them shouted back. Through a few more shouted conversations they claimed she was the one who ordered the attack. Many of the men Zaid was with didn't even know who that was and stood with confused expressions. Zaid had asked them for proof and in response the two groups set up a meeting. The moment they got back Zaid had to tell Nazim.

The woman in question was standing with her mouth hanging open like a dead fish. "They said they have proof, Kinza, and want to meet with some of us to show it. Obviously they are lying, but that is the word they are spreading around the city."

"But, I didn't *do* anything!" she protested. "How would I have even met any of these people? I didn't know any of you even existed."

"I agree that it is a stretch," Nazim said, "but how would they know your name? You just arrived a few hours ago."

"I have no idea, but the only people I talked to are you and the people by the fire I was sitting next to, and none of them have left."

Nazim sighed. "Either way I want to meet with them. Maybe we can find out who is really behind this during the meeting. It's to happen tonight and you are to come with us." Zaid was pleased that Nazim didn't believe this lunacy, but he could see the warriors that tailed him did. The sidelong glances and sneers in Kinza's direction were proof enough of that. He would need to keep an eye on her for the next few hours in case the rumor started to spread that she was the cause of the destruction.

Nazim left them but insisted that one of the warriors stay with Kinza for "protection." It seemed that Nazim's cautiousness hadn't abandoned him despite his beliefs of the situation. Kinza just sat down in the corner under the vines instead of going back to the fire.

"You know I didn't do anything, right?" she asked, looking up at him.

Zaid just nodded, too tired to say anything else. The past few days had been brutal and it did seem like everything tended to revolve around Kinza regardless of the fact she was always unaware. It still made him tired though, he wanted to have *something* be normal.

After a few minutes Khalil and Zaid's mother wandered over. Kinza had dropped her head down to her knees and when she didn't rise Zaid explained what had happened. Ekaja had immediately started shouting reprimands and obscenities that he hadn't heard her use in years. Since Amir. He smiled a bit at the memory of them arguing over something unimportant.

Ekaja sat down and put her arm around Kinza. "They have nothing to use against you, Kinza. There is nothing they could say. You don't know them at all, correct?"

Kinza just nodded.

"Then there," Ekaja said, clapping her hands together in finality. "If they have no proof, then it must be a lie meant to spread hate and fear and distrust."

Khalil nodded, "That would be a good tactic. But that still doesn't answer why? From the looks of it, this attack is only meant to spread chaos. Who would want Rhapta to be submerged in this darkness?"

They all sat silent, not one of them knowing the answer.

As the time ticked by Zaid could hear the conversations around the fires turn from fearful to angry. Parents moved their children away from the fires closest to Kinza and people no longer hid the fact that they glared at her outright.

At one point a man stood in defiance and came over to

Kinza's corner. Both the warrior and Zaid moved to block his path but he stopped a good distance away, hot anger in his eyes.

"You," he said pointing to Kinza, whose head lifted finally from her knees. "You are Kinza Solace."

She didn't reply and just glared back at him.

The man pointed his finger at her, barely-controlled shaking. "If it is true and this is your doing, I will come for you." A few other people rose from the fires and stood staring in their direction. "We will come for you and everyone you've ever loved. If my wife is dead because of you, you will *burn*." The warrior shouted at him to back up and Zaid stayed closer to Kinza, cautious.

The other people were shouting and cheering the man on as embers started floating away from his skin.

Kinza had gotten to her feet. "I didn't do *anything*!" she shouted back at him. Her features twisted in bitter rage. Zaid prayed to the Creator that she didn't choose now to cause one of her explosions.

Zaid moved to stand in front of her, blocking her from view. "Stop," he whispered, putting his hands on her shoulders. People were still making noise. "Don't bother saying anything. This is all going to go away later once we meet with the Unfettered. They are just afraid and taking it out on you."

She turned her angry, dark eyes to him. "It's not fair," she said, shoving him in the shoulder. "Why did you have to take me?" She turned away and sat back down against the wall, leaving Zaid near the point of exhaustion.

The ember man had moved back toward the fires but his words were riling people up. Nazim had gone outside to speak with the warriors and upon coming back in his voice boomed, "QUIET!" The room went as silent as the dead. "We have been shown not a single shred of proof that any of this has to do with Kinza Solace," he said quieter this time. "And until that has happened, you will treat our guest with *respect*." No one spoke in objection, but it was in their eyes.

Zaid sat down and settled in for the long few hours before the meeting.

CHAPTER 6
THE TRIALS

Kinza walked through the dark streets of Rhapta, feeling a lot like a prisoner. It looked like she was going to have a trial after all.

Nazim had come to get her a few hours later and said they were to meet the Unfettered in an open plaza not too far away. There would be ten Unfettered and Nazim was bringing a group of ten as well. Including himself, Kinza, Zaid, and six warriors, he had also brought another man, Rayaan, to act as an additional witness and not directly under Nazim's command. Rayaan was a slight man who looked to be in his early thirties, but she supposed it was hard to tell with Anunnaki. They all aged so slowly. She wasn't sure what his ability was, but he kept quiet and to himself as they walked.

At night, Rhapta was much darker than the blinding lights of Chicago that she was used to. There were no neon lights, or electric billboards, or the constant stream of headlights in the middle of traffic. The only light came from the moon and the subtle glow that came off of the Aurastones. In this quarter of the city, many had fallen long ago or had been taken away. It made sense, why keep an abandoned section of the city lit when the stone was so precious? Either way, the dim light made her feel like she was truly on another planet.

She walked in the middle of the group, with Zaid next to her. Nazim had said it was to keep her safe in case of an ambush, but she knew better. It was to keep her in arm's reach, on the off chance that she was the person behind the attack. It would be easier to capture her this way.

Kinza snuck a glance at Zaid. He walked to her right, looking like a storm cloud, the ever-present scowl on his face. Even if the rest of Rhapta started to believe the lies the Unfettered were telling, she took a small bit of peace knowing that Zaid knew the truth. If it turned for the worse, he could help her get out of the city. If she was a bit more confident in her teleporting abilities, she might have felt a bit safer. Now was not the time to practice though. It would probably look bad if she suddenly disappeared on her way to a trial to defend her innocence. She sighed. How had it come to this?

They saw a light up ahead and the warriors that surrounded their group tensed. She didn't know their names or their abilities, but she trusted they knew when to be on guard.

"That is our destination, the central southern plaza. It looks like they built a fire. Steady now, it's most likely to announce their presence," Nazim said. The warriors relaxed marginally, but kept their spears and swords tight in their hands. "Kinza," Nazim said, turning to her. "I want you to keep quiet at first. I will speak with them first and see what they have to say. They may speak lies, but we must let them talk. Once they are done, you can defend yourself."

She nodded, anxiety bubbling in her stomach.

They came into a large open plaza. The central fountain had dried up and in its place was a roaring fire. A few men added wood, looking bored. Kinza counted ten men, as Nazim said there would be. A man standing in the middle turned and smiled at them. Even in the firelight, she could see how yellow his teeth were. She also noticed one hand was distorted, like the fingers had been broken but never healed right.

"Welcome," he said, stepping closer. Nazim's warriors pointed their spears forward in unison. "No need for that. I said we could talk and I meant it. See? My men do not, and will not, draw their weapons while we speak peacefully. I cannot speak for the rest of the evening though," he added.

Kinza looked around. To the right was a smaller man with disheveled hair. He lounged against one wall, tapping his foot. On the other side of the plaza was a tall woman with rather severe eyebrows and thin lips. The remaining men in the plaza looked like they could easily have been the homeless she so often saw in Chicago. Albeit, with large muscles and sheathed obsidian weapons.

"We will also keep our weapons to ourselves while we speak," Nazim said pointedly to his warriors. They reluctantly drew back. "We appreciate being able to speak in such tense times. Hopefully we can come to some sort of agreement."

The man lounging against the wall shot upright and made to protest, but the man in the middle hushed him. "You'll have to excuse Ojasvat, he doesn't know his place sometimes." He looked at the man while he spoke. Ojasvat swore under his breath and went back to the wall. Turning back to Nazim, the other man spoke, "My name is Zakariah, by the way. And I think you may have misunderstood. I do not speak on the behalf of all Unfettered, so we are not here to make any treaties, if that was what you were thinking. I was told you wanted to know why we have decided to do this and, given the circumstances, I see no issue with answering your questions."

Nazim's brow lowered at his words, but only jerked his

chin. "Very well then. Your men told some of ours the name of your leader, but we have a hard time believing it's sincerity."

Zakariah's eyes finally fell on Kinza with an air of betrayal. "Ah yes, you must be Kinza Solace. It's nice to finally meet you in person," he said, giving a mocking bow.

"What?" Kinza asked, taking a half step back and found Zaid held gently at her arm.

"This is the part where you stay quiet," he whispered to her.

"She has told us already, and we can see clearly now, that she has no knowledge of you," Nazim said. "How can you claim to know her? And if she is your leader, why do you reveal her? This sounds counterintuitive to your actions, trashing the city at her request."

Zakariah scowled now. "She promised us a way out of the city," he said flatly. "A way out without being ubir, and without the impermanence of venari. She has yet to uphold her end of the bargain, and we start to doubt her viability. The Unfettered are a lot of things, but we are not those who would go back on their word. We will still uphold our end of the bargain, even if she breaks hers. Besides," he said looking up and around at the dark city. "Maybe Rhaptans will finally understand they are just cattle and the Elders hold the whip. If their land is attacked, they will only save themselves, leaving the cattle to fend for themselves. Maybe during all of this, some will learn where they truly belong, and that we are only trying to free them."

"There is no bargain!" Kinza shouted. She could not help it, how dare he say such things? Zaid placed a firmer hand on her arm this time, as if willing her to be quiet.

Nazim just glanced in her direction and returned to Zakariah. "Well, this is your chance to explain yourselves. How did you come into contact with Kinza? And when?"

The woman on the other side of the plaza turned a scathing gaze toward Kinza, but Zakariah continued to speak for them. "We were contacted by Kinza Solace three and a half years ago. She spoke telepathically to one in our number, who is now dead, who was venari at the time. She—"

"Sorry to interrupt," Nazim said, clearly not at all apologetic. "But she spoke to you telepathically? In Rhaptan? From where? She is from across the ocean. No one can speak that far."

Zakariah huffed an irritated breath. "If you will let me speak....No, not in Rhaptan, in English. And yes, we had no idea how she was doing it, but yes, from across the ocean, she spoke to one of our men who was *venari* at the time."

Zaid's eyes narrowed at that.

"She told him that she wanted to help us and knew a way to leave the city, permanently, and without becoming ubir. In return, she needed our help. Something very simple, when she gave the word, we were to attack the city. There were some minor details as to when and where, but the request was simple."

"And you risked your lives on the basis of a stranger's promise?" Nazim asked.

This time Ojasvat spoke, "We would rather die free than live a long, healthy life in a cage."

Zakariah didn't reprimand him, only nodded in agreement.

Zaid snorted. "And how have you been doing that? You convince people to become ubir, to kill other people; humans."

Zakariah turned him a scornful expression. "Humans? You mean the humans that would capture, kill, and experiment on us the moment they realized we existed. Have you forgotten why the barrier hides the city in the first place? It is *our* fear of *them*. And you worry about the poor humans?" Zakariah stood. "There are *billions* of them, and they get to explore and roam the rest of the planet while we are stuck here, as our numbers dwindle. If a few humans need to die so our race can survive, then so be it."

"They are not the reason we cannot leave," Zaid shot back. A few of the warriors had become restless at Zakariah's words as well. "We have always been stuck here. Wishing for a way out doesn't make it a reality. It's best you all grew up and accepted that."

"That's enough," Nazim said. "Let us continue with the original line of questioning. What exactly did she say would allow Anunnaki to leave Rhapta safely?"

"She said that the key to leaving was our tattoos. You know how the *venari's* tattoos are temporarily larger? She said she could make it permanent; like hers." Kinza froze, how did he know her tattoo was larger? Zaid had gone rigid beside her as well. "And before you ask," Zakariah said drily, "our man said hers was on her abdomen. It was larger and looked like lace and some fancy beadwork."

Kinza's blood had started to go cold. How? How did he know what her tattoo looked like? The only living people who have seen it are Grams, her best friend Mitra, and Zaid. No one else knew where it was or what it looked like.

Nazim's eyebrows knit together at that. He turned toward her and she was already dreading what he was going to ask. She mentally begged him not to.

"Kinza," he said. "Will you please show us all your tattoo? You do have one, yes?"

She nodded reluctantly, but looked to Zaid. His expression had turned grim this time and she understood there was nothing he could do to help her. So, with no way out of this, she lifted her shirt, just high enough that she knew they could see the delicate tattoo that stretched, larger than any Anunnaki's, across the width of her upper abdomen.

Several of the people in the plaza gasped. Some of the Unfettered had taken a step closer to get a better look. A few of the warriors behind her started whispering telepathically, the noise sounding like static to her.

Kinza dropped her shirt and glared at Zakariah. "I have no idea how you know what my tattoo looks like, but I've *never* spoken to one of your people before."

"This does not prove that she was the one who contacted you, though," Nazim said. "You say only one of you ever spoke to her?"

Zakariah nodded, eyes still glued to the spot on her shirt where the tattoo would be. It seemed to reinvigorate him and he spoke a little louder, so all could hear. "Yes, she contacted one of our men, a *venari,* three and a half years ago. She told him to go to Chicago and meet with a middle man of sorts. I assume she had contacted the *venari* because he was the only one of us that could leave."

"And this man he met with?" Nazim asked, crossing his big arms.

"A man from a line of Ummanu, who no longer watched any portal and was no longer in contact with Rhapta. Our man met him the first time and the man gave him a message from Kinza that she wanted to meet. The message contained a time and a place. Our man returned a few days later, pretending to be out working on a mission for the Elders." He sneered at the last part. "He met Kinza at that time and she explained that she could make our tattoos larger and permanent, thus allowing us to leave. She showed him her tattoo and he described it to us. He brought the information back to us and we agreed to her request. The next time they met, she detailed *what* she wanted us to do, just not when. She said she was waiting for the right time and would let us know when it arrived.

Kinza's blood had gone from being as cold as ice, to boiling under her skin. Lies! These were all lies! Could not they all see that? How could this man say these things with such a straight face?

"And you didn't question *how* she knew how to do any of that?" Nazim asked.

"We did. Our man asked and she said the *why* and *how* was none of our business. So we had our man follow her for a few days. Found out she lived with her grandmother, who was Ummanu, and some of our other men did their own bit of research." He shrugged, "Sounded like some kind of revenge, something about dead parents."

Kinza's heart was pounding in rage and fear. How could they know these things? How could this *complete stranger* know that her parents were murdered? It sounded like he knew why as well. What was happening?

"Over the course of the next few years our man met with her infrequently, waiting for her call," Zakariah said. "It just took a lot longer than expected."

Nazim looked deep in thought, as if trying to piece the events together. "Where is this man? I would speak with him since you say he met with Kinza."

"Like I said before, he's dead."

"What was his name," Zaid said. "I know most of the *venari*."

"Unlikely, as he was away much of the time. But his name was Ghassan Laghari."

Kinza's mouth popped open. The image of a scraggly-haired ubir as he lurched toward her came to mind. There was no way. This was not happening.

Zaid had gone rigid all over again and ground out, "His ability. What was it?"

She held her breath, waiting for a response.

Zakariah turned to the woman and said, "It was....what, like a breeze?"

The woman nodded, "Ghassan could control the wind, but in gusts." She spoke loud enough for everyone to hear her.

Kinza sagged, trying to recount every single thing that had happened, in order, over the last week. Was she going crazy? Was this some long, weird, insane nightmare that just kept on going? She had killed Ghassan just a few days ago, causing him to fall off a roof as he tried to kill her in turn.

Beside her, Zaid was very still, looking as confused as she felt. He was staring at Zakariah and the others in turn, eyes narrowed.

"Anyway, Ghassan grew tired of waiting for her call," Zakariah said, nodding toward Kinza, "as many of us did. He felt like she was stringing us along, like dangling a carrot in front of a donkey. He made the choice to become ubir. We hadn't heard from him in a while after he changed. You know they become unreliable after that." He said it as if Ghassan was a neighbor who forgot to cut his grass for too long. Nothing to be concerned about, just mildly annoying.

Nazim sighed. "And the other man? The one Ghassan met with?"

"Oh, right!" Zakariah said, popping up. "I figured we would need him at some point, to at least tie up a few ends if you know what I mean," he winked. He turned to one of the men behind him. "Bring him," he said quieter.

The man walked toward the other end of the plaza and around the corner and a moment later shuffled back toward the light with a plump man in tow.

Kinza blinked. Now she was sure she had lost her damn mind.

It was Phil, the security guard.

ZAID LOOKED across the plaza at the man who looked vaguely familiar. It took him a moment to place him and when he did, his heart sank. He had seen the man before, twice when he was following Kinza prior to kidnapping her. He had followed her every movement for days, noting where she went and who she talked to, trying to confirm she was his target.

He had seen her talk with this man on her days she cleaned at one of the high rises in downtown Chicago. The man was the night security guard for the building and sometimes the two of them chatted for several minutes while she waited for the bus.

The other pieces of evidence were nothing individually, but adding them up together didn't look good. And *this*....now this person should have had no ties to Rhapta, yet here he was. The man's very presence made Zaid question everything he had seen over the last week. Kinza's powers, her anger and despair at being kidnapped, not knowing how to control her abilities, knowing nothing about Rhapta...was any of it real?

Kinza herself just stared, as if in shock. Was that real, too? Or a ruse?

"This is the middle man that Ghassan spoke with? The Ummanu?" Nazim asked, eyeing Kinza at the same time.

"My name is Phil, sir," the portly man muttered. He looked at Kinza apologetically and she just continued to stare back.

"Phil?" she finally said.

"Sorry, Kinz. They kidnapped me and one of them had a truth-telling ability they put on me. I could not keep a secret to save my life," Phil said. "I tried to lie for you though, I truly did. But I told you I didn't want any funny business and, well, here we are." Zaid thought he really did look sorry.

"You work for Kinza, then?" Nazim asked.

"Yes, sir," Phil replied.

"And how long have you known her?"

"Three and a half years, when she started working at that cleaning company that comes in my building sometimes."

"And when did she first contact you?"

"Soon after she started working there. She just chatted with me at first, but that changed later to her asking for favors. I was shocked when I found out she knew about you all as well and she didn't mention being Ummanu, but I didn't question it too much. My family fell out with you all when the Chicago portal closed twenty years ago." His face was honest, open.

"And why did you agree to these favors?"

Phil sighed. "I really didn't know what she was doing, honest to God. She just asked me to meet a *venari* a few times over the last few years and deliver messages. They were all coded so I didn't know what they said. She would pay me a good deal of money—all cash—for every message delivered. You see," Phil said, licking his lips, "my family never had a lot of money to begin with, and when the portal closed, it's like our luck dried up with it. I've got my daughters, I need the money. I want them to go to college, live a better life. You know?" Zaid listened to his heartbeat. You could tell a lot about whether someone was lying or not based on their heartbeat. But his could not have been steadier.

"And when was the last time you met with her?" Nazim asked.

Phil thought for a second, "About a week ago, at work. Just for a second, she told me to pass a message along to a new person, another *venari*. I hadn't seen the other one in a while."

Zaid had watched her talk to him a week ago. He had seen this conversation. Had he really been this blind as to what was going on?

Nazim sounded less confident by the minute. "And who was this *venari*?"

"I never got a name, sir, but had these yellow-orange eyes and for a second I could have sworn he had sharp teeth."

"That was Agu," Zakariah said. "And before you ask, he died the first night of the attack. I can show you his body if you'd like?"

"That won't be necessary," Nazim said. "All right, anything else? Anything else that can prove you got these orders from this girl," he said pointing to Kinza.

"Ghassan said he saw her teleport once. That's all we have, though."

"Teleport?" Nazim asked and turned toward Kinza; he must have caught Zaid's expression because he just nodded.

Zaid felt sick. They knew she could teleport. How did they know that? He had gone to check on Ghassan's body after he fell. He had been looking for Kinza's as well, but only Ghassan's was there, mangled and broken next to a copse of trees. He found Kinza had teleported safely into a bush a quarter mile away. Did the other ubir, Basma, see Kinza teleport? Had she somehow given the Unfettered that information? That didn't explain how they knew about her tattoo, or her grandmother, or why this man, Phil, said she had hired him.

Zaid let himself consider, just for a moment, that Kinza *had* known about the Anunnaki all along. Growing up, being the only Anunnaki outsider would feel rather lonely. And then having her parents killed by the Anunnaki as well, because they were trying to kill *her*.

He could see where a deep bitterness could take root. Something strong and twisted enough that revenge would be the only way out. But she had saved his life, more than once. Why would she do that if she wanted the Anunnaki dead?

Nazim looked to Kinza. "You are allowed to defend yourself, of course. You may speak if you wish." He appeared skeptical that she could produce anything of worth.

Kinza seemed to finally come out of her shock. She had just stared at Phil, as if trying to reconcile that he was truly there. Zaid's mind warred and tried to find the truth. Was she truly confused, or was this the face of someone who had been caught?

"I never did any of those things!" she lashed out. Nazim closed his eyes and Zakariah's mouth curled up at the outburst. Kinza turned to Nazim and grabbed his arm. "Phil is the security guard at one of the buildings I clean. Of course I see him all the time, but I never knew he was Ummanu! We just talk about—about the *weather!* And his kids, and school. That's all."

She was breathing hard and a few of the Unfettered turned away, as if there was nothing she could say.

"And Ghassan," she spun around to look at Zaid. He could not even look her in the eye. Did she truly deceive him? "Ghassan was one of the ubir that attacked Zaid's friend Haris, so we *helped* him." Her eyes pleaded with him.

"And where is Ghassan now? Is he truly alive and we can speak with him?" Nazim asked.

Kinza looked around helplessly. "Well, no...I...I killed him," she finally said. "But it was only because he was trying to kill me by pushing me off a roof!"

Several of the warriors took a step back, muttering and shaking their heads. Zaid realized that someone was missing. Rayaan was nowhere to be found. Had he gone back to the hideout?

Oh no... Zaid thought. If word got out that Kinza was leading the Unfettered there would be chaos. Was she leading them? He didn't know.

Nazim didn't respond right away, taking a moment to

think. "All right," he said gravely. He looked to his warriors and with an unspoken command, they grabbed her and tied her wrists with *laqueus*—rope that binds Anunnaki abilities. He knew they would have had some with them but didn't expect it to come to this.

Kinza shouted, but they had her tied before she got a chance to react. Zaid moved toward her on instinct, but one of the warriors shoved him back. What was he doing? Should he even be helping her?

Two of them held her between them, not hurting her though. She started saying his name and he hated himself. Either he was letting her down by not backing her up, or he was stupid enough to have believed her lies. Regardless, he had failed. Her or Rhapta, he didn't know which yet.

Nazim turned back to the Unfettered. "I know it is futile, but I ask that you cease this. Cease killing your own people, your own *home*."

Zaid had been too absorbed in his own thoughts to notice that massive group of heartbeats moving through the city like a school of fish toward them. They had gotten close enough that he and the others could hear the shouts and cries of the angry mob as they rushed through the plazas. Firelight danced on the tops of the buildings, and he caught a glimpse of weapons glinting in the moonlight a few streets down. They had caught sight of Kinza bound in the clutches of Nazim's warriors and started sprinting toward them.

Zakariah stood and backed up, the other Unfettered following. "If you knew the question was futile, then why did you ask?" he said with a wink. The group of them took off in the opposite direction, dragging poor Phil along behind. He would be dead before the night was out.

"Sir?" one of the warriors said, looking at the screaming mob of people headed toward them. "What are our orders?" He shifted on his feet and took a step back. The mob was clearly here for Kinza's head, but anyone could get hurt.

Nazim looked sadly at the mob and back at Kinza. She shook her head silently, tears running down her face. "I'm sorry, Kinza." The warriors nodded and stood their ground as the mob approached. They would not run.

Zaid looked back and forth between Kinza and the mob and made a decision.

CHAPTER 7
NO ALLIES

Was this it then? Were they really going to let her be killed by a mob of angry Anunnaki? Somehow the thought didn't hurt nearly as bad as Zaid's silence.

Kinza wept, not knowing what else to do. She had tried fighting back but it was useless. Nazim didn't truly know her and had nothing to go on. The tingling on her neck and the heat in her abdomen had risen the more Zakariah—and Phil—had talked. She was pretty sure at some point she started to feel like she was standing outside her own body. How could this be real? It had to be a dream. In a matter of days she had been kidnapped, found out she had magic powers and that her parents were murdered by assassins trying to kill *her*, and now she's been found guilty of starting a war with a race of people she hadn't even known existed.

That definitely sounded like a psychotic break. In reality, she was probably lying in bed, back home, having a nightmare, and her mind had come up with all of these wild explanations for the problems in her life. It just all felt so real. The emotions, the pain, the betrayal, the frustration and no one believing her. Maybe if she had had just one person to back her up, Grams or Mitra. The thought almost made her laugh. Mitra would have gone headfirst into battle with a suit of armor and a horse for her.

And now the nightmare was going to end. Everyone knew you woke up right before you died in a dream. She just wished it didn't have to be so brutal. Was this really how their laws worked? There was no judge, jury, or attorney, just a group of people claiming she did something that she didn't. And now the executioner was coming at her like a raging bull and she was the color red.

The moment Nazim's men put the *laqueus* on, the tingling in her neck and the heat in her abdomen vanished. The only thing that remained was the whispers in her head that were slowly turning to the screams of the ascending mob. In the back of her mind she noticed that the feel of the silvery-gold rope didn't hurt her like it did last time. But that wasn't important now, she'd wake up soon and have to get ready for class. She remembered she never finished her homework. Damn, she would need to do it in the morning.

Two of the warriors held her on both sides in an iron grip. Despite knowing she would wake up soon, she could not stop her crying and she hated herself for it. It was just a stupid nightmare, she shouldn't be so frightened. Hopefully this wasn't one of those nightmares where she would actually have to experience her death. If she did, she hoped it would be quick.

Suddenly, both of the warriors were yanked to the side and she heard Nazim shout. A half second later something hit her hard enough to knock the breath out of her and threw her into the air, but then she was moving.

Fast.

She tried twisting around to see what had happened, but the shadows of Rhapta's buildings moved by in a blur. Looking down she realized why. Zaid had thrown her, still bound, over his shoulder and was running away. She knew he was fast, but this was mind-boggling. He got to move this fast all the time? A race car would have had difficulty keeping up and he was carrying her. She tried to imagine how fast he got without any additional weight.

At first it looked like he went straight out the other side of the plaza and had kept going, but after a few seconds she felt, rather than saw, him make a complete turn and head back the other way. The sounds of the mob quickly faded. Were they on the other side of the city already? It had only been seconds but they must have gone a distance that would have taken her hours.

Prior to turning around, he had gotten far enough that she saw more lights and possibly a few Aurastone; closer to the center of the city. He headed back into the abandoned areas quickly after that. She wasn't sure, but it looked like he was taking a different route. Maybe to keep them off his trail? She could not imagine anyone seeing him, let alone following him.

He ran for almost a minute with her over his shoulder, heading deeper into darkened streets before they heard a single shout. She could not make it out, but Zaid must have because he immediately turned around and ran a few seconds back and stopped. He deposited her on her feet with a thump that had her wobbling. The sudden change from moving at inhuman speeds to a standstill had her wanting to vomit.

"What happened?" It was Khalil's voice and Kinza turned to see the man walking up to them with worried eyes. He glanced at Kinza's bonds and he nodded in understanding. He must have seen the mob leaving the building and came looking for them. How he had known which direction they would go she could not guess at.

Zaid finally turned to look at her. His expression was unreadable, but he took out one of his obsidian daggers and sliced the bonds and threw them into a nearby alley. His reaction should have made her relieved, but it only made her feel cold. He had looked at her like she was a stranger. Which, to be fair, she almost was. They had only met a few days ago, but so much had happened between them.

Looking away from her, he just said, "let's go," and started running at a pace they could match. Kinza didn't say anything and neither did Khalil. The three of them ran through the streets, avoiding the sounds of people. She could not tell where they were going, but she thought she could see the city wall looming closer the further they got. They were well into one of the abandoned areas of Rhapta. She occasionally had to hop large vines and tree roots that stretched across broken boulevards and between buildings. No Aurastones lit the way, only the light of the moon high above them.

Kinza's lungs burned, but not as much as she would have expected. She kept up easily with Zaid and Khalil, even if Zaid was putting on a much slower pace. How could she be so tired and have so much energy at the same time? Physically she could keep going, but mentally she wanted to pass out.

Finally, she was sure they were at the edge of the city because the wall came into view, but it looked distorted to her in the darkness. The wall near where they had entered the city was probably four times her height, but this section barely made it ten feet. Far to their right, she could somewhat make out a watchtower set into a corner of the wall with a large Aurastone sitting at the top casting a faint glow. She could see a bit of movement across the watchtower and guessed there were guards on duty. But who were they? Unfettered? She wondered if they had started patrolling the perimeter so people could not leave, like birds in a cage.

Zaid and Khalil slowed as they reached the wall and Kinza realized why it looked off to her. It wasn't like the rest of the city's wall; this portion, stretching from the watchtower far to her right and as far as she could make out to her left, was just a large wooden fence.

"You think they won't look here?" Khalil whispered. He was breathing heavily, hands on his knees.

"Not sure where else to go," Zaid said, feeling along the boards until he found one that satisfied him. He tested it a bit with a slight tug, and then with a quick glance at the watch-tower he ripped the board away with a yank. The sound made Kinza wince, but Zaid was ushering them through and gently set the board back in the empty spot where he came through as well.

Kinza looked around and was thankful for the moonlight otherwise she would have probably fallen to her death. The section of fence made much more sense now. Before her sat a massive quarry that descended like an inversely-stacked pyramid into the earth. It was hard to gauge it's exact size in the darkness, but she could not see the other side from where she was and it felt like she was standing on the edge of a cliff. They stood above the topmost level looking down. Was this where all the Aurastone came from? Haris had said the only minable deposit on Earth was here.

Zaid started making his way down a path she hadn't noticed a moment before. It looked like it wound down through the levels of open earth and stone. The two men kept to the sides of each section as they descended, with the occa-sional glance toward the watchtower. Kinza tripped over axes and rope and stray boards as they crept along as quietly as possible. She didn't see any Aurastone, but she assumed if she had they would have already dug it up. They passed a few lean-to shacks that had been set up along the winding paths, but Zaid just shook his head and motioned forward; deeper down into the pit.

They had gotten low enough that only the very top of the watchtower was in view when Zaid entered into one of the small shacks. It was nestled into the side of the path, not far from the edge of this level and faced away from the watch-tower and into the lower recesses of the quarry. There was no door and one chair in the corner next to a pile of tools. Zaid sat in the back corner and Khalil sat near the open doorway, she assumed to keep watch. Kinza leaned back against one of the walls and slid to the floor.

She found she could not say anything at first. The only thing she could do was stare at the wall across from her. So she hadn't died; yet. The run had done her some good. Well, it pulled her out of the weird state she had been in. It felt as if she had been splashed with cold water to wash away the shock she was in from the near death experience. This wasn't a dream or a nightmare. Everything was real and those people really did want her dead.

She thought of the absurdity of the situation. Phil—*Phil!*—was here and had said all of those lies about her. They were definitely lies. It was true she knew Phil somewhat, he rambled on and on every time she, Mitra, and Karin left after work. Had someone bribed him to say those things? She would only slightly blame him if that were the case. His story about needing money for his daughters was true. But how did the Unfettered get him? They had to still have a *venari* in their ranks. Even so, what Ummanu would let them bring a human through the portals? He clearly was not ubir. There were just as many questions and no one seemed to be on her side.

Even if no one else believed her, she knew the truth. She

wasn't mad, she was just being framed. But why? Her moment of clarity had her remembering how Zaid just stood there as Zakariah talked, and how he would not look at her when she pleaded with him. After everything, he really didn't believe her? He just stood there and didn't say a single thing in her defense. Anger seeped into her core and she shoved it down, trying not to react. He must have had a reason for not saying anything. Maybe he was pretending to be on their side so they could get away.

She had a hard time convincing herself.

The silence stretched for several minutes before Khalil spoke. "I take it that it didn't go well?" He sat in the doorway, looking outside as he spoke.

Zaid didn't respond and Kinza's anger bubbled up again. "Why didn't you say anything?" she asked, looking at him in the corner, eyes closed like nothing in the world was wrong and he just needed a little nap. "Why didn't you defend me? You *know* those were lies."

Zaid just stayed where he was, eyes closed and unresponsive. Kinza found hot, angry tears welling back up in her eyes. She felt drained and exhausted and abandoned. So that was it then? He really thought she was guilty? After all that?

"What happened?" Khalil asked, calmly.

Zaid still didn't bother saying anything and it took Kinza several breaths to be able to speak. The moment she started to recount what happened with the Unfettered, she was a sputtering, crying mess again. She had to backtrack several times to explain what *really* happened and ended with telling him how Zaid didn't do a single thing to help her until he grabbed her and ran. Which she still didn't understand. If he thought she was a mass murderer, why save her?

When she was done speaking, she was calmer again, only glaring in Zaid's direction as she sniffled. She was sick of crying, but her tears seemed to come from an endless well. Khalil didn't respond right away, the three of them just sat in the dark while Khalil looked out at the moonlight that lay on the quarry. They listened for the sounds of people, but Kinza could not hear anything at all. The forest surrounding the city had to be on the other side of the quarry, but she didn't know how far away that was.

Kinza thought about what to do next. If no one was on her side then she needed to leave. Could she make it out of the city and back to the edge of the barrier? And then through the forests surrounding Mount Kilimanjaro and then all the way back to America with no money, no passport, and a race of supernatural beings on her tail?

Probably not.

She sighed, allowing herself to wallow in her own misery. Grams would tell her it's okay to just be miserable sometimes, as long as you pulled yourself out of it sooner rather than later. She was good at the first part, the second was harder.

"I remember there being much more Aurastone the last time I was here," Khalil mumbled to himself.

Ekaja had said there were people on her side, but where would she find them? Would they even believe her anymore? Surely the knowledge that she was found guilty by Nazim would spread throughout Rhapta, especially if the Unfettered continued to spread their lies. And now she basically ran when the mob was coming after her. Even she would think she was guilty if she was anyone else.

"Why is there so much Aurastone missing?" Khalil said, sitting up a bit.

Kinza decided she was back to square one. She had to assume she had no one on her side, well, other than the fact Khalil and Zaid haven't turned her in or killed her. Maybe Zaid wanted to give her over to the Elders for a proper trial. He had said that Nazim was only a retired warrior trainer, so the meeting with the Unfettered wasn't exactly legal, was it? Taking her to the Elders was what Zaid had been planning since day one, so it seemed only logical that he would stick with that, even if that just meant she would be executed later instead of sooner. She scowled again at his dark form in the corner.

"Hello? Have I lost my verbal speech as well? Zaid, there is a lot of Aurastone missing," Khalil said louder this time. Too loud.

Zaid finally opened his eyes to glare in Khalil's direction. "What do you want me to do about it?"

Khalil stood up to get a better look outside. "I'm just thinking, the last time I was here there was a ton of Aurastone, huge slabs of it everywhere. And now—I mean I can't see that well —it looks like a ton of it is missing."

Zaid closed his eyes again. "Okay, you go be the Aurastone police and I'll keep watch."

Khalil turned and settled back inside, giving Zaid a droll look. "I just mean that it has to be somewhere. While the two of you were off with Nazim, I spoke with several people in the hideout. It sounds like at least *half* of the population is missing. That's too many to have just wandered out in the human areas without us knowing about it, and there are not enough dead here. So, logically, they would need to be *somewhere*."

Zaid sighed, keeping his eyes closed. "And?"

"Well maybe the missing Aurastone is connected to the missing people and...well...I don't know. At least I'm trying."

"And what are we going to do with that information?" Zaid asked.

"I propose we find them."

"How do you *propose* we do that, oh wise one?"

"I don't know!" Khalil snapped back. Kinza hadn't seen

him raise his voice, or react with anything more than the occasional quiet bitterness.

Zaid sighed again, sitting up more. "Okay, well, what do we do now? Half the city is missing and there are still....things that we don't know." His eyes flickered in Kinza's direction.

She snorted. "Oh, so you're *not* entirely sure I'm a mass-murderer? I'm assuming you want to find the bloody knife first before you're one hundred percent convinced. So by-the-book," she said, crossing her arms.

Zaid started a retort back, but Khalil cut in, "Both of you shut up! It's giving me a headache."

Both Kinza and Zaid sat back in their respective corners and the room settled back into silence. It must have been in the middle of the night because Kinza's eyelids started to droop. It could have been that, or the umpteenth near-death experience she had.

"I think we should find the Apostles of Truth," Khalil said, quieter.

Zaid turned him a scathing glare.

"I know what you are thinking," Khalil said, "but they supposedly have knowledge the rest of us don't."

"According to who? Them?" Zaid asked. "Khalil, you know what they are like. They are just like the Unfettered, luring people in with promises, but those people always end up turning to the blood rite. They just use promises of knowledge instead of freedom."

"Do you have a better idea?"

Zaid was silent and then bitterly he said, "No."

Khalil settled back against the doorjamb. "Then tomorrow we can work on finding them."

Zaid didn't bother answering, just closed his eyes again and went to sleep. Kinza found that regardless of how tired she was, sleep would not come. At least there was some sort of plan set, but it did little to soothe her. She closed her eyes and tried as hard as she could to fall asleep, but thoughts and questions just kept tumbling around in her head.

"How exactly does the blood rite work?"

Zaid wanted to groan in frustration. She could not be quiet for more than ten minutes. He refused to answer her, but to his irritation, Khalil did.

"Hmm," Khalil said, thinking. "I don't remember exactly who the first person was to do it—this was a long time ago—but the rite itself is rather straightforward once the first person figured it out." He was quiet for a second. "Why? Are you thinking of going rogue on us?"

Kinza snorted. "No, I've just heard people talk about it and I'm just curious. I know it's some sort of blood sacrifice thing, but is it magic or something?"

Khalil chuckled. "One could say that our entire race is magic, but no, I'm sure there is science in it somewhere that we just haven't entirely figured out yet." He took a breath. "Basically, when an Anunnaki wants to become ubir, they just have to kill someone and smear their blood over their tattoo. I'm pretty sure the person they kill has to be innocent but we can't be sure. The first time they do it, they can leave the city and I'm sure everything seems wonderful to them. They don't forget Rhapta and they don't become human. They are just themselves. But it only lasts a short amount of time, I'm not exactly sure how much, and they need to kill again. You see, that's the kicker. Just like the *venari's* tattoos, the blood rite only lasts a short amount of time before they need more blood.

"This cycle continues, and the more they kill, the more

infected the tattoo becomes and the more mad the ubir is. It sort of—what's the human phrase—snowballs? The madness just keeps getting worse until they are like addicts, killing even before they need to."

The image of Amir, Zaid's brother, came to mind. It twisted his gut to see his brother's face, smiling as a sense of calmness used to wash over him whenever he was around. Then later on, after Amir had become ubir, and the maniacal glint in his eyes. Zaid had known that Amir must have killed several people before he got that far. Who were those people? Elderly, children, loved ones? *Venari* never looked into the deaths other than to track the ubir. There wasn't any point since it would only attract attention to the Anunnaki and that was what they were trying to avoid. But Zaid did always wonder what happened to them and who they had been.

"Can they ever get better? Like addicts can?" Kinza asked.

"It's rare. This is just a theory, but I believe that the Anunnaki healing that we all have tries to heal the tattoo like any other wound, but the worse it is infected, the harder it is to heal. It follows basic medicinal logic. And keep in mind, a lot of the people who decide to do the blood rite are those who live harder lives on the outskirts and generally had stunted healing abilities to begin with. It just makes it that much harder to come back from becoming ubir. It's really only happened a couple times, ever." Zaid heard Khalil shift around on the dirt floor. He was also trying to listen for heartbeats as far out as he could. He had felt a few come close to the edge of the quarry a few minutes ago, but they faded back again. Otherwise the only other people close were the two guards on the watchtower.

"What happens to the people who recover?" Kinza asked. She had stopped crying. Regardless of what he thought of her, the sound of her crying made his chest ache. He hated himself for it. It was very likely he was sitting next to Rhapta's biggest enemy in a thousand years and he was worried that she was crying? He focused on shoving those thoughts down into that dark place in his mind where he kept similar unsavory items.

"If they do, they are never the same," Khalil said. "They still committed heinous crimes so they are usually imprisoned anyway and to make sure they won't 'relapse.' But generally they are weekended for the rest of their lives and tend to die early. Personally, I think death is much more forgiving."

It was quiet for a minute before Kinza spoke again. "Why would putting the blood of a murdered person on our tattoos affect them? Isn't it just ink?"

Zaid heard a rustle and assumed Khalil just shrugged. "I don't know, Kinza," he said quietly.

It stayed quiet after that and Zaid fell into a deep, dark slumber where even nightmares could not reach him.

CHAPTER 8

PLAYERS IN MOTION

Mikah sat to one side of the stifling tent, as close as possible to the doorway as was socially acceptable. In a circle sat the eleven Elders—minus Hakim—that had escaped the attack, with an additional five apprentices around the edges of the room. Oh, and plus the guards. Mikah wondered which perverse man's idea it was to hold a meeting inside an unventilated tent, with seventeen people, at high noon.

He kept his composure though, no one would ever know how sweat made the back of his legs stick to the chair. Honestly, he was lucky he even got one, a few of the other apprentices were forced to sit on the floor. Council meetings in Rhapta were held in a large, aired auditorium. This was only a fraction of the fifty Elders on the council and their apprentices, but it was quite a step down. He supposed it only reflected their current situation. Like a whipped dog running away, tail between its legs.

The Elders had known about the Unfettered for years, but their numbers were always hard to estimate. The organization was chaotic and had little in terms of organization. The sheer amount of people with black bands that had run through the city, burning it down, had been astounding. Mikah had caught a glimpse from a window before he fled, the image stuck in his mind forever. The Elders had all clearly underestimated the reach the Unfettered had on the people if so many had joined their ranks. In truth, they were probably as much a threat to Rhapta as the ubir were.

Quiet! Elder Minesh called, representative of city planning and roadways. He was a middle-aged man who was only content when he was the center of attention. Mikah was pretty sure it was the only reason the other Elders let him take the lead on this meeting, otherwise he would have been hissing and moaning the entire time.

After Tahir's revelations, the camp had become riotous with anger lasting for hours. It wasn't until someone pointed out that they could not leave yet that people started to calm down and demanded next steps from the Elders. They were sick and tired of sitting around while a literal prophecy was upon them and an outsider was destroying their city.

Hence the meeting.

I am calling this meeting to order! Minesh said, attempting to raise his voice above the others. Unfortunately, broadcasting his telepathic voice was difficult for him and did little to quiet the bickering Elders. Even in Mikah's mind, Minesh's voice sounded nasally and weak.

Minesh's outspoken young apprentice stood from his seat behind him and bellowed, "QUIET!" Kiaan, unfortunately, had a similar disposition to his mentor when it came to being the center of attention. He did, however, have a louder voice. Kiaan came from the outskirts, and while he could hear telepathically, he had a hard time speaking and tended to do so verbally.

It was unusual for people in high positions, such as the

Elders, to take on apprentices from such low birth like those in the outskirts. It was generally due to the lack of string abilities, but there were exceptions. Mikah remembered seeing Kiaan turn a palm-sized stone to mud. He supposed that would be relatively useful for someone whose job dealt with the construction and repair of roads, assuming he could do it on a larger scale.

The noise startled several members in the room and it quickly quieted and the Elders took their seats. Mikah always thought they were like a flock of birds flapping in their white robes, vying to be the loudest until a chimpanzee came in and shut them up.

Have Yuvaan prepare what warriors we have and we can be done with the meeting. The statement came from Elder Sumai, representative of the south quarter. A tall man with a deep voice, he had as little interest in politicking as he did in thinking. Obviously they needed to talk about the what, when, and how, but Sumai hadn't thought that far. It was probably best he had the job he did, overseeing the abandoned south quarter. There wasn't much to do now that no one lived there.

Come now, Sumai. Let us talk this through, Tahir said from his seat in front of Mikah. They hardly had time to speak since the announcement and Mikah was still a bit put off from being out of his confidence, if even for a moment.

This chaos is your fault, Tahir, Elder Urash said. *If Hakim had another vision, and one of so much importance, you should have at least delivered it in a less excitable manner, let alone have spoken to us first.* Mikah was inclined to agree, but said nothing. Urash was the representative of the healers and tended to be more analytical than his counterparts. Mikah did appreciate that he was always the cleanest as well. He probably should have sat next to him because this side of the tent smelled of unwashed bodies.

Many of the Elders nodded along with Urash.

I am deeply sorry for not consulting you first, Tahir said, looking around, *but I thought the people needed to know right away. I have had several people come to both me and my apprentice asking for news.* Several eyes slid to Mikah who lounged in the back. He nodded sagely, but he questioned Tahir's answer. Tahir was the one who said to make himself known to the people, so of course they would come and ask questions. And why could it not wait? Even an hour would not have made a difference.

Mikah could not help but to remember the conversation he had with the prisoner in Tahir's storage tent. Hunar. Despite all the reasonable questions he had proposed, Mikah still could not bring himself to believe the man sitting in front of him was to blame for all of this. He had studied under Tahir for years now and would have known if he was planning something as nefarious as this.

He spent his days following the Elder around, sitting in on meetings, running his political errands, and sometimes his personal ones. Other than the past few days, Tahir rarely left the Grand Hall. All Elders lived and held office inside the massive structure in the Central Plaza, only leaving if they absolutely had to. In Tahir's case, the only time Mikah had seen him leave was to check in on the quarries, which he did monthly. Otherwise the Elder kept to the Grand Hall with the others. Did Hunar truly believe Tahir orchestrated *all this* from inside the Hall? It was laughable.

How do we even know if this is true? Elder Qirin piped in. He was by far the most scatterbrained of all the Elders there. White tufts of hair stuck out at odd angles around his head. It was remarkable he was able to manage the complex waterways and cisterns that ran throughout all of Rhapta. Qirin continued, *I mean, I know Tahir's men saw someone with destruc-*

tive abilities. But how do we know it was actually the prophecy? It could've been anyone.

Mikah saw Sumai roll his eyes, but Elder Harran was the one who responded. *It's irrelevant who this person is. What we know is that someone attacked and we need to do something about it.* He represented the north quarter and was a firm believer that the prophecies were nothing more than hogwash. He did make a fair point though. Arguing about whether the enemy was the one in the prophecy or not didn't really matter. It *may* indicate that a person has a greater set of abilities than the next person, but an enemy is still an enemy.

Hakim's visions are important, Ekbal chimed in. Mikah had never cared for him. Maybe it was because Ekbal never cared for him either. *While I do not approve of Tahir announcing these visions without consulting us first, I do think they hold information that we might be able to use in regaining the city. And Hakim's visions have never been wrong.*

Where is Hakim anyway? Are we able to talk with him directly? The voice came from Qirin's apprentice, Urbarra. Mikah internally cringed at her lack of restraint, and the irritated looks of the Elders only matched his feeling. The meetings were for Elders and the apprentices were only to speak if they were questioned directly. Were all of the other apprentices this incompetent?

In his years under Tahir, Mikah had met a few other apprentices here and there, some came and went. It wasn't unusual for an apprentice to learn under a mentor for a few years, only to find it wasn't a good fit for them. The rare few that stuck around were the ones who would end up taking their mentor's place—whenever that happened. It wasn't unheard of for Anunnaki to live up to two hundred years. He could not remember exactly, but he was sure Hakim had passed that mark recently, too. Changes in position and authority didn't happen often in Rhapta.

Qirin, keep your apprentice in her place, Minesh said. *But, yes, where is Hakim? Is he any better?* he said, looking to Ekbal.

My uncle spends more time within his visions than he does in lucidity anymore, Ekbal said. *I fear that speaking with him directly and gleaning specific information has passed us. We can only take what visions he speaks. I fear that his time with us is slowly running out.*

The room was quiet for a moment. *And what of Hakim's apprentice? Is she ready to replace him?* a voice asked. It was calm, clear, and precise, having come from Elder Balasi. The Elder was a quiet, but watchful man, rarely speaking unless it was necessary. Tahir had told Mikah on several occasions that it would be best to keep Elder Balasi in their good graces. He held a position very different from the other Elders, representing their relationship with humanity.

Rhapta's involvement with the humans was nothing like it used to be, but its citizens knew that we had *some* influence over them; they just didn't know how. Balasi knew about every human culture, country, current politics, trends, movements, wars, etc. While Hakim had still been coherent, they had worked together to guide humanity as best they could, keeping the details from the rest of Rhapta. No one truly cared that Rhapta's involvement in humanity was shrouded in secrecy, it's not like the two peoples ever connected, but Rhaptans knew the power Balasi held in such a position.

Ekbal didn't immediately respond to Balasi, instead turning to look behind him. Mikah just noticed one of the apprentices sitting cross-legged on the floor with her eyes closed. He had seen her once or twice, but didn't know her name, only that she was Hakim's apprentice. She was tiny, with big eyes and delicate features. She reminded Mikah of the sprites and fairies in the stories his mother used to tell him when he was young.

Eta? Ekbal said. *You may speak.*

The young woman, Eta, opened her eyes but kept them downcast, as if shy. Her voice, however, was quiet, but strong. *I have trained under Hakim for a few years now. I have many visions and have learned from Hakim how to decipher them, but....they are not as strong as his own. I fear that I will not be having any on such a grand scale anytime soon.* She didn't look up and rested her hands on her knees.

Qirin sighed, *Well, what do we do now?*

We can't let them have the city, Sumai said.

I can talk with Commander Kartik and see the status of the warriors we have, spoke Elder Yuvaan. Mikah was surprised he hadn't managed to open his trap this entire time. He usually had an opinion—or seven—that he wanted to announce.

If the prophecy is true then we need to prepare for a counterattack, Urash said.

His own apprentice, Riku, started to protest, but Urash shushed him. Mikah had met Riku on a few occasions. He found the younger man to be rather hot headed for a healer, if overly dedicated to his work.

The other Elders looked grim but nodded. Mikah noticed Tahir hardly spoke up and let the other Elders squabble. Knowing him, it was probably a tactic to make him seem less rash. But what he had done earlier *was* rash, wasn't it? The way he announced Hakim's vision, it was like he wanted the people angry. What purpose did a crowd of enraged Rhaptans serve?

Do we know how many people are left in the city? How many alive and how many dead? Are some of our warriors still there? Hakim's vision said this woman, Kinza Solace, is there, but is she with anyone? These questions came from Elder Utu. He was almost as old as Hakim was, with twice as many wrinkles as any man in this room. Mikah remembered meeting him when he was a child. Utu oversaw all childhood educational services within the city. Every subject, every teacher, all the funding, it went through him. It was only natural he had so many questions.

Tahir finally spoke again. *My man that just got back said he saw quite a few people, but he didn't get a headcount, nor did he keep an eye on Kinza Solace.*

That was a lie. Mikah looked sharply at Tahir. Just a few hours ago Mikah had walked in on Tahir and that man was talking again in his tent. Years in politics had sharpened Mikah's ears to listen for details and he knew without a doubt they had been talking about the numbers that remained in the city and had mentioned the woman's whereabouts. Why lie?

He shook his head, trying to clear the confusion. Damn that Hunar for putting necrotic thoughts in his head. It was too bad that Mikah could not remove his own thoughts. How convenient that would be to remove the useless information.

What if we sent someone back in, a larger group this time, to get a head count and spread the word so when we are ready for a counterattack, our people are ready as well? In the meantime, we can have Commander Kartik prepare our warriors for what they do best, Harran said.

Trying to do my job for me again, are we Harran? came the sour reply from Yuvaan.

Well, if you won't—" Harran started to reply but was cut off by another Elder. And so began the squabbling for another five minutes. Mikah rubbed at his temples, the heat giving him a headache. What would not he do for a cool breeze right now?

Tahir spoke up again, a little louder, *I am happy to send my apprentice, Mikah, with a unit of Kartik's soldiers to start?*

Mikah perked up at that. He would get to go back? Oh, thank the Creator, he was so awfully bored here. Not that this wasn't a trying time for them all, but he was so used to the lively activity of the Central Plaza and people he could talk to and errands for him to run. He was pretty sure he had walked the circumference of the camp twenty times in the last few days.

A few of the Elders nodded, digesting the idea. *I could see if Kartik could spare a team,* Yuvaan said, surprisingly helpful.

That's not a terrible idea, Utu said. *We could let the people know to prepare for our return within a week and to fortify what buildings they can. Once we get a count of where the Unfettered are we can make the final plans.*

That sounds wise, Utu, Tahir replied. *But I would make one minor adjustment. We should prepare them for an attack tomorrow.*

The room erupted in outrage again at the aggressive time-line. They could not have their warriors ready by then, there would be no time for planning. They know basically nothing, they can't be ready by tomorrow. The conversation turned to the timeline needed for these events to happen.

Mikah closed his eyes and waited it out. Tahir, logically, brought up that the camp is only temporary and won't hold forever. The longer they stay here the more dangerous it is, all the while, the enemy is ransacking the city. Something about the weakening psionic barrier, blah, blah, blah. Mikah's head was pounding. Maybe he would find some more of that *guakal* wine when this was over.

Qirin brought up all of the bad scenarios he could think of if they attacked too soon or too early. Urash recounted the number of healers he had in camp and noted it would not be nearly enough in an attack. Harran and Yuvaan were at each other's throats again, and the apprentices Urbarra and Kiaan ended up in a rather unsavory shouting match. In fact, the only people other than himself who remained quiet and let the chickens squawk were Tahir, Balasi, and the apprentice Eta.

Mikah thought about Hakim for a moment. What *would* happen when he died? So much of Rhapta's decisions were based on the old man's knowledge and foresight into the future. In fact, Hakim had been around long enough that he was a young boy when the last Rhaptan king was still on the throne. Who would fill that space when he was gone?

He glanced over at the woman on the floor again, Eta. Just as before she sat still, eyes closed and hands on her knees. As if the leaders of their civilization weren't hooting like a gang of baboons. She had said her visions were nothing compared to Hakim's, but did that mean they would always be that way? As far as he knew, no one else in the city had been presented with a similar ability, so she would naturally have to take Hakim's place, regardless of what kind of power that did or didn't give her.

Tahir had taught him to befriend those in power whether or not you liked them. It was better to have someone you disliked on your side than to have another enemy to deal with. Maybe Mikah should start building that bridge. You never knew when you would need one.

Enough! Minesh shouted as best he could. *That's it then. We have at least some kind of plan. Tahir's apprentice will go tonight with a team of Kartik's men. They will attempt to locate Kinza Solace, get a head count on the Unfettered, and prepare what citizens they can for an impending attack—whenever that may be.*

The Elders were silent now, some in agreement and some wanting to reevaluate, but regardless, they all nodded in unison and that was that. They weren't going to get any closer to a unified agreement without more concrete knowledge of what was going on inside the city. Without another word they all filed from the tent.

Mikah braved the heat just a moment longer to linger at the back of the exiting group, sidling his way up to Eta. She had stood quietly and waited patiently for the old men to leave. As Mikah walked up, he actually had to look down to talk to her, she was at least a whole head shorter than him.

It's Eta, right? I'm Mikah Sultan, he said, giving a slight bow and then extending a hand. *I wanted to formally introduce myself since it seems we are most likely going to be working together in the future and I would love to get some sort of working relationship going now.* He waited for her to shake his hand, but instead she looked at him like a dung beetle had got up on its hind legs and started speaking. She left the room without a single word.

He dropped his hand. *Or not.*

CHAPTER 9

FRIEND OR FOE

Kinza woke to bright sunlight and a kink in her neck. She groaned as she sat up. Zaid and Khalil were already up and talking and she tried to stretch out her stiff muscles. It took a moment, but the events from the night before hit her and she stifled a scream. She had hoped she would wake from this nightmare, but it looked like she wasn't going anywhere anytime soon.

"It's on the other side of the city, Khalil," Zaid was saying. "We are bound to run into someone at some point. We might as well lower those odds by going through the western quarter."

"We don't know who's over there though. At least we have already been through the east and know what to expect," Khalil replied.

"Where are we going?" Kinza asked, standing up.

She wasn't surprised that Zaid didn't respond to her nor even look at her. "I have a friend who is a scholar that I think we should try to find. We can ask him about the Apostles of Truth since they are just an underground movement of scholars themselves. The problem is he lives on the other side of the city."

"How do you know he is even there?" Kinza asked.

"I don't," Khalil said with a sigh. "That being said, Zabu tends to keep to himself and rarely leaves home. I would not be surprised if he went into hiding as soon as the fighting started and stayed there."

Zaid stood up, "Let's get going. We'll have to be careful of the watchtower now that it's daylight. Stay as close to the sides as possible." He walked outside.

Khalil gave Kinza an apologetic look and followed him out. She did as she was told and kept to the sides of the quarry. Now that the sun was out, she could see how truly massive it was. She could faintly make out the other side and the wooden fence that lined it, but it stretched far to her left and quite a bit deeper than she imagined. It could have easily taken hundreds of workers over many years to dig this. In some areas trees had grown at the bottom and she remembered this quarry theoretically would have been here for thousands of years, the Anunnaki slowly chipping away at it.

Right now it was abandoned with the attack on the city, other than the guards up in the tower. She wondered if they were the Unfettered looking for escapees, or just regular citizens looking for Kinza to have her killed. They probably weren't actually guarding the quarry itself and she hoped their gaze was turned inward toward the center of Rhapta and away from her.

They stayed as low as they could and crept back up the pathway. When they were still a few levels away from the top, Zaid motioned for them to wait a moment. He vanished up ahead and came back down a few seconds later nodding. They eventually made it back to the same board Zaid had ripped out the night before and slipped through the fence, placing the board back in the spot to cover the hole.

Kinza could see they were in a narrow pathway that stretched along the fence both ways and wound behind the backs of several abandoned buildings. From what she could tell, these were abandoned too.

"Where are we exactly?" she whispered.

No one answered at first and Khalil gave Zaid a pointed look.

"The southwest corner of the city," Zaid ground out and walked in-between one of the buildings. Kinza wanted to scream. She was the one who was being framed, but he acted like *she* was the one who betrayed *him,* when he was the one who hadn't defended her the night before. If she ran now and tried to escape, he would only catch her in a matter of seconds like he always did. That, or she would be captured by one of Rhapta's many inhabitants who wanted her dead.

With no other options, she trudged along behind Zaid. The city must have truly been huge because she recognized none of the buildings around them from the day before. Yes, they all had the same crumbled walls, mossy pools of water, and choking vines, but many of these were smaller. She imagined they were houses for poorer people and rows of long abandoned shops. Weeds wound up through the cracks in the limestone streets and she could hear birds chirping in the morning sun.

They walked for nearly an hour in silence before Zaid stopped to listen. Without saying anything, he motioned the two of them into a nearby building. It looked like it could have been a home similar to Ekaja's and they went up the stairs to the upper apartment. Kinza crouched beside a window with Zaid on the other side. She knew enough now to keep quiet, and within two minutes she started to hear voices in her head like whispers again.

They were speaking in Rhaptan and Kinza got that they were talking about what they had done the day prior, but none of the details or the tone. By the firm set of Zaid's jaw, she figured they weren't chatting about the weather, which had cleared the choking smoke from the city the night before. Kinza wondered how long it would take before she understood Rhaptan clearly.

She chanced a peek out the window before Zaid yanked her back down and glared at her. She had caught a glimpse of a man and two women, all in ragged and bloodied clothing that looked like it might have been beautiful recently. None of them had the black armbands that the Unfettered wore, but one of them had a flock of tiny birds following behind her like a train.

If they hadn't been looking for her Zaid would have already gone down to talk to them, but he stayed where he was and kept silent.

Great.

They waited nearly ten minutes before he deemed it safe to keep moving. They continued to walk through more abandoned buildings, heading north. The sun had started to beat down and sweat beaded on Kinza's neck. She desperately wanted a shower and a change of clothes, but that would have to wait.

The sun was high in its arc when the buildings started to spread out and they entered onto one of the wide boulevards that ran through the city. It slowly changed from an area of abandonment to an area of order. The buildings were all long and wide and well-kept. The streets were swept and no vines crisscrossed across the buildings.

"What is this area?" she asked, curious. Before they could answer they turned a corner and a large ring came into view, the middle filled with sand and a low fence around the edges. It looked like some kind of training area.

Khalil kept silent so Zaid was forced to answer again. "Technically we are in the north quarter now, but it's just called the warrior's quarter because their buildings cover most of it."

Despite how quiet it was now, she could see this place teeming with life had it been a normal day. Boxes and crates were stacked neatly against walls, racks where swords and spears were kept leaned against the fence. She guessed that many of the long, low buildings surrounding the ring were barracks.

"Why does Rhapta even have an army if no one knows about them? Like who are they going to fight?" Kinza wanted to hit herself the moment the words left her mouth.

Zaid just turned around and gave her an incredulous look. Khalil had a bit of mercy on her, though. "Thousands of years ago, Rhapta wasn't hidden and the rest of the world knew about us. While, at the time, we could not leave, there were the occasional invaders, so we did need the warriors back then. It is true that when we sealed up the city and left human society the warriors became less of a necessity, but they were still part of our society and our culture, so we kept training them. Now it's more of a prestigious position. They act as guards, jailers, scouts, and overseers now. A lot of them are also just an honor guard for some of the Elders."

Kinza tried to imagine what life had been like when the city was known to the rest of humanity. Haris had said that during the time of Mesopotamia, Anunnaki had been like leaders and worshiped by humanity. It was a strange thought, somebody worshipping her. She saw what happened to celebrities, she could not imagine someone being worshipped like a living god and remaining sane.

"Do the *venari* train here as well then?"

"No," Zaid said tersely. *So touchy.* "The *venari* have unmarked buildings toward the center of the city."

Kinza didn't ask any more questions and the three continued on in silence again. As they started moving to the east and wound through more buildings, it looked like Zaid was trying to keep them an equal distance between the wall far off to their left and what she assumed was the center of the city to their right. From where they were, she could not see anything special off to the right, but she assumed it was there.

Kinza started to pick up on more whispers in her head. Most of which were in Rhaptan, and too far off to make out what they were saying anyway. But Zaid must have noticed and was even more tense than usual. Khalil kept his eyes on the tops of the buildings as well.

"Zaid—" Khalil said suddenly, but Zaid cut him off.

"Inside! Now!" he whispered furiously and shoved Kinza and Khalil into the nearest building. It looked like nothing more than a small shop. There were boxes of cloth toward the front and a long counter going across most of the back, with a closed door that she assumed went into a back storage room. The three of them ducked behind the counter. Zaid looked confused as he watched the front door, which was ripped off its hinges. Khalil looked confused as well, but Kinza didn't ask what was wrong.

A few moments later a large group of people moved through the street, all of them in near-complete silence. It was so eerie seeing such a large group of people moving so quietly, goosebumps ran up her arms as she ducked back down so they would not see her. Would they even hear them if they came into the shop?

A couple minutes went by and Zaid motioned for them to stay. He still had the confused look on his face when he crept out front and into the street. Kinza didn't immediately hear any screams, but she didn't think she would have either. Khalil shook his head and walked out as well, to Kinza's silent protest. She sat back against the counter in a huff.

I can't believe they just left me, she thought to herself.

At least five minutes passed and they hadn't gotten back and she was getting worried. She decided to get up and just take a look outside. She moved as quietly as she could toward the front of the shop.

She was just about to peek out into the street when a hand clamped around her mouth and another went around her throat and squeezed. It happened so suddenly that Kinza didn't even have a moment to feel the panic. On instinct she threw her head back and heard a grunt behind her as the two of them fell to the ground in a crash. She rolled as quickly as she could and tried getting to her feet but the person lunged at her, tackling her back down.

It was a woman, she realized, with long hair, but it looked like she had no weapons. Kinza quickly took that thought back when the woman's hands started heating up and soon came close to *burning* her. Her hands were on Kinza's throat and she scrambled around feeling for something to help her. A piece of broken crate was on the ground above her head and she grabbed whichever part was closest and threw it into the woman's face.

A crack resounded and the woman yelped and fell off of her. Kinza gasped for breath and got to her feet. She was pretty sure her throat was burned. There was barely a second to breathe before the woman came back at her with malice in her eyes. Kinza noticed a black armband tied around her bicep. The Unfettered.

Where were Zaid and Khalil?

Kinza didn't have time to move before the woman barreled

into her and slammed her against the wall. Unfortunately for her, that's when Kinza's abilities decided to show themselves. Instead of her usual white-light explosion, a wave of fire erupted around her like a bonfire and she was in the center of the flames.

The only other time Kinza's fire had come out, it had happened in the forest outside of Mount Kilimanjaro. Her explosion that had saved both her and Zaid's lives had caused the trees to start on fire, but that was all. She hadn't even thought it was a separate ability, thinking it just a result of the explosion. And it had been nothing like *this*. The three-foot flames that wafted around her now shocked her to a standstill. The woman had immediately cried out and stumbled back-ward, writhing in pain and trying to put out the flames that had caught in her hair.

Kinza didn't feel a thing, and tried not to panic as the crates around her caught fire. Soon the entire interior of the shop was an inferno. Kinza ran out into the street, not knowing how to make the flames that swirled around her stop. She had an inkling that Stop, Drop, and Roll would not work here.

She spun around looking for something, water maybe, but caught sight of the brawl just a few yards away. Zaid and Khalil were fighting in the center of the large group of people they had seen a moment ago. They were still entirely silent though, which was why Kinza hadn't heard anything.

Khalil had a long gash down one arm and was down on one knee. Zaid was moving insanely fast, whipping back and forth trying to defend them both, but it was a losing battle.

The entire group of people stopped when they saw her, wreathed in flames. She heard garbled whispers that she didn't understand and the group immediately moved back. The screaming from the woman in the shop had stopped and Kinza tried hard not to think about it and failed. The entire shop was consumed now, burning as hot as the flames around Kinza, but she didn't know how to make them stop. Her heart had started beating wildly at the panic of having no control.

The group of Unfettered moved back, away from Zaid and Khalil, while still staring at her. Zaid moved to put one arm under Khalil who looked ready to pass out. One or two of the Unfettered took a few steps toward her and stopped. They said a few words she didn't quite understand, something about 'allegiance.' Then they placed fists over their hearts and *bowed* in her direction. Kinza backed up, afraid of starting anything or anyone on fire.

The group slowly backed away and disappeared down the street.

The shop fire continued to roar, as did Kinza's panic. How to put these out? She patted at her arms and legs, realizing the flames didn't touch her clothes. In fact, it looked like the flames really only started a few inches above her. But no matter what she did they would not go away.

"Kinza, what are you doing?" Zaid said, setting Khalil down gently and coming toward her cautiously.

"I can't—" she took a breath, "I can't make them stop. They won't stop!" She spun around looking for water, but the buildings were too close and she didn't want to burn anything else.

"Stop moving for a second," he said.

She had a hard time complying, the anxiety making her shake. What if the flames never went out?

"You started them, you should be able to stop them," Zaid said. He was now just standing a few feet away, not moving. Wasn't he going to help her?

"I didn't start them on purpose, it just happened!"

His face was skeptical and his doubt hit her in the chest. He heaved a breath, "The flames are responding to your panic. If you stop panicking, they should go away."

Kinza tried to slow her breathing, but watching him just stand there, not caring, made it worse. She crouched down and put her head in her arms and closed her eyes, trying to think of something else. Grams, Mitra, school, work, her neighbor's cat, the ice cream shop around the corner from her house, the green nail polish she had bought a week ago, her favorite pair of pants.

After a few minutes, her heart slowed and she braved a look around. The flames surrounding her had indeed gone away, but the shop still burned. She didn't think she could put those ones out, so it was a good thing there was some space between the next buildings.

Zaid still stared at her with a closed expression and then turned around and went back to Khalil.

Khalil tried waving him off, "I'm fine, I'm fine. I'm a *healer*, I'd know if I was going to die." Zaid still helped him to his feet and put one of Khalil's arms around his shoulders. The two of them trudged down the street toward her, and then right past her and kept going.

Kinza could do nothing else but follow.

Zaid shuffled down the street, holding Khalil up. He had lost a lot of blood in the gash on his arm and took a pretty hard hit to the head, but the healing was working fast. Out of instinct he kept his senses open, listening for more heartbeats.

Mentally, he laughed humorlessly. Why bother listening? All the Unfettered *bowed* to Kinza now. He had been sure he and Khalil were about to die. Someone in their group had to have some sort of sound-suppressing ability that somehow kept him from sensing heartbeats as well. He had walked headfirst into the group of them, followed moments later by Khalil who picked up a rock and did his best. Khalil was a healer and not a fighter, so he went down quick.

They had been surrounded when a literal inferno stumbled out into the street. He didn't even need to look to know it was Kinza. Of course it was her. Anunnaki had a very wide range of abilities with an even wider range of skill, but nothing close to the absolute fireball that stood in front of the Unfettered. It had taken them a moment to realize who it was, but they retreated nonetheless, bowing to her as they left. Their precious leader.

So why did he help her? Why let her follow? If she was truly leading the Unfettered then he should kill her, or at the very least, turn her in. Something about her panic while the flames refused to go out made him hesitate. Why? He continued to allow himself to be fooled by this woman.

Regardless, she hadn't tried to kill him or Khalil yet, and he still needed to find the other Rhaptans. He supposed that *he* didn't need to be the one to do it, but he was less likely to get killed than most other people. Most of the people in the hideout would not have lasted more than ten seconds against that group of Unfettered. They had some pretty gruesome abilities among them, one of them made it so it felt like his nails were being peeled off without even touching him.

"How far?" Zaid asked.

"Two streets up, on the right. Third door into the square," Khalil grunted. They walked in silence the rest of the way, the sound of Khalil's shuffling footsteps the only sound. Zaid didn't need to glance back to know that Kinza stayed behind them, her heartbeat was steadier now.

It was only a block before Khalil could walk again, and the gash on his arm started stitching back together. He glanced at Zaid sidelong, "Why didn't you get hit?"

"I'm fast," he said. The two of them chuckled before becoming somber again when they turned into the correct plaza. Like many others, the contents of the home that lined the area were strewn about the street. This plaza ended in a dead end and was surrounded only by homes. These were single family homes for some of the wealthier citizens and were close to three times the size of Zaid's mother's home.

Khalil went up to the door and knocked lightly. There was no answer and he looked toward Zaid.

"There is someone inside, just one person though," he said. He could sense the heartbeat toward the back of the house.

Khalil nodded and pushed the door open. "Zabu? The interior of the house was not as trashed as some of the others and Zaid could see the wealth this man had. Much more than his own family, but not quite as much as the inner plazas. Deep velvet couches sat in what must have been a living room, with rows of bookcases lining the walls, stuffed with books. In another room was a wide desk, polished to a shine and intricate tapestries lining the walls.

They moved into the house, careful to not make too much noise. Zaid moved ahead, following the heartbeat to the back of the house to the kitchen. Unlike most Rhaptan homes, Zabu's kitchen floor was made of wood and covered in rugs. Zaid flipped one to the side and found a trapdoor underneath.

"Maybe we should—" Khalil started, but Zaid just ripped it open to find a startled man beneath.

"Khalil?" he asked from below.

"Hi, Zabu," Khalil said. "You look well."

"I've been better."

"As have I."

Zaid rolled his eyes and moved to let the man up. He was short and rather round, and looked as if he spent most of his time indoors. "I'm surprised you aren't dead," Zabu said.

"So am I, and honestly I would be if my friend Zaid hadn't arrived."

"Ah yes," he said looking up at Zaid, squinting a little. "Khalil's mentioned you before, nice to finally meet you. Please have a seat," he said, indicating to the fallen table on the other side of the kitchen.

"Right," Zaid replied, helping to right the table. "Well, we actually came here to ask you—" Zabu jumped as Kinza walked in, she had been lingering in the hallway.

"Oh, right, sorry Zabu. This is our other friend, Kinza. If not *also* for her I would definitely be dead," Khalil added.

Zabu's heart stuttered a moment, but the expression on his face didn't change as he looked at Kinza. "It's nice to meet you as well, Kinza. Please, have a seat, I think I have some fruit somewhere." He started digging in the kitchen through baskets and cabinets and pulling out ceramic bowls and some fruit.

"So tell me," Zabu said. "You have come to ask me something? I hope it's not who is behind this attack," he said with a chuckle, "because I have no idea. I don't even know how many people are alive." He placed the fruit in a bowl and made to bring it to the table, but stopped and reconsidered. He pulled a large knife out of a drawer and started slicing up the fruit instead.

"It's a long story really," Khalil said, taking a seat. Kinza sat on the other side of the table, against the wall. "I need to know if you know anything about the Apostles of Truth."

Zabu looked up sharply at that. "*Well,* that's certainly not what I was expecting. I am a scholar after all, but you know I don't fraternize with those types. I keep records of the cisterns." He continued slicing and Zaid could not help but notice his heartbeat pick up its pace ever so slightly.

"I know that, Zabu. I just...well, we need to find them. It's a long, complicated story and they have information we need.

We are just having a hard time finding them. Have you heard anything at all?" Khalil asked.

"I'm sorry to be a disappointment, but I really don't," Zabu said. He had just finished filling one of the bowls and started on another. "Kinza, would you be kind enough to grab these bowls for me?"

Kinza looked up, startled that he was talking to her directly. "Oh, sure," she said, getting up from behind the table. She walked over to where Zabu was at the counter, he smiled at her as she grabbed the bowl and she gave an awkward smile back. As she turned back to the table, Zabu's eyes snapped toward her back and plunged the knife in her direction.

The bowl shattered on the ground as Zaid shoved Kinza to the side and tackled Zabu to the floor. If he hadn't been watching, even superhuman speed would not have helped him get there in time.

Zabu howled in pain and Khalil shouted in surprise. Zaid shouted for rope and Kinza scrambled across the kitchen and began digging through boxes. She came back with a long coil of twine. It would have to work.

"What in the hell are you doing Zabu?!" Khalil yelled. Kinza gave Zaid the twine and backed across the room, breathing hard and eyes wide. A few strands of dark hair had fallen into her face.

Zabu struggled and let out a garbled scream as Zaid bound his hands and hauled him across the kitchen into a chair. The man didn't have a hope of overpowering Zaid, but he was still large. "It's her!" he yelled. "*She's* the leader of the Unfettered, you idiots! She's the one who attacked us. The one from the prophecy! Why are you helping her?!" Zabu struggled some more, but Zaid had finished tying his arms and legs to the chair and he could only wiggle it a little.

"So your plan was to, what? Stab her with a kitchen knife?" Zaid asked.

"Yes!" Zabu exclaimed as if it was obvious. Zaid heard footsteps and turned to find Kinza stalking back across the house and outside.

Zaid let out an exasperated sigh. "Well this was a dead end," he said to Khalil and followed Kinza out.

"Oh, Zabu," Khalil muttered and followed as well, leaving the scholar to shout for help, deep inside his expensive house.

CHAPTER 10
NOWHERE TO GO

Khalil followed Zaid as they wandered back toward part of the abandoned western quarter. Kinza walked between them, eyes cast down.

They had left Zabu tied up, it was probably for the best. Someone would come find him and in the meantime he would not be able to follow them. What a mess that turned out to be. If Zaid hadn't been watching they would be carrying a body right now. Khalil was pretty sure Zabu was lying as well. The reason he had suggested going to see them was because he had once seen him talking with a few people that were known to be Apostles of Truth. Khalil didn't think Zabu had actually joined them, but he most likely had some information that might help them.

Whatever information he did have was lost to them now. They had no plan now, no way to contact the Apostles of Truth, no way to find the missing Rhaptans, and the remaining Rhaptans were out looking for Kinza while defending them-selves from the Unfettered. Everything was a mess and he desperately wanted to check on the state of the outskirts. From his estimation, most of the people who potentially escaped would have been from the inner or northern parts of the city. People from the outskirts would have either fled to human lands, went into hiding, or died.

He did wonder if a few people decided in a moment of panic that becoming human would not be so bad. Many of the people in the outskirts were halfway human already, himself included. The stunted abilities, lack of Aura connection, and predisposition to disease would help them fit in well. How many went? What would happen when a group of people walked out of the forest not remembering where they came from or who they were? It made him sad wondering who might have done it.

And Zabu! His poor, misguided friend had always been fearful and overly cautious, never wanting to leave his house unless he needed to. He had actually gotten a special permit to work the ledgers of several of the Elder's accounts from his home as he was too scared to leave. Khalil shook his head. It looked like his friend had succumbed to that fear, but that did tell them something. If Zabu had found out about Kinza's presence already, that meant two things. One, that the rumor of Kinza's presence and involvement in the Unfettered's attack had spread, and two, that there were enough people in the city to spread it around. If the people in Nazim's hideout were the only people in the city, it would not have spread that fast.

It gave him hope that others were still alive and hiding as well.

Khalil considered the puzzle at hand. What to do next? He tried thinking through it in a myriad of ways. Maybe there was someone else who knew where the Apostles were. Maybe the missing Aurastone in the quarry had nothing to do with the missing Rhaptans. Maybe the people *had* gone into human lands and the news just hadn't gotten to them yet. That would have been a disaster. Thousands of people just appearing coming down a mountain with little memory of where they came from. All this thinking was giving him a headache.

The one thing he did know for sure was that Zaid could be as blind as anyone else when a seed of doubt was planted in his mind. Over his years of studying and practicing as a healer, Khalil had gotten very good at realizing when someone was faking an illness or an injury. Despite the fact he could literally see their Auras—which could say a lot about someone's health—he slowly picked up on mannerisms, facial expressions, and tones of voice when someone was pretending. He had inspected hundreds of children pretending they were sick only to avoid going to school. Looking at the facts before him, Kinza Solace did not seem to be pretending. He could not say for sure, that would be naive of him, but there were too many things that didn't add up in the Unfettered's story.

Why were some of them revealing Kinza's identity, while others bowed to her? Why was she so terrible at controlling her own abilities? Yes they were powerful, but she had problems containing both the explosion and the fire. Why go through this entire farce with Zaid at all if she was planning on destroying the city? And who sent Zaid to capture her like an ubir, and why? There were just too many loose ends and Khalil liked things to be neat and clean.

He didn't know what happened between the two of them on the way here, but there was always some kind of tension in the room when both of them were there. They bickered and yelled like wild cats, but defended each other when they were in danger. He had caught them sneaking glances at each other, did they think he was blind? It was almost insulting. The urge to throttle them both was strong, but sadly that would not solve any of his many problems.

There were too many things for him to evaluate and he was dead tired.

The gash on his arm had hurt worse than he had let on. Several times he had nearly lost consciousness and the chances of finding another healer now were slim. The gash had healed over, but he desperately needed to sleep to allow the healing to finish its job. He knew too well that sleepless nights made an Anunnaki's healing slow considerably. He didn't have any of his herbs with him either. Even though the healing ability worked miracles, sometimes herbs helped focus that healing and speed it along.

For some of those who lived in the outskirts, the occasional medicinal herb did things their stunted healing could not. He should have brought *something* with him when they left his workshop, but he hadn't had the foresight. All he had been thinking about was getting out before the Unfettered found them. What if he ran into someone who needed help and he was weak or tired or out of herbs. He could hear his old mentor chastising him for being so careless. 'You had to fill your own cup first, before you could fill others.'

He thought of his parents and his grandparents and hoped they were all right. He tried not to think of them as dead, and thankfully none of the bodies he had found were theirs, but it was nerve-wracking not knowing. He had just seen them a few days before. During the initial attack, on his way back to his shop, he had stopped at his parents' home. It was a small place on the outskirts, but it was empty, things scattered around on the floor. He hadn't had time to look for them. Were they even here in the city? He sighed, trying to figure out where they were drained on him as well.

They didn't see anyone for over an hour and Zaid eventually turned them into one of the abandoned plazas they used to play in when they were kids. He wasn't sure if Zaid chose this one consciously or not, but he was satisfied. The plaza was surrounded by several connected buildings on three sides, most of the doors boarded up and missing shutters on the windows. Khalil didn't have to look to know Zaid was going to the last building in the corner, shoving the old wooden door aside and stepping through.

When they were younger and wanted to skip school, they would come here and hide for hours, playing games in the empty halls and trying to catch birds. The temporary freedom made their punishments worth it.

Inside was much darker, the only light came from the cracks in the boards and a hole in the middle of the long ceiling. He wasn't sure what this building had been used for, but it was too big to be a house and there was an old cracked fountain in the middle. Birds nested in the corners and sang to them as they sat down at different sides of the room.

In an almost unspoken agreement, the three of them said nothing and Khalil soon drifted off to sleep. He dreamt of silly things, his medicine cabinet in his workshop, the bottles labeled incorrectly. A version of Rhapta without the walls, no outskirts, only city. Instead of people, different colored Auras walked around, speaking to each other through shared understanding instead of words.

He woke abruptly sometime later, the light having moved across the room and glowing a deeper orange now. He had to have slept for hours.

What had woken him?

He looked around and saw Kinza was curled up in a ball within a bundle of vines on the floor, sleeping soundly. He was still trying to figure out how she had been able to reach his Aura when his telepathy had diminished years ago. The answer would present itself eventually, he was sure. All truth came to light at some point.

Now where was Zaid? Khalil looked around and realized he could not find the dark form that was his friend. That wasn't entirely unusual, Zaid didn't always tell people what he was doing before he did it. Khalil sat up and stretched his arm, which was entirely healed now. The tiredness was still there, but it was less of a burden than it had been earlier.

A sound rustled at the other end of the room. There was a dark hallway that extended on the other side into another larger room connected to this one. He and Zaid had explored it as kids and found it was almost entirely closed off except for one window high up. They didn't check it when they had come in this time, but Zaid would have heard a heartbeat if anyone had come in that way.

The sound came again followed by an undignified protest, and then Zaid came stumbling through the hall with a body struggling in his arms. The odd thing was the body, a woman, was appearing and disappearing as she struggled, but she stayed visible when he dropped her to the ground.

Kinza woke with a start from her bed of vines. She looked more exhausted than Khalil had been and that was saying something. The hair that had been shoved back into a ponytail was escaping slowly and dark hollows sat beneath her eyes. He wondered if Zaid had noticed.

"I'm not here to hurt anyone!" the woman protested. She looked to be in her middling years, but still as she got to her feet quickly. She had a shawl wrapped around her shoulders and tugged it back into place.

"Then why were you sneaking around back? And *invisible*?" Zaid shot back.

Khalil had gotten to his feet and made his way over to Zaid and the woman. He racked his hands through his own unkempt hair. "And who are you?" he asked.

"My name is Tiamat, and I'm a friend of your mother's,"

she said pointedly, looking at Zaid. He relaxed slightly at that, but still was cautious.

"Why are you here? Is she all right?" Zaid asked warily.

"Yes, Ekaja is just fine." She took a deep breath as if readying to launch into a story. "While you and she," she said nodding to Kinza across the room, "were still with the Unfettered, the man Rayaan came back to tell us what happened. It is true that many people became enraged as Rayaan did not wait for Nazim's word, only interpreted Kinza's guilt on his own and spread the word. People left in a mad rush and Ekaja was worried about you, Zaid. She sent me to find you and make sure that you were still alive."

Zaid rubbed the back of his neck. "Yeah, still alive," he said with a sigh.

Kinza had walked over and Tiamat turned to her, "My dear, I do not know whether you are innocent or guilty, but I do believe in a fair trial, and that was not something you have been given. I'm sure yesterday was a horrifying way to be introduced to Rhapta and its people, but I assume you know not all of us are so quick to judge."

"Thank you, but it seems the odds are against me," Kinza said, rubbing her arms. It would be night soon and the evening chill had started to come early.

"I must be getting back to my family, but Ekaja did also send me with something..." she dug around in a cloth bag she had slung across her shoulders. "Ah, here!" she said, handing over a small red leather book with gold lettering on the top.

Something about the book tickled the back of Khalil's mind. Did it look familiar? He had spent a lot of time around books, but this one was small, the size of a diary or journal. It was very distinct. Zaid, on the other hand, looked dumbfounded, as if that was the last thing he had expected Tiamat to pull from her bag.

Tiamat was still standing with her arm outstretched so Khalil took the book instead. "Your mother also wanted me to give you this. We are still trying to find out what is going on and where the other Rhaptans are and there are many dark theories. Some people are even speaking out against the Elders, as if they did this." She shook her head. "Ekaja said she didn't truly understand Rhapta's politics as much as others, but she said your brother used to, and that this was his."

This was the item Ekaja grabbed when she was fleeing her home in the middle of the night during an attack? Khalil was doubly disappointed in himself for not grabbing his herbs when she had remembered this book.

Zaid nodded slowly, still staring at the book. "He was looking for that the last time I saw him." Khalil knew that could not be true, Zaid had captured him later and had to be the one to execute him. He supposed it was the last time he saw Amir while he was still himself. The next time Zaid had seen him, Amir had been an ubir and deep into the madness. But what secrets did it hold? And how truthful could they be? After all, Amir did make the choice to complete the blood rite.

Tiamat shrugged. "Maybe it's nothing at all, maybe it'll help. I remember your brother was getting mixed up with all the wrong people after he started his apprenticeship. But he was so smart and it's possible he knew things that could have helped us now."

Khalil handed it to Zaid, not wanting to read it if it was personal. It could have very well been a journal of the last thoughts of his brother before the rite. "Yeah, he probably could've helped," Zaid said, brows knitting together as he flipped through the pages.

Khalil remembered distinctly the change in Zaid after Amir was gone. It was like something had snapped in him. Zaid had always been a little moody, but when Amir was around Zaid had at least smiled. After Amir was gone it was like he took Zaid's happiness with him. Not that he blamed him. Khalil believed the Elders did both good and bad, but what they did to Zaid was unforgivable. Enacting a long forgotten law that hadn't been in place for decades, forcing him to execute his own brother. Khalil never found out which Elder it was, and he wished he never did.

"Ekaja said she could not read it," Tiamat said. "Like it was encrypted or something." She looked around at the dying light. "Look, I need to go now. I wish you the best of luck. Please stay safe and I will tell your mother you are all right."

Zaid and Kinza nodded. "Thank you," Khalil said. The woman then vanished. He heard footsteps and light scuffling, but the only movement was a slight bit of shifting sand on the floor headed toward an open window, and then it was gone.

"Do you think it will help?" Kinza asked. "Can you read it?" She was trying to peer over Zaid's shoulder without being too obvious, but was failing entirely.

"I don't know, and no," Zaid said, temporarily forgetting he didn't want to talk to her. He was too absorbed in trying to read the book, but didn't seem to be getting anywhere.

"May I see it again?" Khalil asked. He had spent some time with ciphers as a kid. Nothing extensive, but the puzzles interested him.

Zaid handed it back and Khalil flipped through the pages. It would definitely take some time if he really wanted to crack it. He closed the book again, looking at the outside. It wasn't the interior that tugged at him, it was the cover. Gold lettering on a background of scarlet, where had he seen that before? He swore he had seen several people with a similar copy. Maybe back when he was still a student and spent a lot of time with the scholars in...

"That's it!" he cried, a smile blooming across his face. "I know where the Apostles are."

"You do?" Kinza asked, arching an eyebrow. They clearly weren't as excited as he was.

"Yes, I believe so," he replied, handing the book back to Zaid. How had he forgotten? He had seen so many of them before while studying alongside other young scholars. Not everyone had one, but he would catch glimpses of them within the arms of students, wedged between stacks of books.

"Where?" Zaid asked, brow furrowed. He had a particular dislike for the Apostles of Truth, but they were still their best option in finding more information.

"Where else would you find a bunch of scholars?" Khalil asked. It was so simple he almost laughed. Right under the nose of the whole city! Oh what the Elders would do if they realized one of the most prominent groups of rebels in the city was filing in and out right next door.

Zaid and Kinza just stared at him, not putting it together.

"In the library."

CHAPTER 11

THE APOSTLES OF TRUTH

Kinza was glad she had gotten sleep back at the ruins, otherwise she would have been dead on her feet now. She, Khalil, and Zaid crept through the city toward the center; the only place she really hadn't been yet. Khalil had said he had an idea where the Apostles of Truth were and he was practically giddy with excitement. Were the Apostles not a rebel group out to get the Elders, or something like that? She had no idea what to expect, maybe they would try to kill her too, everyone else was, so hey, why not? But if it gave Zaid and Khalil a chance to find the missing Rhaptans and hopefully push back against the Unfettered, she would do it.

She was surprised to realize she didn't hate Rhapta and its people. Yes, she was angry, and confused, and scared, and so, so tired. But *they* were the ones who were attacked in the dead of night, many of their family members having been murdered. Despite most of them hating her now, she still found she wanted to help them.....and hopefully not die in the process.

The feeling she had the night before, at her "trial" kept coming back. All throughout the day it would come and go, the feeling like she was watching her body from above and felt as if all of this was a nightmare she could not wake up from. Even the events prior to arriving to Rhapta felt years behind her.

Was it truly just yesterday morning that she and Zaid were happily driving up the mountain, music blaring and the wind in her hair. He had looked so relaxed and had actually laughed. Now he would hardly look at her, and when he did speak to her it was with clipped words and short sentences. It was worse than when he had thought she was ubir. What had she done to deserve this?

She sighed and stepped around a fallen block of limestone. They were getting closer to the Central Plaza, as Khalil called it. Nazim had said that is where the majority of the Unfettered were camped and at the time had counted roughly a hundred of them. It was wild to think only a hundred people could cause this much damage. She did notice as she trudged along that the houses and buildings were becoming less abandoned the closer she got to the center of Rhapta.

Kinza had started to notice larger shapes in the distance as they walked, but it was hard to tell in the dark. Khalil had said the library was on one side of the Central Plaza, but they probably needed to sneak in the back to avoid the Unfettered. The problem was that with so many Unfettered, and just angry Anunnaki in general, it was hard to know what abilities people had. It was very possible someone else could have an ability to the Unfettered they had seen earlier who could silence the sound of an entire group. What other kinds of abilities were there?

After what felt like forever, Zaid finally stopped, causing Kinza to run headfirst into his back. He turned to glare at her but didn't say anything. She would have rather he yelled, then they could at least fight about it. This near-silence from him made her feel small and insignificant.

He motioned for them to follow, but to be careful. Many of the Aurastone had been cracked and subsequently smashed to pieces as well because there was very little light and no painful ringing of the Deathstones. They turned a corner around a large building and Kinza had to stifle her gasp. There were *at least* a hundred people gathered around too many bonfires to count, all around a vast open space before her. It was chaotic and unorganized, especially since they had gotten so close without running into patrols or anything like that.

She could vaguely make out a massive building on the other side of the plaza that she assumed was the Great Hall. Instead of heading into the camp of Unfettered, Zaid took them further down the street, a few blocks south and away from the light. He had them dodging and doubling back a few times, she assumed because he heard people coming their way.

Before she knew it, they were crouched behind the back of another huge limestone building. Khalil pointed out something to Zaid and he nodded. Staying low, they moved along the side of the wall until they got to a door. Even in the darkness, Kinza could tell how smoothly Zaid's movements were compared to her crouched waddling. It took him only a second to pop the door's lock with one of his knives and they were inside.

"Khalil, I hope you know where you're going because I can't see a thing," Zaid said. A second later a fire lit on the end of a torch and Khalil's face came into view.

"I do." Where had he gotten that? "I've spent hours and hours here and I have a pretty good idea where to go. This is the workers hallway that runs the perimeter of the building. Just follow me," he said.

Kinza followed with Zaid at the rear and Khalil took them out of the dark hallway into the main library. Kinza nearly choked at the sheer size. The ceilings stretched high above her and massive windows near the ceilings let in the light from the bonfires on the other side of the building. There were rows upon rows of books on shelves that wrapped around the walls and created a labyrinth on the main level. There was another level above them with a balcony that extended out all the way around. More books and some smaller seating areas sat up there.

A lot of this level was trashed, books pulled out and thrown on the ground, but it didn't look like anyone was here.

"So, you said the Apostles are supposed to be here, right?" she asked. It looked pretty empty.

"Not here, downstairs," Khalil replied and marched on ahead. He went straight down to the back wall and Kinza saw a wide open doorway. The path through the doorway slanted down and around and they found themselves on a low level right below the first. It did look more like a basement in here, but there were things other than books. Scrolls, tablets, and even some artifacts lined many of the shelves and some sat in cases. It reminded her a bit of the lost Library of Alexandria.

Khalil, again, went toward the opposite wall and turned down a row of shelves. They passed three or four columns before they got to the side wall of the building, the back of the wall had a bookshelf set into it as well. They were rather efficient with space here.

"Okay, I think it's here," Khalil said.

"Um, where?" Zaid asked.

"Here. When I was still studying to become a healer, I spent a lot of time down here reading and every once in a while I would see a scholar carrying one of those books," he pointed to the red book in Zaid's hand, "and they would come down this hallway, but they would not come out."

"Ah, okay..." Zaid said, looking around.

"So there must be a door or something?" Kinza asked.

"I think so," Khalil said and started feeling around underneath the shelves and pulling books back. Kinza was starting to feel like this was a dead end as well when a voice spoke behind them, startling her.

"Who are you?" Kinza and the others whirled around to find a man wrapped in deep blue robes levelling an obsidian-tipped staff at them. "I said, who are you?" he asked again, more insistently this time. How had Zaid missed this guy?

"We are looking for the Apostles of Truth," Khalil said, cautiously.

"That's not what I asked you," the man said, shoving the spear closer. Zaid looked like he was about to end this conversation in a rather unpleasant manner, and Kinza really just wanted to get this over with.

"Our names aren't really import—"

"My name is Kinza Solace," she said, cutting Khalil off. "If you want to kill me, just get it over with." She had come to expect the hostility from the Rhaptans, so the stranger's sudden change in demeanor had her furrowing her brow.

He stood upright in realization, snapping the spear to attention and gave a small, but gracious, bow. "Well, then," he said with a huff. "We have been waiting for you for a *very* long time, Miss Solace. Please follow me." He pushed past them, eliciting an irritated glare from Zaid, and felt along the back wall. There was a faint click and the entire bookshelf swung inward on silent hinges.

He took a few steps in before realizing the group wasn't following him. Kinza and Khalil were standing open-mouthed at the tunnel and Zaid continued to practice his glaring.

"Well, come on!" the stranger said and headed into the darkness.

Life underneath the library was very different from what was going on above ground. The stranger took them down a dark winding passageway that eventually opened up into a large room that branched out into several hallways in many directions. Tons of people, most garbed in the dark blue robes, hurried to and fro throughout the hallways, usually with stacks of books in their arms and chatting to the person next to them. It was surprisingly well lit with small Aurastones embedded into the stone walls at regular intervals.

The occasional person would glance in their direction as they passed, but most were too absorbed in their own work to take notice. Similar to aboveground, the network of tunnels seemed to be set up with intersections, like the plazas, connecting them together. Many doorways they passed were filled with rooms full of even more books, tables, scrolls, and so many *people*. Maybe she had grown accustomed to the empty streets of Rhapta, but there seemed to be so much life down here.

"My name is Tammuz, by the way," the man said, veering down another hallway, nearly knocking into two more people coming the opposite way. How big was this place? Kinza didn't get a chance to ask when the man said, "Ah, here we are." He stopped in the doorway of a rectangular room. It had a long table down the middle surrounded by several men in what looked to be some sort of meeting. They leaned back from the books they were inspecting when they saw Tammuz in the doorway. He didn't say anything and just looked pointedly at a man with graying hair who was standing at the head of the table.

The man stood and smiled. "If you will all excuse us?" he

said. A few of the men looked irritated but packed their things and left, some with confused glances at Kinza on their way out. "Please," the man said, "come in and have a seat. I'm so glad you've found us Kinza. Thank you Tammuz."

Tammuz nodded and left the room. Kinza noticed one other man had stayed. He looked like he was scowling but something in Kinza wanted to bet that he would be the first person to laugh under the right circumstances.

"You know my name?" Kinza asked, sitting down in one of the vacant chairs. Khalil sat across from her, but Zaid remained standing by the doorway, eyes boring a hole into the two men. What was his problem?

"Of course! My name is Sa'id, and this grouch is Nimatullah," he said, gesturing to the other man.

Proving Kinza right, he barked a laugh. "No one has called me that in fifty years. You can call me Nim."

"Soooo, you're not going to kill me then?" Kinza asked.

Sa'id and Nim looked at each other and roared with laughter. "No, Kinza," Sa'id finally said once they caught their breath. "I don't blame you for asking. It sounds like there have been quite a lot of rumors about you recently, but I suppose there have been quite a lot of rumors about us too." His eyes twinkled as he said it.

"Does that mean you know why we are here?" Khalil asked skeptically.

"We know that the—" Sa'id looked down at a piece of paper on the table. "—one from the prophecy has arrived and they are apparently the leader of the Unfettered and here to kill us all. Also her name is Kinza Solace." He looked up, scrutinizing Kinza. "You don't look much like the Unfettered."

"I'm not!" Kinza exclaimed. She closed her eyes and took a breath before starting over. "All of the Unfettered people are claiming I am their leader and that's a total lie, because a week ago I didn't know any of you existed or that I'm Anunnaki. And Khalil noticed there was a bunch of Aurastone missing in the quarry and thought it would be a good idea to find you guys and see if you knew about it since you apparently know a lot of stuff you shouldn't and maybe it relates to the missing Rhaptans." She was breathing hard by the time she finished.

Both Sa'id and Nim's eyebrows went clear up to their hairlines. "That's quite a lot of information. And you were right to come to us, we probably have more information about you and what is going on than anyone else in the city. It might be best for us to start at the beginning," Sa'id said.

"Why don't you start with telling us who *you* are," Zaid interjected from his spot by the doorway.

"Oh, well, I'm the head scholar within the Apostles of Truth, and you are in our only safe haven," he said, gesturing around them. "I thought that was obvious."

Zaid just scoffed, but didn't reply.

"Are you sure you would not rather sit?" Nim asked Zaid. "This might be a long conversation, boy."

"I'll stand."

"Fine, be that way," Nim muttered.

"Rhapta used to be ruled by a monarchy up until two hundred years ago."

"Yeah I know this part, there was a king that died and the heir went missing."

"Yes, exactly! When one of the advisors went to go look for Prince Malik to tell him his father had passed, he was nowhere to be found. The entire city was scoured and even the forest surrounding Mount Kilimanjaro. There were even less *venari* back then, but they were told to keep an eye out in their travels and the word passed to the Ummanu as well. The prince was just gone.

"Rhapta had never been without a king and this, we found

later, was a problem because the line of Rhaptan kings had some unique traits. Among having several powerful abilities, their Auras were massive, so large that their psychic energy alone could sustain the barrier surrounding the city if need be. Without this power source, it's been draining ever since.

Everyone knows what happened next, the king's advisors stepped in and for what is now the Council of Elders that we know and love. Most of Rhapta accepted them wholeheartedly while still mourning the loss of their prince, but no one questioned why. Why did the prince vanish? What happened to him? Several scholars started to question this, wanting to know what really happened, but they were met with fierce retaliation from a few of the Elders, only stoking the fire, so to speak. Thus the Apostles of Truth were born.

"Shortly after these events, a young boy who we now know as Grand Elder Hakim, had a vision. This one you should know." He winked.

"The prophecy," Khalil said.

"Yes," Sa'id said, leaning back and crossing one leg over another. "The foretelling that one day an outsider would come to Rhapta and either save it or burn it down. The Apostles continue to question why. Why did this prophecy only come *after* the prince had vanished and the Elders had assumed power? In itself it implies that we need to be saved as well, yet the Elders continued to spread word that all was well, nothing was wrong. Here we are two hundred years later, our population has dwindled to a fraction of what it used to be, the psionic barrier is weak, and people have become restless, turning to the blood rite for an escape."

"And you aren't a catalyst for that?" Khalil asked.

"Absolutely not!" Sa'id said, leaning forward and placing both hands on the table. "It is yet another lie spread intentionally by some of the Elders to tarnish our name. We bring in those who seek knowledge and truth, and as you saw on your way in, we have flourished in recent years; there is much truth to be discovered apparently." Nim nodded beside him.

"You think the Elders have some sort of evil plan or something, right?" Zaid asked, not bothering to hide the contempt in his voice. Kinza could see why Zaid was mistrustful of *her*, but why was he so distrusting of the Apostles as well? They were presenting some solid evidence and hadn't tried to kill or kidnap anyone yet. That was saying a lot in this city.

"Only some of them," Nim said. "Don't misunderstand us, boy, we don't believe all of the Elders have vile ambition, but they did stand to gain great power if the monarchy suddenly crumbled."

"Hakim is the only one who was alive at that point, everyone else came into office later. The last I heard, Hakim was practically senile now," Khalil pointed out. Kinza was trying to keep track of the timeline of events, but it was difficult when you had to remember the Anunnaki lived so long. This wasn't ancient history to them, it was the time of their parents and maybe grandparents at best.

"As you can see, there are a great many questions that need to be answered," Sa'id said. "Just because we don't understand something doesn't mean it didn't happen."

"Why are you telling me this?" Kinza asked. How was this relevant?

"Because it is the foundation for the events that are happening now!" Sa'id said, eagerly. "For years we studied the prophecy and hypothesized what it could mean. We've looked into the Elders and have found disturbing secrets among them. And now the city has been thrust into a civil war and one side claims *an outsider* as their leader. The same outsider whose parents were assassinated at the order of one of the Elders."

A shock ran through Kinza, the image of her mother's lifeless hand on the carpet. "You all knew about that?" First the assassins who came for her said they were given orders to kill her mother, and subsequently her father, and now these Apostles knew as well.

"If you think Tahir did this, you can tell your minions they are looking in the wrong place," Zaid said, voice low. "I know Tahir, he has been something of a mentor to me for years."

"And some of the worst pains in life are betrayals by those we trust most." Sa'id's voice was sad as he looked at Zaid, who only glared back.

"So you do know about the missing Aurastone then?" Khalil asked, moving them along.

"Oh yes, of course," Sa'id said, coming out of a momentary reverie. "Overseer Walid has been carting slabs of it out of the city in the middle of the night for a few years now."

"Whole slabs?! That would only create giant Deathstones," Khalil cried.

"That's what we thought at first, but with a host of missing people we are starting to rethink that theory." Sa'id leaned back again, thinking. "What if, say, someone knew they would need to leave the city safely in the future? It's never been done before on a large scale, but there would need to be some sort of psionic barrier to keep us both hidden and prevent us from becoming human. We have long theorized that the source of the barrier, our abilities, the Anunnaki themselves, *everything* comes from the stone. If someone figured out how to move it, it's possible they could create a satellite city of sorts; a camp, if you will."

"So you're saying that the missing Rhaptans could just be hiding out there somewhere? How would they know to escape there?" Khalil asked. Kinza tried to understand, geographically, what that would look like. Zaid had told her that the barrier kept Rhapta almost on another plane of existence while still remaining in Tanzania. Would the camp also be in Tanzania, or someplace else?

"I'm not sure, but that is our foremost theory at the moment," Sa'id said. "One of the most concerning things we found, though, is that almost all of the warriors made it out. If they are all indeed safe, they could be planning to return in force. With the tension growing there could be an all-out battle in a matter of days. Someone did this, that we know for sure. Someone is inciting chaos by framing you, Kinza."

"What do we do then? Leave? Well, I guess you can't leave," she said, feeling guilty for even suggesting it.

"And they will just send *venari* after you," Sa'id said, shaking his head. "No, I think the best course of action would be to convince the Elders—the ones who truly want the best for Rhapta—that you are not a threat, while keeping people as safe as possible. I cannot deny that the Elders hold consider-able power over Rhapta and if they believed you not to be a danger then I think that would pour water on the real enemy's plan."

"The people need an outlet for their anger," Khalil said. "So many people have gotten hurt and it will take a long time to rebuild what has been destroyed. Even if Kinza's name is cleared by the Elders, I don't think the people will accept it without knowing who really did this."

"Yes, yes you are right." Sa'id sighed. "We will also need to expose them as well. And we do have considerable evidence, despite what some may think."

"This is a load of crap," Zaid muttered.

"Zaid!" Khalil chastised.

"Don't worry," Sa'id said. "I didn't expect him to trust us. Yes, I know who you are, Zaid Hatem, and why you have no faith in what I say. Amir would have been a brilliant scholar, but he learned too much too fast."

Zaid's face only darkened at that. "You admit then, that you were the ones who pushed him into the blood rite, effectively killing him?

"No, you misunderstand," Sa'id said. "Amir spent much time looking into Elder Tahir and he was the one who discovered many dark things. I believe it was his worry for you that stoked that fire, knowing that Tahir was becoming a close figure in your life. Amir, against our wishes, went to confront Tahir. I don't know what happened, but someone saw Amir going to speak with the Unfettered shortly after that, and then we never saw him again."

"Amir was losing his mind before he left, and it was right after he got involved with you!" Zaid shot. Kinza knew what had happened to his brother, but she hadn't really talked with him about it. Seeing his anger now made her want to reach out to him, but that would only make things worse.

"I am sorry, truly, for what happened to him," Sa'id said and then looked around. "I think that might be enough for tonight. Please, I have several empty rooms here and you are more than welcome to stay the night. We have food and hot water as well."

At the mention of a hot shower, Kinza nearly melted into the floor.

Nim brought them through winding hallways, past more scholars hurrying along. Did none of them ever sleep? They entered what Nim said was the residential wing with rows of doors set into the stone. They were given three rooms next to each other and Nim showed them how to find their way out if they needed to leave.

"My room is right down the hall if you need me," Nim said and then looked at Zaid. "Please don't kill me in my sleep," he said dryly and left.

Kinza's room was small but more than she could ask for. The floors and walls were made of the same limestone that made up the rest of the city. There was a bedroll in the corner with a pile of blankets and pillows, a writing desk, and several baskets and chests. She dug through those and found a collection of women's clothing and additional blankets.

On the other side of the room she found, to her sweet relief, a bathroom. Indoor plumbing was indeed a thing here, but at first she could not understand how the shower worked. There was no shower head and just a few ropes hanging to one side. After some experimenting she realized it was a pulling system and if she pulled the right one, hot water would flow down from tiny holes in the ceiling.

She spent way too long under the scalding hot water, washing away the dirt, grime, and tear stains of the last week. Her hair was a matted mess, but there were little bowls of some almond-scented soaps and she scrubbed everything clean. Grams would have been pounding on the door with how long she was in there, she thought wistfully.

When she was done, she wiped the steam from the large mirror that leaned against the wall and took stock of herself. Somehow she looked healthier and sicker than she had ever been. Her soft brown skin glowed, but still the dark circles hung beneath her eyes. Her muscles were more defined than she remembered, but she swayed slightly from exhaustion. Her hair had returned to its normal curly state. Ringlets of varying sizes hung down to her shoulders, dripping water.

Digging around in the chests, she was pleased to find a pair of loose pants that cinched at the ankles and a cropped shirt, both the color of sand. If she moved in the right direction, she could just get a glimpse of her tattoo. There was even a pair of soft shoes just her size. She could not have asked for more.

Looking at the bedroll longingly, she turned to leave. She needed to do something first. Just down the hall, a few doors down, she knocked at a similar room to hers. The door opened and she found Zaid and her heart sputtered for a moment.

He stood there in nothing but a pair of dark pants and skin still damp from the shower. The Aurastone lights in the hallways made the angles of his muscled chest more pronounced. Unfortunately, the ever-present scowl was still there. Hadn't he been smiling at her just a few days ago?

"What do you want?" he ground out.

"I just wanted to talk—" the door slammed in her face. She stood there for a full minute contemplating her situation before heading back to her room. She grabbed a long deep blue scarf and wrapped it around her head. It was large enough that it acted as a shawl, covering any hint of her tattoo in the front as well. Hopefully she looked like any other Rhaptan woman, she had seen several of them wearing clothes just like this.

She made her way through the winding halls, remembering the way Nim showed her, and found her way up a spiraling staircase and pushed out into the night.

She needed some air.

CHAPTER 12

A STROLL THROUGH THE DARK

Mikah took a deep breath, inhaling the scent of Rhapta. It always smelled faintly of water to him for some reason. They weren't near any large bodies of water, but it just felt *coastal*. Maybe that was his internal longing to see other places, the sea for example. Rhaptans scorned the *venari* for many reasons, but Mikah believed they were just jealous. They were the only people who got to leave and see the rest of the world. Yes, the reasoning was gruesome, but they still got to see it. No, Mikah disliked *venari* for other reasons, and he was loath to run into that particular reason.

Before he left, Tahir had briefed him on what to look for. The abilities Kinza Solace would have, and who she was with. Apparently she had not come into the city alone, instead she had managed to snag an escort. Mikah supposed it made sense, otherwise how would she have known where to enter? Honestly, he didn't know how she had gotten in contact with the Unfettered in the first place. Doesn't being an outsider mean that she was unaware of Rhapta and its people? Who had told her it was here?

Oh, Zaid, Mikah thought to himself. *You always were the dumbest person in the room.*

Mikah and Zaid had never played well together, just cut from very different cloth it seemed. While Mikah was elegant swaths of silk, Zaid was a sheet of bark someone ripped from a tree.

Unfortunately he was Tahir's favorite, even if the man claimed not to have favorites. Even Zaid wasn't that blind. Had he not been tapped to become *venari,* Tahir would have wanted him as his apprentice. Honestly, what did Tahir see in him? He was too quiet, and when he did speak he was rude. Asking him to smile was like asking the dead to return. And, oh, how slow he was, it took him forever to put two and two together. Could he understand the strategy of battle? No. What about people and their motives? Also no. Politics? Definitely not. He would have made a horrendous Elder. He was even past his tenth year before he acquired his abilities. That had to say something about one's genetics.

Now here Mikah was, sneaking through a dark, broken city with a team of Kartik's best men, hoping to find just that man and the woman he was with. Mikah wondered what she would be like. An old hag? No, no, she was supposed to be young. If she was an outsider that must mean she looked different from them. How else would people know she wasn't Rhaptan? Mikah sometimes liked to compare people's personalities to their faces, you could tell a lot from someone's features. This woman would probably have boils and a menacing grin.

He shook his head; his imagination was getting away from him.

Tahir said that Zaid would have probably been fooled by

the woman into believing her lies. That honestly wasn't that surprising, but Tahir wanted him to *help* Zaid; break the woman's hold on him. If he was stupid enough to believe her then so be it, let him go. All wars have casualties. No, if Tahir found out Mikah failed to bring Zaid back when he could have, it would only harm his chance of becoming an Elder in the future. He had been an apprentice with Tahir too long now, and Zaid was *venari*. Zaid was not a threat anymore, just a nuisance.

Mikah sighed into the darkness. They had entered through the north quarter with the intent of staying away from the Central Plaza and the Unfettered there. It looked like the fires had long ago burned themselves out. Anything still burning would have been recently started. Tahir's man had said the Unfettered were still going through the streets, occasionally beating or killing people they found and burning homes and buildings to the ground. Right now it was deathly quiet and they didn't see a soul. When he had escaped into the tunnels out of the city people had been screaming and shouting. The sounds were eerie within the walls, generally you didn't hear verbal speech unless you were on the outskirts.

They walked for a while and only ran into one or two Unfettered, which they dealt with quickly. Mikah stayed out of the way when that happened. He knew what his ability was and wasn't good for. Hand to hand combat? Not so much. Besides, one of the warriors in his group had skin that turned as hard as iron when he wished. All he needed to do was walk up to the enemy, there wasn't a whole lot they could do to stop him. Another warrior's spit was acidic and Mikah really wanted to stay out of range in case of splash back.

They hadn't found any of the larger hideouts yet, but those would probably be in the abandoned areas of the city so they started to head into the western quarter. He didn't really expect them all to be in one place, more likely they would have gathered in smaller groups that were easier to hide. There was a good chance there were more people in the outskirts, but they didn't have orders to go there so they stayed within the walls.

The abandonment of this area was a reminder of how much potential the Anunnaki people had, yet it was wasted. Such a shame, they could have been so much more. For the millionth time in his life, Mikah wished he had been born in the early days of Rhapta, when it wasn't hidden and humans worshipped them as gods. Even if they could not leave, humans could come in, bringing wealth and stories and art.

As they made their way south, the captain of the team of warriors decided they were too close to the plaza when they ran into a larger group of Unfettered. Again, Mikah stayed out of the way, but it took the men a few minutes longer to deal with this group. Despite the Unfettered's strength, they weren't trained. They didn't move in a coordinated unit, nor did they know how to assess a fight, when to move forward, when to retreat. Every move they made was at one hundred percent power, leaving vulnerable areas exposed. It was a good sign, for when the rest of the warriors arrived they would have the upper hand. The only reason the Unfettered got away with the first attack was because they had surprise on their side.

Let's move further west, deeper into that quarter. His men gave curt nods.

Mikah was getting bored again and walking through more broken streets sounded less than exciting. *I'll check this way,* he said, heading east. The warriors were not in charge of him, so they really could not say where he went and what he did.

But—

Don't worry, if I die you can tell Tahir I disobeyed orders, Mikah said, cutting him off. Before the captain could protest again he walked away. He was careful not to meander too close to the center, and did have to hide in one of the buildings when a group of voices went by. It looked like four of five Unfettered, the black armbands tied around their arms. The ground shook when they walked by and he wondered if whoever had that ability could turn it off or not. If they could, they were only announcing their presence and were probably doing Rhaptans a favor. Still, he made sure to keep still, it was hard to tell what abilities other people had. Mikah did have a small obsidian knife tucked into his belt just in case, but he was better at avoiding confrontations to begin with.

He was walking by one of the dead-end plazas a few streets west of the Central Plaza and almost had to do a double-take. This one was surrounded by low buildings coated almost entirely in vines, trees, and roots. It looked like one tree had even started growing on the low roof, sending long flowering vines down to the broken stone street and throwing half the plaza into shadow. In the center was one of the familiar large fountains and this one still had water in it and was surrounded by several tall bushes. What he had almost missed in the darkness was the woman that sat on the edge of the fountain, looking into the water. Mikah inched closer, trying to see what she was looking at. In the reflected moonlight he saw shapes moving. Fish. There were little orange and black fish swimming around.

Unfortunately his movements caught her notice. She immediately jumped up with a gasp and took a step back. He mentally berated himself for not making himself known. The best way to get attacked was to startle someone.

I'm not Unfettered! Mikah said quickly, putting his hands up. He truly hadn't meant to scare her, but he was glad he could see her face now. Even in the dark he could see she was beautiful. Clear skin, dark eyes, and black ringlets sticking out of the blue scarf she had draped around her head. What was a woman doing out here alone? She didn't look like she would be Unfettered, but he checked her arm anyway and didn't see one of the black bands. She was the first Rhaptan he had seen since he got back into the city.

Her eyes narrowed at him. *See?* he said, showing both arms. *No bands.*

She looked hesitant to speak. *You could be pretending,* she finally said in his head. Her voice was both bold and gentle, an unusual combination that had him wanting to hear her speak more.

Yes, I supposed I could, he said. *But then you could be, too.*

She seemed to see the logic in that and nodded, but kept her eye on him. *Sorry, it's been a rough few days.*

I understand, he said and came closer to the fountain. It no longer cycled the water, the statue in the middle just the visage of a long-dead Rhaptan king. He wondered who put the fish there. *Are you and your family well? Where are you hiding out? I saw the Unfettered were still going through the streets.* Maybe she could lead him to one of the larger hideouts. That would make his life easier.

Um, yes, my family is okay, she said, wandering to the other side of the fountain. *And I know, I think the Unfettered are just trying to keep people scared.* She thought for a second before asking, *Do you know where everyone is? It's a ghost town.*

Mikah put his hands into his pockets hoping to look less threatening. *Yes, that's why I'm here. I'm here to warn people.*

Her brow furrowed. *Of what? The attack already happened. You know where everyone is?*

He had to be careful just in case she was Unfettered. He didn't want to give away their position; he didn't really think she was one of them though. *Yes, when the fighting started, Elder*

Tahir got as many of us out as he could. Grand Elder Hakim had a vision just before the attack. We have a camp just north of the city and the Elders who escaped are planning countermeasures. Myself and a few warriors snuck back in to tell everyone to prepare. Are you sure you are safe where you are staying? I can help you.

Surprisingly she didn't seem interested in the fact that there were Anunnaki outside of the city for the first time in history. Instead she absently picked at the top of a fern. *Oh, no, we are just fine and my mother isn't a big fan of strangers in her home. When, um, when is this going to happen? I want to make sure we are ready.*

He took a few steps up to the fountain, but she stayed where she was on the other side, both holding her position and not coming closer. He found he liked the contradiction. *Soon, within the next few days, the Elders haven't decided on a day yet, but I'm guessing as soon as they get enough information. We are trying to get an idea of how many Unfettered there are. Their numbers are much higher than anyone realized. Have you seen many of them?*

I—" she paused, *"we've been hiding at home, but I did hear that they are camped in the Central Plaza. No idea how many, though. I should get going..."* she trailed off, looking around toward the plaza's exit. Truly, she was mesmerizing in the moonlight.

Right, of course, sorry, he turned to leave but remembered why else he was here. *Oh wait, one last thing,* she turned to look at him with those eyes. *I'm not sure if you've heard, but the leader of the Unfettered is a woman named Kinza Solace. She would have some pretty dangerous abilities, and several of them. You haven't seen someone like that, have you? The sooner we find her, the sooner we can stop the Unfettered.*

At the mention of the Unfettered's leader, she stiffened. It was very possible the Rhaptans still in the city had found out about the prophecy on their own and rumors spread like wild-fire within the Anunnaki; in the midst of an attack or not. That, or this was her first time hearing about the Unfettered's leader. *Oh, um, no I haven't seen anyone like that. Like I said, we've been staying inside.* She sounded like she was trying to be braver than she really was. He hoped he hadn't frightened her.

Oh well. *Okay, that's probably for the best.* He paused to think before saying, *You have a really beautiful voice by the way. Where are my manners? He* came halfway around the fountain, letting her decide if she wanted to come closer, and stuck his hand out. *My name is Mikah. What's yours?*

He thought he was about to get rejected for the second time in twenty-four hours—a record for him—when she reached out and grasped his hand as well. Her fingers were slender and warm, and gripped his hand tightly. *It's Mitra.*

It was nice to meet you, Mitra, he said with a smile. *And don't worry, we'll catch her soon and the Elders will return. Are you sure you don't want to come with me?*

I'm sure, thank you. I really need to go now, she said, tucking the scarf more firmly in front of her.

Well, then, it's been a pleasure, Mitra, he said and gave a short bow. He left first, so she could watch him leave and Mikah kept on his lazy walk through the dark streets.

Kinza's heart was beating wildly as she hurried back to the library. She could hardly believe it, she had spoken Rhaptan, an entire conversation! And she had understood the man she had spoken to enough to respond. He hadn't said anything about how she was speaking, so she must have done a good enough job of it.

She needed to tell the Apostles what she heard right away. How stupid had she been though? Going out into the city, alone, while everyone and their mother was looking for her. That was not exactly smart. Grams would have yelled at her for being so careless.

The ache at missing her grandmother came back. She wished she had taken Zaid's offer to call her the other day. She could have at least told her she was okay, but Grams must think she was dead now. If she ever did get back, they would have to have a long conversation. Was the old woman really Ummanu? She did have the mark on her door, and a Death-stone, and seemed to know why Zaid had been there. But if she wasn't ubir, then why would Grams think they would come for her? If Grams knew about the prophecy too and didn't tell her she would scream. It felt like everyone but her knew. It would have been nice to have been prepared. She could have used stronger deadbolts or something...

She mentally berated herself for thinking about things she could not change. There were so many things in life that she wanted to be different but it was a waste of time trying to make it so. The best she could hope for now was to survive this civil war, convince the Elders that she wanted nothing to do with Rhapta, and go home and live her life in peace. Could she really do that though? Could she live the rest of her life with these abilities, knowing that there is an entire race of people out here like her? She would also outlive anyone she let into her life by close to a hundred years. The thought of it was....lonely.

Just more things that she could not afford to think about now. The fact that there were people still alive outside the city was a good sign, confirming that the Apostles' theory had been correct. The bad news was they somehow knew about her too and were coming to kill her. The entire city was really against her. This was bad. Really bad. They needed to come up with a plan, and fast to convince the Elders she wasn't trying to harm them, let alone lead an army against the city.

If only they knew exactly when the Rhaptans would return. It was nerve-wracking not knowing when they could show up. If the scouts just got here then surely they would have a few days at least. She looked up at the sky, wishing she could at least find a clock. The moon was on its descent, so it had to be really late, or probably early the next morning by now. She would tell Sa'id or Nim what she had found out after she slept.

Within minutes she found the secret door set into the wall of a building a few blocks away from the library. Nim had said the network of tunnels under the library were extensively spread out like a tree's roots and there were a few doors that led out into the city, but they kept an eye on them from below. No one but the Apostles knew of them, so telling Kinza, Zaid, and Khalil had been a risk for them. There also apparently were other similar networks of tunnels around the city, but these were the only ones they had located. The Apostles didn't have the number of people the Unfettered did, despite how lively it was down below. They needed to prioritize their work on the most important things. She pulled the door open, making sure to look around in case anyone had followed her.

Despite the fear of being caught,, the conversation with that man, Mikah, had definitely been the most pleasant of any she had had here so far. Even though she had been panicking the entire time that he would figure out she wasn't Rhaptan, she had almost enjoyed the chance to speak to someone like that. It was like she was a normal person, not some prophe-sized hero-murderer. It was nice for a change, and it didn't hurt that he was kind of cute.

That smile...

She made her way through the tunnels, getting back to the

brightly lit hallways of the residential wing. It had finally quieted down, but it seemed activity would never come to a full stop. She saw a few people, some in the blue robes and some not, talking in one of the meeting rooms and a few more chatting sleepily down the hall.

She finally got to her door, desperate for the sleep she had put off for too long.

"Where the hell were you?" Kinza whirled around to find Zaid standing behind her, thankfully he had put a shirt on but was hovering a little closer than usual.

"Oh, now you want to talk?" She rolled her eyes and opened her door. Seriously, the man was like night and day.

He yanked the door shut before she could go in. "I asked you a question. Where were you? I heard you leave."

"And you didn't bother following me? Wow Zaid, you are getting really lax in your stalking abilities." Precious minutes of sleep were being wasted on this conversation.

He moved to lean against her door. "You said you wanted to talk, so talk."

"Not about this!" she exclaimed, getting irritated. Why could they not have had this conversation an hour ago? "I wanted to know why you are so stupid as to believe them." She tried shoving him aside but he just pushed her away.

"Hey—!"

"I *saw* you talking to that security guard, Kinza," he whispered, eyes narrowing again. "I watched you for a week before I took you."

"Oh, how nice of you," she said, throwing her hands up. "Clearly you didn't listen as well because if you had you would have heard the normal conversations I had with Phil." She started ticking off all the things she could remember. "How his kids were, what kind of tv dinners he bought this week, his crazy ex-wife calling again. Those kinds of things."

"And how did they know about your tattoo? They just happened to guess exactly what it looked like?" He crossed his arms. "And Ghassan? You disobeyed my orders and left the truck when we were at that resort. Why did you go looking for Ghassan?"

"Because I was worried about you!" She tried to help save him and now he thinks she is some kind of maniac? "Ugh!"

"Right, and you just so happened to kill him in the process. Zakariah said he was getting fed up with you. Killing Ghassan seems like a good way to solve that problem."

"He was going to push me off the roof! What did you want me to do?!" The Apostles down the hall had turned to look at them.

"Stay in the truck, Kinza!" he yelled in her face. "You should have stayed in the truck!"

"This is stupid and clearly a waste of time. You're already set on not believing me." She tried pushing him aside again, only to get shoved back. "Move!"

He just kept talking. "You're telling me you don't want revenge on the Elders or whoever it was that had your parents killed. Because I would believe it if that were the case. A little Anunnaki girl, all alone in the world and her parents were murdered. It's a slippery slope to revenge from there."

"I didn't know about the Anunnaki at all!" she yelled. The mention of her parents stung and she *was* angry that her parents were murdered. Of course she wanted revenge from the happy life she could have had with them, but in a put-the-perpetrator-in-jail kind of way and not murder-an-entire-civilization kind of way. She didn't tell him that, he would only find a way to reinterpret her words.

The door to her left was yanked open and Khalil stepped out, one eye open and the other squeezed shut against the light. "Can you two please be silent? Some of us actually need sleep to exist."

Kinza used the momentary distraction to shove Zaid to the side and entered her room. "Goodnight, Zaid," she said and slammed the door in his face, cutting off whatever retort he was going to say.

CHAPTER 13
RALLYING THE TROOPS

Mikah and the warriors made progress the next morning. They had seen a few Rhaptans who ran upon seeing them, but they followed their trail. The captain had them walking to the south quarter for an hour or so when they found signs people had been nearby.

The night before, after Mikah had left the woman in the plaza, he walked nearly the entire western quarter until he found the team of warriors. They had grabbed him at first, thinking he was one of the Unfettered, but quickly realized it was him and muttered their apologies. They camped in one of the abandoned buildings and went back out at dawn. Mikah didn't tell them about the woman he had talked with, Mitra. It wasn't like she had given him any pertinent information anyway.

The group of them turned down another boulevard and saw a large building up ahead, a few warriors standing guard. One of them ran inside when they saw him and his group. A moment later a stream of warriors poured out as well as a tall bald man with a thick beard. He stormed over to them with wary eyes, his warriors had their spears pointed toward them. Mikah's own warriors held their hands up as he did.

Who are you? the man demanded.

We are here at the Elders' request. My name is Mikah Sultan, I am Elder Tahir's apprentice. There is a large camp of us outside the city that escaped, he said pointing back north. *We came back looking for survivors.*

Outside the city!? the man exclaimed. *And you are not ubir?* His warriors exchanged glances.

It's a long story, but yes, Mikah said. *Elder Tahir was able to craft a small satellite city, really just a camp, barely big enough to hold us within a temporary barrier, but it won't last. The escaped Elders are planning countermeasures as we speak. We snuck back in looking to see who is still holding out here and if we can work together to expunge these Unfettered. I assume you have realized it's them?*

Yes, the man said, rubbing at his beard. *We've learned other things as well. You had better come in. I am Nazim.*

Nazim's warriors lowered their spears and began chattering amongst their lost brethren, relaxed now they knew they hadn't defected. *Ah, yes, you used to be one of the warrior trainers?* Mikah asked.

Yes, Nazim said, nodding. *That was some time ago.* He took them into the building. Mikah had thought it was two floors, but it was just a vast open space, probably used for food storage a long time ago. Now the room was packed with people. So many that there was not much left for room. If any more were found they would need to expand elsewhere. A few fires were lit in worn braziers and people huddled around, some with their morning breakfast.

You have quite the group here, Mikah said. He hadn't expected this many people to have banded together, and had planned on having to give his spiel to several smaller groups. This would make his job a lot easier.

Yes, we've done our best to keep the Unfettered at bay, Nazim said as they strode all the way to the back where a few other warriors gathered. *It's less like they are trying to kill us now and more like they are taunting us. You say many people made it out?*

Yes, most of the missing are in the camp, thousands. Mikah thought of the cramped tent he had been in just yesterday and the gaggle of people that had pressed him the moment he got outside. Too many people in too small a space.

I cannot imagine a marvel that you were able to leave safely and remain Anunnaki. Nazim did look both impressed and confused at that. But now was not the time to discuss the mechanics of rocks and psychic barriers.

Well, you can thank Elder Tahir for that one when they return. You say you have learned things? I would hear of them.

Nazim stopped and looked at him, glancing around at the people in the room. It seemed clear that he was the leader here as many people kept their eyes trained on him—and Mikah— as if waiting for news. They looked scared and worn down, as was to be expected. *Yes, if you hadn't heard the whispers, a group of people arrived yesterday. Two men and a woman, the woman was an outsider.*

Mikah's eyebrows went up. He already knew what the man was going to say, of course, but wanted him to feel as if he had accomplished something.

Yes, it is what you think, Nazim said, lowering his voice. *The old prophecy is upon us and it has turned for the worst. We were able to speak with a group of the Unfettered and they claimed she was their leader. She pretended not to know them or of us, but the evidence they presented....it was ironclad.*

That was something he definitely did not know. The enemy was pretending to not be their enemy? Some of the Unfettered working against her yet still attacked. Tahir needed to know this, especially if Kinza Solace was trying to play both sides. *What happened?* he asked. *Is she here now?* He looked around for someone bound in chains or *laqueus,* but didn't see anyone who met that description.

One of the men took her and ran off, he has a speed ability, there was no way to catch him. The other man disappeared in the mob. Zaid. Internally, Mikah growled in frustration. That idiot *venari* was hiding her? It looked like Tahir was right again; Zaid must've been fooled by her. What could she have said to make him sway to her side? On second thought, he would've believed anything. Mikah would probably need to remove his memories of her as soon as he found him, otherwise it would be a pain trying to get to her if she was being carted around by a man who could move at the speed of sound.

Mob? he asked instead. He hadn't expected that either.

Oh yes, the people here found out she was the one behind the attack and went wild with rage, stampeding down the street to get her before she was zipped away. We ended up scuffling with a few of the Unfettered and several of us didn't make it. But the noise brought out more hidden Rhaptans and our numbers have grown. That explained why there were so many people packed in here.

I assume you've tried looking for them?

Yes, but it is difficult to do so and keep out of sight of the Unfettered. What word of the Elders? Nazim asked.

They are preparing the warriors now to strike back within a few days at most, Mikah said. *I can't say when. They want as many people here ready as possible, boarding up buildings for fortification, readying weapons, finding out who can fight, all of it.* He was glad to see there were several warriors here. It was nothing compared to the host in the camp, but it was better than nothing.

I can help but I think the people will need to hear it from you as well.

Of course. Mikah had expected as much. He followed Nazim back to the front of the room. He raised his arms for silence, but the people had been watching him and Mikah speak and quieted quickly.

Quiet now! Nazim said. He had a booming voice, good for speeches, bad for secrets. *I have with us Mikah Sultan, apprentice of Elder Tahir who escaped the city safely. He has brought us news of the missing Rhaptans. Please give him your silence.* People whispered momentarily at hearing about the escaped Rhaptans, but did as Nazim told them.

Thank you, Nazim, Mikah said. *It is true,* he said, addressing the crowd now, *myself along with thousands of other Rhaptans escaped on the night of the attack due to Grand Elder Hakim's foresight. He had a vision shortly before it happened and Elder Tahir ingeniously came up with a way we could make a small, temporary camp north of the city.* The whispering broke out again and people exchanged furtive glances. Of course the knowledge that people left the city would shock them. But he had an agenda to keep to.

Yes, it's true and we can look into that more later. Right now I, along with several of Commander Kartik's warriors have returned to see how many survivors there are and prepare you.

For what? a man said from the side of the room. He lounged with arms crossed, expression concerned at Mikah's words.

The Elders in the camp are planning a counterattack that will take place anytime within the next few days. They will most likely return from the north, where we escaped. The majority of the warrior force is with them now and is preparing. What the Elders ask is that you get yourselves ready. Fortify a stronghold, marshal your best fighters and those with offensive abilities. Use what we have here to get ready. Questions started popping up left and right, people wanting to know details that he didn't have. The talk in the room turned excited but worried. He knew the feeling; at least they would be able to do something instead of just sitting there.

I also learned that many of you have uncovered who the leader of the Unfettered is; the woman, Kinza Solace. Her name sparked anger among them, spreading like a forest fire. *Do not worry. We will capture her as well. If anyone knows her whereabouts it would help us greatly.*

A few people spoke up, mentioning places they thought they saw her, but none of them had consistent answers. Another woman stood. She was graceful and looked slightly familiar, speaking with a strong voice.

Some of us are not convinced by the lies the Unfettered are spreading. There was no public trial and much evidence has not been proven. Mikah hadn't considered there would be people who didn't believe Kinza Solace was their enemy. It didn't matter though. He would prove it to them momentarily, it was good for them to let a little steam out.

How can you say that!? another woman cried as she got to her feet. *Nazim was there and witnessed everything. And she ran. Does that not prove her guilt?*

No it does not! the first woman shouted back, not the least bit cowed. *Last time I checked, all criminals in Rhapta are allowed a fair trial, not a mob of screaming children sent after them.* This wasn't incorrect, Mikah just felt that now wasn't the time to be digging into the semantics of Rhaptan law. The enemy would come barging through your door whilst you sat negotiating what to do when you caught them.

You have not lost anyone so you do not feel the pain we do, another man countered. It seemed there was as much bitterness here as there was in the camp. He would have to tread lightly, giving the people tasks to outlet their rage instead of inciting another riot as Tahir would've done.

Please! Be quiet, Mikah said, raising his arms and the people settled down. *I have more news. While at the camp, Grand Elder Hakim had another vision. It was unfortunately one confirming the leader of the Unfettered was Kinza Solace. Unless Hakim's visions are suddenly wrong after two hundred years....*

It must be true then! the second woman cried out. Many others nodded with her. At least they didn't start screaming for blood this time. That gave him such a headache.

We need to hurry, he said. *The camp will not last much longer and our people need to come home. The only way to do that is to push back against Kinza and her army of Unfettered. They are strong, but they do not have our sheer numbers. We will not leave again!*

The people mostly cheered, a few of them looking sour at the prospect of a battle, but the room bustled with activity. Men and women lined up before Nazim, some clambering for jobs, others offering their abilities. They were working together, chaotically, yes, but at least they were focused.

Mikah sighed. Now to find the enemy.

CHAPTER 14
SEARCHING FOR TRUTH

Zaid stood in front of Kinza's door for a solid five minutes, trying to cool down.

A few hours ago he had heard her leave her room and had assumed she went to talk with the Apostles again. After thirty minutes she hadn't come back so he went looking for her. It didn't take him long to wander through the network of hallways asking people if they had seen her until one man had said he saw someone with her description head outside. Zaid decided not to follow her. He didn't know where he stood with her anymore. At first he had been her captor, and then he might have considered himself her friend, but now... now he didn't know what to think.

Her footsteps shuffled down the hall a few hours later and he had shot out of bed, ignoring his relief that she wasn't dead in favor of his anger. She was in a city full of people trying to kill her and she just wandered outside?

Before he realized it, he was blocking her from entering her room, demanding to know where she had been. He kept waiting for an explanation, something that would shed light and clear away all the messiness of the last two days. Her anger had only fueled his more. It didn't help that she looked gorgeous, yelling back at him while wearing Rhaptan silks and scarves, and smelling like orange blossoms. It only made him more confused.

As he stood in front of the closed door, he had the sudden thought of what it would have been like if she had been born here; if they had grown up in the same city. If there was no prophecy, no attack on the city, no ostracization, would they have been friends? Or would she have looked at him the way the rest of Rhapta looked at venari? He couldn't imagine her face twisting into the familiar wariness and disgust he received from others. He shook his head, drawing himself back into reality, where he didn't know who she really was and Rhapta was at war.

Zaid turned and stalked a short distance down the hall and let himself into Khalil's room. The light from the hall illuminated the bed and Khalil shot up in exasperation.

"What?!" he yelled, squinting at the light. Zaid could see the sallowness in his face, even in the half-light.

"Keep an eye on Kinza, I'll be back," he said.

"Wait, what—?" Khalil started to say but Zaid closed the door again before he could reply. He didn't want to have to explain, but he made a decision. There were too many questions and not enough answers for him to make his next move. Would he continue to help Kinza? Would he turn her in? Was she really the leader of the Unfettered or was she being framed? The questions swirled in his mind as he moved through the hallways again, foregoing sleep in search of truth.

If the Apostles had more information, they would have told them; not that he trusted their word. The assassins that had been sent to kill Kinza all said they were sent by Elder Tahir, and now the Apostles were claiming Zaid's own brother had been working against Tahir as well, and that was why he was killed. Amir was no longer here so the only person left was the man who had befriended Zaid years ago, the man who had helped him and his mother in times of need, and who had mentored him when his first years of training became over-whelming.

As he neared the outer hallways he noticed a few scholars standing by the stairwell that led up to the door, one of them had clearly been outside and they both whispered furiously. They glanced at Zaid as he neared.

"Is there news from above?" he said, jerking his chin to the stairwell.

They looked at each other before one of them caved and said, *Apparently some of the missing Rhaptans have been found. A group of them was discovered by one of the holdouts in the south quarter. We were right! They were staying in a camp outside the city somehow. It's amazing!*

Just a group of them? Zaid asked. *What about the rest?*

Yes, one of the Elder's apprentices and a few warriors, that's it. They are spreading the word to those of us still here that there will be a counterattack within a few days at the latest. The Elders want us to prepare for war. The two men looked grim, but Zaid found this to be good news. Maybe he could find them and find out where Tahir was.

The war has already started, he said and moved past them and up the stairwell.

The night air was a relief from the walls of the library. He ran as quietly as he could, away from the camp of Unfettered in the central plaza and headed south. Nazim's group was defi-nitely the largest he had seen over the past couple of days, so it was probably going to be his best bet.

The sky was already lightening as he ran, making it easier to see the streets with no illumination from the Aurastones. He did his best to avoid smaller groups, listening for the heart-beats until the familiar mass of beats came from a few plazas up. He slowed to a walk, not wanting to startle them as they would still have patrols wandering this far out. His steps veered to the right and slowed as a group of warriors took notice of him.

Stop! they called and ran to him. Zaid raised his hands in a sign of peace, but still found his feet stuck to the ground—one of the warrior's abilities then. It was a good thing that one didn't come with them the night of Kinza's trial, otherwise things would have ended very differently.

I'm not one of the Unfettered, he said, hoping to calm them. Spears up, they encircled him instead, drawing out a long length of *laqueus.*

We know who you are, Zaid Hatem, one of them sneered. *Where is she?*

I want to speak with Nazim, Zaid replied. *Also, I need to talk with the Rhaptans who returned. Who was the apprentice that made it back?* he asked.

You do not get to ask the questions, one of them said. *We are taking you to Nazim and he can decide what to do with you.*

Zaid sighed as his arms were pulled behind him and the *laqueus* was wrapped around his wrists. He had been bound by *laqueus* before—all *venari* had to train with it—but he never enjoyed the stifling silence he felt in his head with it on. It didn't remove his ability to communicate, but telepathic speech sounded far away, with little ambient sound as if he had stuffed cotton in his ears. The part that unnerved him was his sudden unawareness of the surrounding heartbeats. He never realized how much he relied on them until they were gone. It was almost as bad as if he had gone deaf. He knew that if he tried to run he would do so only at the sluggish pace of everyone else. Hopefully Nazim and the apprentice listened to him, otherwise he wouldn't be returning to Kinza and Khalil anytime soon.

They walked him back to the familiar long building, but didn't bring him inside. One of the warriors went in, presumably to get Nazim. Zaid noticed stockpiles of obsidian spears , swords, and various other weapons piled in the small plaza before the building. A few people walking in pairs were coming and going, even at this early hour. They glanced at him but kept to themselves, some giving him angry glances as they walked by. They all seemed to be carrying bags or baskets filled with things from the surrounding neighborhoods. It looked like the Apostles were right and the Elders were readying the citizens for battle.

It was only a few minutes before Nazim came storming out, his large form towering over the warriors trailing behind him. Gone was the friendly disposition he had shown Zaid a few days ago only to be replaced with stony fury. Zaid didn't expect any less.

You have a lot of nerve coming back here, Nazim said coming to a stop before Zaid. The other two warriors flanked him on either side. In the twilight of pre-dawn, the red paint on their skin was as dark as dried blood.

I need to speak to the apprentice that arrived, Zaid replied.

Nazim shoved a finger in his face. *You don't go demanding any—*

It's all right, Nazim. I'm happy to speak with him, a smooth voice came from behind them. The group turned to look at the man striding out from the building, the ever-present charming smile stretched across his face.

Zaid inwardly groaned, letting out a long string of mental curses. Out of all apprentices, why in the name of the Creator did it have to be *him*?

Mikah walked up looking at Zaid as if he were king and

Zaid a peasant who had come to beg for mercy. *You look....alive,* he said, curling his lip.

Where is Tahir? Zaid said, ignoring the jab. *I need to speak with him.*

Mikah's eyebrows rose slightly. *Do you now?* he said, voice tinged with mirth.

Zaid had successfully gone the last two years without taking a swing at the other man's face, but he started to wonder if he was going to break that record today. They had known each other for several years now, but Zaid knew Mikah had a bitter jealousy of Zaid's relationship with Tahir. Unfortunately, it didn't stop Mikah from making one of his oh-so-clever comments meant to set Zaid's teeth on edge.

Mikah, Nazim said. *This is the man I was telling you about, the one who took Kinza Solace from her trial and ran off with her.*

Mikah looked at him in mock surprise.

You were going to just let an angry mob kill her! Zaid shouted. The warriors behind him tugged on the *laqueus* a little to restrain him. *And since when are you judge, jury, and executioner?*

Mikah's head swiveled to the other man with a dry gasp to match his expression.

These are unprecedented times! Nazim shouted back. *People are dead! Or have you not noticed? I did not think she seemed the type to do this, but there was just too much evidence against her that she couldn't explain away.*

That doesn't mean you let a mob maul her to death, Zaid spat. *You could have kept her bound until the Elders came back.* He shook his head. *This is stupid. I need to talk to Tahir, it's really important,* he said, turning back to Mikah.

Mikah had one hand half covering his mouth, failing to hide his amused smile as he watched the men bicker. They were talking about people being murdered and all he could do was stand there and smile? Zaid wanted to smash his teeth in.

And why would you need to talk with Tahir? Mikah asked. *Has that woman gotten into your head? Oh yes, I've heard some wonderful rumors about how she brainwashed you. Tell me it isn't true.*

I can't explain, but it's about things that happened while I was bringing Kinza in, and I—

Nazim let out an exasperated huff. *You shelter the leader of the Unfettered, but expect to be granted permission to see an Elder? Do you think we are dumb of mind? We can't risk Elder Tahir's location if you are just going to bring that information back to that woman.*

Yes, I'm going to need a little more than that, Hatem, Mikah replied. *Are you implying you are* not *allied with the Unfettered?*

Zaid growled in frustration. *No, I'm not allied with the Unfettered. But I was sent to retrieve Kinza as if she was ubir, by Tahir. And then....things happened on the way back to the city that I can only speak with Tahir about. Look,* he said, eyeing their skeptical faces, *I don't know what to believe right now, but I trust Tahir and need to hear the truth about her from him.*

He hated that he was practically begging Mikah for access to Tahir. The other man knew Tahir would want to see him and was only dragging out this conversation to satiate his bitterness against Zaid. But Zaid needed to speak with Tahir, there wasn't any other way he was going to get answers about this whole situation.

If Tahir said Kinza was innocent, then so be it. If not, then he would deal with that when the time came, but being in the dark wasn't helping anyone. He realized that more than anything right now, he wanted to know where he stood with Kinza and hated every moment that he didn't just *know* the right decision.

*I don't believe—*Nazim started to say but Mikah cut him off.

Fine.

Nazim crossed his arms. *What do you mean 'fine'? Are you giving away the location of the remaining Rhaptans now?*

A few of our warriors can take Zaid to Tahir; we have news to send the other Elders anyway, Mikah said, eyeing the people hurrying around the plaza, preparing for war. *If Tahir finds him untrustworthy*—he shrugged—*then they can deal with him there. I do need to ask, Hatem. Where is Kinza Solace?*

No idea, he said. *She and I got separated while escaping from the mob.* All three of them knew it was a lie, but the idea of anyone finding Kinza while he was gone made his stomach twist.

Mikah rolled his eyes. *You leave now then. I'm sure Tahir has all the time in the world to listen about your little adventure.*

Zaid hoped Tahir had answers as well.

CHAPTER 15

BATTLE PLANS

The faint sound of whispering woke Kinza from a deep sleep.

She shot up from her bedroll thinking someone was in the room, but upon blinking away the bleariness, saw it was empty, only a sliver of light coming in from under the door. The whispers were just the telepathic speech from the Apostles going about their work, scurrying up and down the halls just outside her door. She sighed and flopped back down in a heap of blankets, curls falling across her face.

There were no clocks or windows in the underground room so there was no way to tell what time it was, but based on how rested she felt and the time she had gone to bed, it must've at least been late morning. Thoughts from her argument with Zaid came tumbling back. She felt a little guilty for slamming the door in his face, but she couldn't take the way he had been looking at her. His familiar face had been distrustful and his rumbling voice had been filled with doubt about where she had been. She so desperately wanted him to believe her but everything she did and said only made it worse.

She wiggled her fingers in the darkness, remembering the flames that had wreathed her in a fiery corona. Why couldn't she have had some sort of memory sharing ability? Or at least something useful. If only Zaid or the Elders could look through her life they would find she was innocent and had done nothing wrong. Instead, she had these destructive abilities she couldn't even control that only made her seem like a creature of vengeance.

She rolled over and half screamed into her pillow out of frustration before getting up. It wasn't as stress-relieving as she had hoped.

Before she had gone to bed she had found a smaller Aurastone—the size of a melon—in a closed box that acted as a sort of lamp. She removed the lid now letting out the faint light it emitted. The blue of the stone almost looked like it swirled as the light wavered like a candle. Without thinking she placed her hand on the stone and was surprised to find it had a faint energy coming off of it, almost like a humming. It did far more to relax her than the pillow scream had, so she took a deep breath and got dressed.

There were multiple sets of clothing similar to the ones she had on the day before in the chest by the wall. She picked out a set that was a deep golden color with intricate stitching in the same color, giving it a textured appearance. It only took her a moment to wash her face in the small bathroom and tie back some of her curls before she went out into the hall to explore.

Several Apostles in deep blue robes hurried back and forth, some holding piles of books and scrolls, and others in deep conversation about the Unfettered camped practically above them. Kinza passed Khalil and Zaid's rooms, both empty, and made her way to the kitchens. Nim had given her vague directions the night before, but she could have just followed her nose. She followed the scent of spices into a large room with low ceilings packed with many low lying tables and cushions. Each of the tables had platters of fruits, sweet breads, strips of glistening meat, and teapots filled with the source of the spicy scent she had followed. It was relatively empty though and it was easy to spot Khalil sitting at one of the tables in the corner with his nose in a book.

"Good morning," she said with a yawn. The silk cushions rustled as she sat down across from him and peered at the food on the table. With the emergence of her abilities over the last week, she had noticed a decrease in her appetite. Anunnaki only truly needed to eat once every three days or so, and it seemed she was getting close to that. While the food smelled delicious, she had no interest in eating any of it at the moment; opting instead for a cup of the spiced drink.

"Good morning, Kinza. Or I should probably say good afternoon soon," Khalil replied after swallowing a mouthful of some kind of yellow fruit.

She gave a wry smile and sipped the drink. It was indeed heavily spiced, almost like chai but had a sharper taste. "I guess I was tired."

"At least one of us slept well."

"Sorry about last night," she said with a frown and looked around. "Where is Zaid anyway?"

"He left." Khalil was still reading his book as he consumed another piece of the yellow fruit. She couldn't read it, but the writing on the cover looked to be Arabic.

"He left? To go where?" Irritation bubbled up and she didn't bother stomping it down. He yelled at her just last night for leaving and going out into the city, and now he was doing the same? She took another gulp of the spicy tea, letting the heat trickle down into her belly and soothe the ever-present tension there.

"I have not the slightest idea where he went off to, but he left last night," Khalil replied.

She set her cup down. "Is he coming back?"

"No idea."

"Do you know *anything*?"

"Yes, that he left." Kinza couldn't tell if he was irritated with her or with Zaid so she just sipped her tea in silence.

Had Zaid left for good? It was a slightly odd feeling as she had been near him for so long now. She had gotten used to his dark form always present nearby with sharp comments and demands for her to stay put or to keep quiet. Maybe he had finally decided that he couldn't trust her and had gone back to Nazim's group. Kinza couldn't entirely blame him for wanting to be with his family. He had gone through hell the past week and all of the problems revolved around her but his absence felt abrupt and left her feeling sorry for herself.

Stop it, she said to herself. *He could be just going for a walk and will be back in an hour. You're being dramatic.*

Grams would tell her to stop leaping to conclusions, but she couldn't help it. She sighed and glared at the table.

"Ah, there you are!" boomed a voice behind them, causing Kinza to jolt, tea sloshing over the edge of her cup. She turned to find Nim striding up. His grouchy face split into a grin as he looked down at them. "Did you sleep well?"

"Yes," Khalil said. "Some of us better than others."

"Good morning, Nim," Kinza said. "Yes we slept well."

"Great. Let's go," he said and turned around and immediately started walking back the way he came.

"What?" Kinza started, scrambling to her feet.

"Where?" Khalil asked, doing the same but taking his time.

"The Unfettered have not stopped while you were sleeping and there are plans to be made," Nim said. Other Apostles scrambled out of his way as he ambled down the network of hallways, Khalil and Kinza following close behind.

"Ah okay, yeah sure," Kinza said. "Maybe we should, um, wait until Zaid gets back..."

"I don't think the gloomy one will be returning," Nim said.

"Why?" Kinza asked, trying to keep up. His large body moved much quicker than she expected.

Nim turned to glance at her. "I assumed he had talked with you first. A few of our men saw him leave last night and followed him to a large group of people in the south quarter. He was bound, but it looked like he turned himself into them."

A shock ran through Kinza but she said nothing. Turned himself in? To Nazim's group? That was it then. She felt her stomach twist and her heart drop; he had really left her, which meant he really thought she caused all of this. She heard Khalil question Nim on Zaid's actions, but Kinza wasn't paying attention. She was focusing on keeping the tears from welling in her eyes and shoving the swirling mess of emotion down as much as she could. She could think about Zaid later, right now she needed to focus on the upcoming battle and not getting killed.

Nim took them to another room a little larger than the one they had been in the night before. Several long tables were crammed inside, most spilling over various books, maps, cups, and Aurastones to leave little room for walking.

She found Sa'id sitting at the head of one of the tables. He looked up and gave them a warm smile. "Kinza, Khalil, I'm glad you are both awake, I hope you slept well."

"Yes, very well!" Kinza got out before Khalil could mutter his dissatisfaction at his quality of sleep for the third time that morning.

"That is most wonderful. Please have a seat. I'd like to introduce you to a few other Apostles," he said, indicating to two men that sat on one side of the table. The first man was very small and appeared shorter than Kinza and looked like he would blow away in a stiff wind. He sat ramrod straight in his chair but smiled as they entered. "This is Jabari," Sa'id said, indicating the small man. "He has been with us for about a decade now and has done great things for the Apostles of Truth." Jabari nodded politely, but said nothing else.

"And this is Jabari's apprentice—" Sa'id started to say, but was interrupted when the other man lurched across the table and stuck his hand out to Kinza.

"My name is Badr. It's a wonderful pleasure to meet you!" he said. He looked younger than the other man but was much taller, giving Kinza the impression of a string bean. She shook his hand and he gripped hers in both of his and shook vigorously.

"You as well," she said. "My name is—"

"Kinza Solace! Oh, I know all about you already. I can't believe the prophecy is happening now and the outsider is finally here, but I knew it would. This is all so exciting."

"Oh, um..."

"Badr, sit down you buffoon," Nim said, pushing past him to take his own seat. The younger man sat back down, seeming not at all admonished.

Khalil nodded. "It's a pleasure to meet you, I am Khalil." They took seats where they could amongst the cramped room. "Have there been any updates from above?" he asked Sa'id.

Sa'id frowned. "Yes, unfortunately, there have been some developments overnight. A few Rhaptans returned and are in the city."

"What?" Khalil said, leaning forward.

"Oh my gosh!" Kinza cried, realizing she had entirely forgotten about her conversation with the man, Mikah, she had met in the square the night before. She had planned on telling them about it right away but she had been so preoccupied with her fight with Zaid that she had forgotten.

"Kinza?" Sa'id said, the group turned to stare at her.

"I, um, kind of went for a walk last night and met a man who said he was one of the returning Rhaptans and I was going to tell you about it last night, but I was a little, um, distracted and forgot." She gave a sheepish smile, hoping to dull her forgetfulness.

Khalil let out a pain sigh and put his head in his hands.

"You went out?" Nim asked.

"By yourself?" Badr said. "That seems a little...rash."

She heaved a sigh. "Yes, well, I really needed a breather. Either way, the man told me he and the rest of the missing Rhaptans were staying outside of the city and a few of them returned to warn the rest of the survivors here that there will be a counterattack soon and to prepare. He had no idea who I was. I gave another name and I didn't think he knew what 'Kinza Solace' looked like."

"That was a dangerous move, young lady," Nim chastised.

"I know, I'm sorry. I made sure he didn't follow me though, so no one knows where this place is."

"How exactly did you speak to them?" Sa'id asked. "Didn't they notice that you couldn't speak Rhaptan?"

"Yes, um, I guess I kind of learned the language since I got here?" she said, her voice coming out almost as a squeak.

"What?" all three of them asked at the same time, staring at her in confusion.

"You just got here, correct?" Badr asked.

"Yeah," Kinza said, glancing at Khalil. "I noticed it soon after I got here. I couldn't understand at first, but over the last two days or so, I've been just *understanding* what the words mean, even though I've never heard them before."

"That is highly unusual," Badr said.

"More than a little," Sa'id said. "I'm guessing that is an ability, but let's table that for a moment. I want to focus on what that man said to you."

Jabir nodded and spoke for the first time, his voice was measured and precise. "It is in line with the information we have received. The group that came back is warning the survivors here and telling them to prepare for war. It sounds like they are trying to rally people to fight the Unfettered as well, but that will only cause more violence."

"Which is why we need to come up with a plan," Sa'id said, glancing around the room. "The Rhaptans who escaped the city could be here at any time now, as soon as tomorrow, but we are hoping we have a few days. Unfortunately, it sounds like most of the city believes Kinza is the leader behind the Unfettered, who also aren't ceasing their attack."

"What about the Rhaptans outside of the city? If we could get to them, then maybe we can appeal to the Elders that Kinza is being framed," Khalil asked.

"Unfortunately, that won't be possible," Jabari said, appearing grim.

"Why?" Kinza asked, realizing the four Apostles were looking at her.

"Well," Nim said, "Grand Elder Hakim has had a vision that was announced to the camp outside the city. The vision claims that...you," he said nodding to her, "are the leader of the Unfettered. Hakim's visions are never wrong, which means those people in the camp are not going to be much help either."

"That can't be right?" Kahlil said. "How can he have that vision, yet all of us don't believe that is true, right?"

Badr nodded eagerly. "Oh yes, we know that," he said with an appeasing smile toward Kinza. "The problem is Tahir, again, of course. It follows the same pattern, you see. Hakim's health has been declining over the past few decades, but many of his visions are not actually announced by the man himself. Those close to him claim that he is too weak—and frankly, near senile—to be making public statements anymore. So, they are generally announced by his attendants, his nephew, Elder Ekbal, or Tahir. I have a list of dates here with days that Tahir announced Hakim's visions and the subsequent events. I wrote it out in a diagram, let me find it…" he said, trailing off as he dug through a stack of papers.

"I don't understand," Kinza said. "So what does that have to do with his current vision of me?"

"You'll have to excuse my apprentice," Jabari said, referring to the younger man. "His ability is complicated and he sometimes leaves out details the rest of us need to grasp a complex concept. He's saying that we think Tahir announced a false vision on Hakim's behalf to cause further chaos."

"Ohhh!" Kinza said, the pieces falling together. "So we are back to the theory that this Elder—Tahir—is the one behind everything, right?" The others nodded. "I'm curious, what is your ability? If it's not rude to ask?" she said to Badr.

"Oh, not at all!" He seemed excited that someone was interested in him. "I see patterns in events, repetitions, waves that repeat over days, months, years, decades even. The problem is trying to explain what I understand in relative terms and with logic that someone else could understand and comprehend." He scratched the back of his head.

"And it makes for an excellent scholar," Sa'id said with a smile. "But yes, that is our main theory."

"So what do we do?" Kinza asked, toying with an errant curl. "Should I, I don't know, leave? I can't go home to my grandma and have someone follow me back to her."

"No," Nim said with a grunt. "No, I would not recommend that. While we can keep you safe here, Tahir and some of the other Elders have some of the *venari* and assassins in their employ that would just come after you. If I were you I would just do what you were supposed to do."

"Um, and what is that?" Kinza asked.

"Save the city."

A slightly deranged giggle escaped Kinza's lips. "Right, sure, I'll get on that. I hadn't even considered that."

Sa'id cleared his throat. "I think what Nim is trying to say is that the prophecy was clear in the fact that the outsider would be able to bring Rhapta to the ground *or* save it. Meaning that there has to be a way that you can fix this."

"I understand that part, but how?" she asked.

Sa'id gave a faint shrug. "We figured you would know. Do you mind if we ask you a few questions?"

"Sure, shoot." Kinza didn't have anything to hide, but she also didn't think there was anything she knew that would help them.

"Growing up did you know anything about the Anunnaki?" Sa'id asked.

"No, nothing at all. But based on recent events I think my grandma might be Ummanu. We have the Ummanu symbol on our door, but I never knew what it was. I was kidnapped almost a week ago by Zaid and my grandma had a Deathstone, but I had never seen it before then."

"And your parents?" Nim asked.

"They were killed ten years ago." While Kinza didn't mind answering their questions, she didn't want to relive the painful details of her parents' death and didn't want to get into it unless they asked.

Nim pursed his lips but nodded. "You have a mark, yes? Does anyone else in your family?"

"I do have one, and it's bigger than everyone else's. That was probably the only odd thing in my life. I've always had it, but my parents told me they took me to get it when I was little. No one else in my family has one."

They were all quiet for a moment; contemplative.

"What about your abilities?" Badr asked. "Did you receive them as a child?"

"No, actually I had no abilities up until last week."

They all leaned forward at that. "Go on," Sa'id prompted.

Kinza took a breath. "I had started having these nightmares last week of Rhapta, even though I didn't know what it was at the time. On the seventh night I was kidnapped by Zaid, but at the same time I was scared because of my nightmare and that's when my first ability came out." She thought for a moment on how to explain it. "I—I thought it was an explosion at the time, like a bomb, but there was a burning in my abdomen where my tattoo is, and then a white light followed by this *force* that kind of ripped through my bedroom. It happened a few more times by accident after that."

"That sounds...cool!" Badr said.

"I can assure you, it's not as thrilling to be in the middle of," Khalil said drily.

"Okay, that sounds like quite the ability," Sa'id said, scratching his jaw. The stubble there was graying just like the hair on his head.

"Yes, that one is one of the scariest," she said looking down. She didn't want them to think her dangerous. She was, but she didn't want to feel like an outsider anymore.

"You have more?" Jabari inquired. "You mentioned understanding Rhaptan. Have you ever just understood other languages?"

"No, never," she said with a shake of her head.

"Anything else?"

"Oh, yeah. Um, a couple of the times I exploded, I also started a fire. Just the other day it happened again and I was literally on fire and couldn't put it out. And then one time I fell off of a roof and teleported into a bush, and that's only happened one other time. And then the passive abilities, the healing and needing less food and hearing the telepathic speech just came within the last few days."

The Apostles all stared at her slack-jawed.

"So you have some kind of explosion, a fire ability, and teleportation. And you just happen to know a language that is only spoken inside a city that has been hidden for thousands of years. Is that correct?" Badr asked.

"Yes...oh and I did kind of heal Khalil," she said turning to him, "but we aren't sure if that was actually me or if he was helping me." Khalil nodded absentmindedly.

"Right. Okay. That is....a lot." Sa'id sat back in his seat and steepled his fingers before him, thinking. "There is only one person in Rhapta who has more than two abilities, but hers are nothing like yours. This is definitely an anomaly and would only confirm that you are the one from the prophecy." He paused for a moment. "How much control do you have over your abilities? Are you able to fight with them if it came to that?"

Kinza blanched. "Nope, definitely not. There was only one time that I made one of them happen on purpose and that was because Zaid and I were literally going to die. Otherwise they just *happen*. I'm more likely to hurt someone than help stop a fight."

"I might be able to help with that," Jabari said quietly.

Sa'id looked to him and nodded. "Yes, that might not be a bad idea."

At Kinza's expression Jabari continued, "I have a fire ability, like you. I might be able to help you control your abilities as they seem to be on the more destructive side like mine."

"That would be amazing," she said, thankful that she

wasn't the only person whose abilities caused pain and chaos. It made her relax an inch that there was hope for some sort of stability.

"Good, good. We have that going for us, but it won't stop the battle and the Rhaptans rage against Kinza," Sa'id said.

"Do you think I should talk with the Unfettered?" Kinza asked. "To see if maybe some of them will listen to me and stop the attack?"

"No!" Nim said. "That would be a bad idea. Since they don't have orders from you, that means they are coming from someone else—probably Tahir—who told them to continue the attack. You talking with them would only fuel the fire."

Sa'id exhaled a long breath. "The only way to calm the waters is to get to the Elders—the ones not controlled by Tahir—and prove to them that you are not a threat." He looked like he was going to continue, but a soft rap came at the door and a young woman in scholar's robes came in. She hurried over to Sa'id and whispered in his ear, he nodded and she hurried back out.

"And how is she supposed to get to the Elders?" Khalil asked. "During the battle? And how is she supposed to convince them?"

Nim shrugged. "Either we expose Tahir or get him to admit his own guilt. The problem is he is very good at hiding evidence and keeping his inner circle to a minimum. It has taken us decades to even suspect him, let alone gather information; it's how he has lasted so long without anyone finding out what he has been doing. And getting him to admit his own guilt is a far cry. I honestly don't know what you should do Kinza, but if you don't convince them, I'm not sure what will stop the Anunnaki from coming after you."

Kinza wallowed in her misery while Nim turned and whispered to Sa'id, discussing the messenger that had come in.

Kinza was starting to feel a faint tinge of panic in her chest. She didn't want to be in a battle, or find a bunch of old men and convince them she was a good person. She wanted to go home and watch reality tv with Grams and complain about the noise their neighbors made at night. She wanted to be in her own bedroom with Grams just down the hall. She wanted to wake up from this bizarre, exhausting nightmare.

"I wish we had more time to discuss this, but the Unfettered are on the move," Sa'id said.

"What happened?" Khalil asked, raking a hand through his hair.

"They are spreading back out through the city. Their main force is still in the central plaza, but they are setting up around the walls of Rhapta as well. They must have gotten the word about the escaped Elders' impending attack and are preparing. A few of our scouts were hurt in a skirmish and I must attend to them," Sa'id said standing.

"If you need me to take a look at them, I am happy to," Khalil said.

"That would be much appreciated. Kinza," Sa'id said, "I think it's best that for now you stay here. Jabari can work with you on your abilities in the meantime." Jabari nodded in agreement.

Kinza wilted at the lack of a plan. "Yeah, that sounds good."

CHAPTER 16

FALSE FRIENDS REUNITED

The camp outside of Rhapta was far larger than Zaid had expected. He couldn't even see the other side from where he entered through the trees. His hands were still bound in *laqueus* and no less than four warriors surrounded him, but he looked around at the thousands upon thousands of people that were packed together in groups under the sun.

Mikah had been true to his word and Zaid had been sent with Mikah's warriors into one of the tunnels that extended beneath Rhapta. The one they entered was new to him and they walked it for what felt like an hour. When they did come out, it was within a copse of trees. Just beyond that was the massive ring of Aurastone slabs sitting in the middle of a field. There was only twenty feet at most between the end of the tunnel to the edge of the camp, but it still made him nervous being outside the barrier.

He didn't see any humans around, but on the chance there had been, they would see a group of people appear, only to disappear a few seconds later. He couldn't imagine what it would have looked like during the initial attack and escape.

It was an immense relief to see so many people here, though. How Tahir had managed to build this place and then get so many out safely was a wonder to him. It was almost surprising that the Unfettered hadn't found this place. They had been patrolling the city the last few days, but apparently they didn't bother going down into the tunnels, otherwise this place would have been swarmed—or blocked off.

The warriors steered him through the groups of people, many of them staring at him as he was the only person bound. Soon the staring turned to glares of outright hostility or disgust. It could have easily been due to the fact he was *venari* or maybe they thought he was bound because he was one of the Unfettered. Zaid met their stares with one of his own, but couldn't help looking around.

These people looked angry and afraid and miserable. Some cooked and others soothed children. Tents were erected haphazardly to escape the hot midday sun, but others had bedrolls laid out on the ground. Warriors stalked between the groups attempting to maintain some order of people, but Zaid could see that many were restless. As they got further along he could see others sharpening obsidian blades and warrior pupils as young as fifteen running drills. Would they really have children in battle? That was insane, there were more than enough warriors here, practically the entire force. The Unfettered were far less numerous and had won the initial attack due to surprise. If it did come down to a battle it looked like the camp here would wipe the Unfettered out in minutes. But who was he to speak? He never trained in the art of war; only to hunt and capture.

The warrior's brought him to a larger tent stationed close to those of many other families. Pushing aside the flaps, they shoved him inside. He had to bite back a retort as it wouldn't help him here. He was a prisoner until Tahir deemed him otherwise. The inside of the tent was richly furnished, at least by camp standard. There were piles of silk cushions, elaborate chests, and silver trays with bottles of *guakal* wine. He thought he would just have to wait in here but the warriors pulled a chair from the side of the room, shoved him into it, and retied his hands around it's back.

Seriously...? Zaid muttered. One of the warriors slapped him on the back of his head. *Can you tell me if Tahir is coming? I really need to speak to—*

The warriors didn't even look at him and walked back out of the tent. Zaid growled in frustration. Zaid waited, at first for just minutes, then eventually he was sure it had been over an hour. He listened to the muffled sounds from outside the tent of people chatting, some yelling and some crying. No one came back until the flap was pushed aside as the familiar form of Tahir strode in.

Tahir! Zaid said, finally happy to be getting somewhere.

Tahir took one look at him and barked an order at his guards to untie him. Zaid watched in satisfaction as they scurried to obey their master's orders, but he didn't mock them, only rubbed his wrists where the annoying *laqueus* had been. The mental sound of conversations became much louder as soon as it was removed and he exhaled in relief when he could sense heartbeats again. It was an odd sensation to hear so many around him when he was in a field, but it wasn't too different from being inside a city.

Zaid stood and Tahir embraced him firmly. *Zaid, my boy, I am so glad you are here.* He pulled back and held Zaid at arm's length, looking him over. *Are you hurt?*

No, Zaid said. *Just confused.* He sagged a little at the admission.

I understand, son. Come, sit with me and tell me what happened. It's hard to believe it's only been a few weeks since we have spoken. He ushered Zaid over to the many cushions on the floor, and poured himself a glass of the wine and handed one to Zaid. He didn't like *guakal* wine but took it anyway.

I don't even know where to start, Zaid said. *But I came because I need answers, Tahir.*

Tell me what happened with your last target, the now-infamous Kinza Solace, Tahir said.

That's exactly what Zaid did. He told Tahir about his trip there and how he watched Kinza for a whole week before taking her. He told him about the ubir in northern Michigan and travelling through the portal to Moshi. He told him about the assassins that were following Kinza and almost killed both of them had she not killed them first. He left out the part about Aisha and how she had helped them instead. But he told Tahir the rest as well, coming to find Rhapta destroyed and finding Nazim's people. And then he told Tahir about Kinza's trial and the evidence that was stacking up, and about how confused he felt after spending days with her.

Tahir looked at him with sadness, as if Zaid were his own son and Tahir was forced to watch his child in pain. *You have gone through as much as the rest of us these past weeks, Zaid. I can only commend you for what you have done.*

Tahir, I really don't know what to believe. Everyone says that Kinza is behind the attack, but I watched her for days. *She had never seemed like a murderer, much less the ubir I was told she was. And those assassins....*He shook his head and looked back up at the older man. *I need to ask you something.*

Anything, Tahir said, concern in his eyes.

Zaid took a deep breath. *The assassin that came after Kinza, just before they were going to kill us, one of them told us that their orders came from you to kill her. They also said that they had similar orders ten years ago to kill Kinza's parents. She had told me her parents were murdered ten years ago and she never knew why, so that made sense to me. That part that I couldn't believe was that the order came from you.*

Tahir's eyebrows were furrowed as he said, *The order definitely did not come from me, Zaid. Hmm, but that does mean it had to come from someone. They weren't ubir?*

No, for sure not ubir, which means they had to have tattoos like venari, which means someone had to give it to them.

Tahir nodded slowly, thinking. *I have a couple of thoughts then. The first being that someone—either an Elder or Savar—had to give them the tattoo. The second thought is that it was very likely Kinza herself orchestrated this.*

Zaid started, not expecting him to say that. Kinza? Plan her own assassination attempt? *To what end?* he asked.

Tahir shrugged. *We can't know the motives of a madwoman. There must have been some reason at some time, but the one thing I do know for sure is that you were deceived. I'm not sure if you heard, but Hakim had another vision recently confirming that Kinza was the leader of the Unfettered. I'm sorry for what happened to you Zaid, but whatever she made you believe is a lie.*

Zaid nodded, he saw the sense in that. Hakim's visions were never wrong, but the image of Kinda in the forest, sobbing as the assassins were about to kill him and make her watch played over and over in his mind. And he had blacked out, only to find she had gotten him out of the forest. What would be the purpose of saving him if she was just going to destroy the Anunnaki anyway? His memory of her trial came rushing back as well. All the arrows had pointed to her, there was even that security guard he had *seen* her talking with and he had said she was behind this. Tahir was probably right and Zaid had seen what he wanted to see in her.

Tahir, why did you give me orders to capture her in the first place? I know that you gave Savar the order to give to me, but it was odd to begin with. We never get names when we get our targets, and she definitely wasn't ubir.

It was Tahir's turn to take a breath and he almost looked guilty. *Yes, well, about a month ago Hakim had a rather vague vision and it was ominous in nature but the only thing we got out of it was Kinza Solace's name and location. Nothing else. I talked to a few other Elders as well as Savar and we agreed it was best to bring her in, but with as much discretion as possible. Just in case. We didn't want to alarm anyone and thought it best to send the order out as if she were ubir.* Tahir's eyes pleaded with Zaid. *Will you forgive me for not telling you? I know I put you in a dangerous situation, but we were only acting out of caution.*

Of course, Zaid said. *Maybe that vision was just another warning for us.* He shrugged and let out a long exhale. He didn't let himself think too much about Kinza, if he did the box inside of his mind that held all of the things he never wanted to feel would burst at the seams. He didn't think he could handle that right now. A battle was going to happen soon and his people needed every able body to stamp the Unfettered down. The warriors seemed to be ready, but Zaid couldn't just sit here twiddling his thumbs.

An attendant had poked her head in the door and whispered to Tahir who said he would be out in a moment. *If you'll excuse me—*

Is there anything I can do to help? Zaid asked, standing.

Tahir gave him another sympathetic look, as if he knew the restlessness that was itching under his skin. *Give me an hour and I'll be back. There is much to do and I'm sure no one would turn away your skills. Please,* he said gesturing around the tent, *feel free to rest a bit and I'll be back.*

Zaid nodded and sat back down as Tahir left with the attendant. He would just have to wait. With nothing else to do, he took a gulp of the *guakal* wine, gagged, and spit it back into the cup.

He forgot how much he hated it.

TRUE TO HIS WORD, Tahir returned within an hour.

Zaid had spent the time pacing in the tent, he was still too restless to sleep even though he was sure it had been over a day since he last slept. He ate a handful of fruit and flipped through Tahir's books, but was glad when he finally returned.

Come, he said, waving Zaid out. *Let's take a walk.*

Zaid followed him out into the bright sunlight. A warm breeze that hadn't been there earlier ruffled his shirt. They walked through the groups in silence for a while. The looks directed toward Zaid were more muted with Tahir by his side. They passed the sections where food was kept and Zaid saw it was dwindling. People were probably becoming nervous, the camp didn't look like it was meant to last long, regardless of how impressive it was. Some people came up to Tahir to ask him questions, always making sure to keep away from Zaid.

He had gotten used to the treatment of the *venari* a long time ago, but sometimes it still stung that people looked at him the way they did. In truth, he had probably gotten used to it before he had been tapped, back before he had received his abilities after he should have. He wondered what it would have been like to have a normal job within the tribe, something that he could do and no one would sneer at him. Something that would allow him to make more than the occasional friend. He really could only count two, and one of them wasn't even Anunnaki. Loneliness was his third friend now.

Did Elder Ishar make it out? Zaid asked. Ishar was the Elder representative of the bounty hunters, despite the fact that Zaid had a closer relationship with Tahir.

I'm afraid not, Tahir said with a frown. *Most of the Elders are still in the city. Only about eleven of us made it out.* Tahir paused for a moment. *Tell me, why exactly did my warriors have you bound when you arrived? They told me they were my apprentice's orders, but I can't see why Mikah would send you to me in laqueus.*

Ah, well, after Kinza's trial there was a mob headed for her and Nazim was going to let them beat her to death. I panicked so I picked her up and ran. Nazim and the other's didn't trust me after that. I guess you could say it's my fault she isn't bound right now, Zaid said.

That makes a bit more sense, Tahir said with a chuckle. *Mikah can be very thorough. But fret not, the people will learn soon how brave you were. In fact...* Tahir paused in the intersection between several groups and raised his hands. Most people had their eyes on him anyway, but Tahir called for people close by to listen. *I know many of you watched one of our venari arrive this morning bound!* he called. *I know many of you think him an enemy but it couldn't be further from the truth.*

Zaid wanted to dissolve into a puddle. Couldn't Tahir see there was nothing he could say to magically make them like him?

My close friend, Zaid Hatem, Tahir called as he placed a hand on Zaid's shoulder, *went out into the world to try and capture our enemy, Kinza Solace, before she could arrive and he nearly died in the process! For a time he had her, but her numbers were overwhelming, too much for one man—even a venari—to take on by himself. When you see this man walk through the camp, know that he almost gave his life trying to save you!*

Zaid avoided people's eyes, but to his surprise many of them no longer looked at him with hostility. None of them were running up to hug or thank him, but it was a start. Several men and women came up to Tahir to thank *him*, but looked gratefully in Zaid's direction as well. If that's all he was going to receive, he would take it.

What is all this about? a nasally voice said. Zaid and Tahir turned to find Elder Minesh waddling up to them, eyebrow pointed downward in a "v." Behind him was a brute of a boy who was probably a few years younger than Zaid. He assumed that was Minesh's apprentice Kiaan.

Minesh, Tahir said pleasantly. *I hope you are well. And I am just telling our people what Zaid here has done for us.*

Minesh looked Zaid up and down and visibly sneered in distaste, but it was Kiaan who spoke, and out loud. "A *venari*? Are they even Anunnaki with the amount of time they spend with humans," he scoffed.

Silence, Kiaan, Mines said, waving him off. He turned to Tahir instead. *I would speak with you, Tahir. We have important matters to discuss.* He said the last part quietly but it only managed to make his already nasally voice go up an octave.

Very well, Tahir said. *Zaid, feel free to walk around the camp for a while. I'll have a tent set up for you by evening.*

Zaid nodded. Minesh didn't even bother looking at him as he passed, but Kiaan got close enough to ram his shoulder into Zaid's. He debated throwing Kiaan to the ground for half a second before thinking better of it. It wouldn't have been much of a fight. Kiaan was clearly from the outskirts which meant he must have had weaker bones and a slower healing ability. Instead he just rubbed his shoulder and kept on his walk.

Word spread a little ways about what Tahir had said about him and Zaid noticed as he got a few curious looks instead of hostile ones. There were several faces that he recognized, a *guakal* vendor from the main boulevard, a miner who lived down the street from his mother, an old woman who Zaid was pretty sure was one of his school teachers from his childhood.

None of these people were close to him, but they were familiar. He felt a kinship toward them that he never felt when he was in human cities.

For the rest of the afternoon, he walked around the camp, never stopping to talk, just to listen. The sounds of his people, even in war, made him feel at home.

CHAPTER 17
ALL THE PRETTY LIGHTS

Kinza followed Jabari and Badr through the network of tunnels under the library until they got to a steel door. That in itself was an oddity here as she usually saw doors of wood or other lighter materials. It wasn't locked and Jabari lifted the lever and the door swung open to reveal a dark staircase headed down into the earth. He took one of the makeshift torches she held—made of smaller Aurastones attached to short sticks—and headed down.

"After you," Badr said with a smile.

Kinza nodded and focused on her feet in front of her. "So, where exactly are we going? Couldn't we train in one of the rooms upstairs?"

"It really depends on each person's individual ability, and since yours tend to be destructive in nature, it's best to train where no one will get hurt," Jabari replied from in front of her. The staircase was winding down further and further and it felt like it wouldn't end until they reached the Earth's core.

"Ah, gotcha. Makes sense," she replied, trying to focus on

not falling. The steps were short and narrow and she didn't know how far she would fall if she tripped.

"This is the way to the cisterns," Badr continued for her. "There are a lot of them throughout the city, but the one under the library got blocked off a long time ago and now it's just a big empty room. I've never been down here honestly."

"You didn't train down here as well?"

He laughed. "No, my training is the kind that is best done in a library, you know, seeing patterns and all."

"Lucky you," she muttered. When she was starting to think they really were getting below the tectonic plates, the stairs finally came to an end in an archway. Beyond that she could only see a single beam of light coming from somewhere high in the ceiling, but below that was darkness. Jabari went around the corner and she heard the creak of metal. Suddenly the room was illuminated when the beam of light hit the round bronze plate that Jabari had adjusted and bounced around the room, hitting similar plates and ricocheting the light around.

"Oh, snap," Kinza said at the sheer size of the room. It was massive enough that even with the light she couldn't see the ceiling and only saw a vague outline of the other end of the room. It looked like it was made of the same limestone that made up the rest of the city, but it was hard to tell. A few gigantic pillars stood to the sides of the room, but otherwise it was completely empty. A perfect place for training.

"All right," Jabari said, setting the Aurastone torch down and striding further into the room. As they got closer to the middle, Kinza saw that there were deeper recesses on each side, looking almost like empty pools but dropping down twenty feet. They stayed to the middle of the room. "You only gained your abilities last week so you are at a bit of a disadvantage compared to other Anunnaki children. It shouldn't be a problem though, as long as you are not prone to childish tantrums."

"Got it," Kinza said, still looking around. Badr took a seat by one of the pillars and pulled out a book, giving her two thumbs up. "No tantrums. I have to tell you, I don't know how well this is going to go because I really only ever made my abilities work on purpose once. Every other time was an accident."

"That's what we are going to try and change," Jabari said, looking nonplussed by her declaration. He turned to look at her with a serious expression—as if the rest of his expressions weren't serious. "I received my ability like most other Anunnaki, when I was ten. One evening my mother told me I needed to stay inside to complete chores, but I wanted to go out and play with my friends. When she wouldn't let me go, I started screaming and crying and my ability decided to manifest itself. The house caught on fire so fast we barely made it out and my baby sister nearly burned to death. She was fine, mind you, but as you can imagine it was a traumatizing experience."

"That's so scary," Kinza said. "But I think that's what's been happening to me. Whenever I get scared or angry, my abilities come out like they are trying to protect me."

Jabari nodded. "It's very common for Anunnaki abilities to be tied to emotion. That's why I wanted to tell you that story, so you get a full understanding when I say that you need to learn to control your emotions." Jabari chuckled at Kinza's wrinkled nose. "I don't mean you shouldn't feel anything, but you should be able to experience emotion without having it control you."

"Okay..." Kinza said. It was one thing to say that, but when you are being pushed off a roof or angry men are swinging blades at your head it was hard to pretend you weren't scared.

"Let's start with your first ability, generally that one is

always the strongest. Tell me again about your first experience."

"Well, I was having another one of my nightmares—"

"The ones about Rhapta?"

"Yes, but that started before my abilities did."

"Hmm," Jabari said. "I wouldn't be surprised if that was somehow another ability, but that would put you at four if we don't count your healing incident with Khalil. Let's skip that for now. Go on," he urged.

"Well, I was asleep, but it was very vivid, and I was scared, like really scared, and confused. Anyway I woke up right as I was about to die in the dream but that was when the white light and explosion happened."

"Are all of these 'explosions' like that? In a dream?"

"Oh, no. The other times I could tell it was about to happen. I start to feel a tingling in my neck," she said, touching the back of her neck as if prompting it to happen. "The feeling grows and spreads down to my abdomen, under my tattoo, and heat starts to pool there. If I'm really scared it will just keep building until the white light erupts and everything around me explodes. They've been getting bigger, too."

"This tingling," Jabari said, pacing back and forth. "Is this the only time it happens? Just before the explosion?"

Kinza thought for a moment, remembering the bus ride with Mitra and the man draped in shadows. "Well, I think it might've happened once, the night I was taken. A man was following me on the way home and I got this tingling but it went away when I got home."

Jabari stopped to assess her. "That is definitely another ability, I have a second cousin with something similar, but she has more of a cold sensation. It's a more passive ability that lets you know when danger is present, but it will also appear when you *believe* you are in danger, even if you are not. Can you see where I'm going with this?"

"Maybe, so you think this is part of me controlling my emotions, like fear?"

"Yes, exactly. You were right before that many Anunnaki abilities act to defend the person they inhabit. So if you believe you are in danger—or if you actually are—it would signal the 'explosion' to happen."

Kinza nodded slowly. "That actually makes sense." Now she just needed to not be scared when an entire race of powerful beings is determined to kill her. Easy.

"I think we should test your abilities and see what we've got to work with," Jabari said.

"Um, I disagree, but okay."

"I don't suppose you can make yourself scared, can you?" Jabari asked.

"Ahh, no?" she said.

"All right, come here," he said, waving her over. She followed him toward one side of the room, where the deep empty recesses were. As they got close he said, "I think there is a quick way to—" and shoved her over the edge.

Kinza didn't have time to scream as she dropped to the bottom. With a sharp inhale, she screwed her eyes shut, waiting for pain. The ground did come, but faster and less impactful than she had anticipated. She hit the floor on her right side in a heap. Groaning and the sharp pain in her hip, she opened her eyes.

"That was so cool!" Badr shouted from across the room, clapping like she had put on a show. His voice came from the wrong direction though. She opened her eyes to see she had indeed teleported to the far end. Jabari was standing by the recess, grinning, to her surprise. He walked over to her as she picked herself up.

"Why did you do that?!" she yelled. She was more shocked than in pain. She had probably only fallen a couple of feet before she teleported, making her fall much more bearable. The pain was already receding in her hip, thanks to the healing.

"I wanted to see how responsive your abilities were and which ones would come out," Jabari said. "It seems like falling triggers your teleportation. Now let's see about the others." He stalked toward her and Kinza took a step back on instinct. The tingling on her neck started up as fire sprung from Jabari's hands. Not the inferno that she had been engulfed in, but twin flames controlled in each hand. Regardless, fear sparked in her as he moved closer.

"Don't!" Kinza said, backing up. "This is a bad idea!" There was only so far for her to back up before she hit the wall but Jabari's mouth was set and he kept coming. A small obsidian dagger appeared in one hand and heat pooled in her abdomen. Her back hit the wall finally and panic washed through her as Jabari came toward her, fast. With nowhere to run, the heat in her built quickly and before she could shout again the familiar white light shot out around her, followed quickly by a force that sent Jabari to the ground like a ragdoll and the wall behind her to rubble.

Kinza had crouched down, covering her head, but stood up. Dust was clearing from a fifteen foot radius around her. Badr had dropped his book and came running over but Kinza backed away from the still crumbling wall. What if the whole cistern collapsed?

Laughter came from somewhere in the dust. Kinza turned to find Badr helping Jabari to his feet, a gash on his cheek and one arm held tightly to his side. She was about to yell at him when he started laughing again, like a child who had just seen fireworks for the first time. She and Badr stared at him, wondering if he had gotten hit in the head.

"That was exceptional," Jabari said, wiping tears from his eyes. "That's enough, Badr. I'm fine."

"Fine?! What the heck was that?!" she yelled. "I could have killed you!" She was breathing hard, keeping an eye on the wall. It's disintegration had slowed and a massive pile of rubble sat where she had stood moments ago.

"How do you feel right now?" Jabari asked, stretching his arm and wincing.

"What?" she asked, bewildered. Was this man crazy?

"How do you feel right now?" he asked, punctuating each word like she was a child.

"Fine," she spat. Was taunting her supposed to be stress-relieving or something?

"Good."

"Why is that good?" Badr asked skeptically.

"Because we have learned several things from those two incidents. One," Jabari said, holding up a finger, "we learned that anger doesn't trigger your abilities in the same way that fear does. I'm not saying that it never will, but in both instances you were scared and your abilities reacted. But now that you are angry, nothing." He took a breath and the gash on his cheek started to heal. "Two, we learned what your 'explosion' actually is."

"We did?" she asked. She was still upset with him, but wanted to know what he learned because she definitely learned nothing new.

"Yes," he said, back to his seriousness. "That light is your Aura and you are using it as a physical force."

Badr's jaw dropped. "That was an Aura?" he said, going up an octave.

Jabari nodded. "I've never seen anything like it, but that would explain why no one has been able to see yours," he said looking at Kinza.

Kinza remembered all the times Zaid had looked for her Aura and had found nothing. It was just one of the many anomalies about her, but now she finally had an answer. She felt like grinning and screaming at the same time. She had answers! But not the ones she wanted. Why couldn't she just be like anyone else?

"Okay…so what? It just hides until I need it?" she asked.

"I'm guessing that your ability is actually that you have some control over your Aura, and the explosion is more of a reflex. In the same way that you automatically jerk your hand back when you touch a hot pan. I'm guessing there are other things you could do with it in time, but I really don't know. I've never heard of anyone being able to control their Aura other than being able to display it or not. Yours seems to be more physical."

"Wonderful," she said. "How do I stop it from killing people?"

"Control," he said, seriously. "Come," he said, waving her over. At her hesitancy he said, "I'm not going to push you off a ledge again. Come sit." He sat down on the floor cross-legged and Kinza sat across from him. Badr sat a few feet away to watch. Apparently his book was less interesting.

"All Rhaptan children learn some form of meditation and —don't give me that look—it takes years of practice, but it does help you to control your emotions." To emphasize his point, a dark red light started to glow around him. In echo, Badr had a dusty blue light ring him like a halo. "Let me ask you something. When were your abilities at their worst?"

Kinza thought for a second. "On the way to Rhapta, there

were a few assassins trying to kill me. They caught both me and Zaid and there was a moment when they were going to kill him and make me watch. The explosion thing happened along with the fire. It was so big it killed three of them on impact and started a forest fire." The thought of Zaid put pressure in her chest.

Instead of acting shocked, Jabari nodded his head knowingly. "Our fear tends to be highest when those we care about are in danger. More so than when we are in danger ourselves. I'm going to tell you right now, Kinza, that you being in control of your own emotions will help you to take care of those that matter to you far more than lashing out will."

She nodded but had a hard time seeing the truth in his words.

"What I want you to do is close your eyes. We are going to try to loosen your Aura." She had closed her eyes but they flew back open. "Don't worry. We aren't going to trigger your explosions, we just want to get the light to come out. This is something any Anunnaki should be able to do and it's a good starting point to gaining some measure of control. Now close your eyes again."

She did as she was told, but didn't think it would help at all. It's not like there was anything else she was supposed to be doing right now.

"All I want you to do is pay attention to your body. Start at your toes and work your way up through your legs, your stomach, arms and neck, to the top of your head. Feel each limb; where you have pains, where the muscles are tense, and where you are slouching. Now try to relax as much as possible. You don't need to do much else, your Aura should come out on its own."

Kinza felt it through her feet and legs and hips, but after

that she got distracted. She could hear Jabari breathing across from her and Badr fidgeting a few feet away. Her mind wandered to Zaid and she wondered where he was.

Was he a prisoner with Nazim's people, or had they accepted him back in? Ekaja would be happy to see her son again and know that he was all right. Was Zabu still tied to the chair in his house?

She was angry that he had tried to kill her, but the thought of leaving him there to die didn't sit right with her. She wondered if she should talk to Khalil about going to check on him. She thought about Haris, alone in his little house in the woods, tending to the grounds around the inn. He must be lonely there with no one to talk to. She thought about Mitra and how worried she probably was. Her best friend had disappeared a week ago, kidnapped in the middle of the night. Kinza hoped she hadn't cried too much. She thought about Grams waiting by the window, hoping that she would walk through the door.

Her throat constricted and Kinza opened her eyes to stop herself from crying. "Did it work?" she asked in a huff.

Jabari frowned at her. "No, were you even trying?"

"Yes," she said, rubbing her face. She had hardly done anything so far today and she was exhausted.

"Maybe try praying," Badr said from his spot.

"What?" she said. Her only experience with religion was a tear-filled affair after her parents' funeral. She hadn't liked how the big room made everyone's sniffling echo; like she couldn't get away from it.

"That's a good idea, Badr," Jabari said. "We have a few temples here in Rhapta dedicated to the Creator, but everyone's Aura appears when they pray inside the temples. I don't think you actually need to be in the temple for that to work, I think it's more the state of mind."

"I'm not exactly religious though," she said.

"It's less about religion and more about good thoughts. Think about it. What do people pray for? Health of their loved ones, peace and prosperity, a good outcome on difficult tasks, and thankfulness. Try thinking about those things."

Kinza was still skeptical, but would try anyway. She closed her eyes again, this time not avoiding the thoughts of her family. She remembered her mother walking her to the bus stop on the first day of kindergarten. Her backpack had been huge compared to her five-year-old self and her mother had laughed and said she was adorable. Kinza's mind flashed forward to the day she had found Grams crying in the living room, and her mother's hand prone on the floor.

"Stop feeling sorry for everyone and think about the good things," Jabari said quietly, so as not to break her concentration.

Kinza pursed her lips but did as she was told. Her mind wandered to Grams and instead of imagining her lonely and sad, she imagined Grams tidying up her room and getting ready for Kinza to come back. She would be humming to herself and would probably stick a few of her dead flower bundles in her room for good luck. She almost laughed at that. She imagined Grams happy to see her when she got home, ready with a mug of lavender tea and a hug that would crush the air out of her lungs. Kinza realized how thankful she was to have Grams in her life, because despite the loss of her parents, she and Grams had made a happy life for themselves and Kinza wasn't alone.

"Kinza..." Jabari said quietly.

She opened her eyes to peek at him and he nodded toward her hands. Looking down she saw there was a faint white glow emanating from her skin. Nothing like the violent light during her explosions, instead it was soft and gentle. It immediately dissipated but she was already grinning like an idiot.

"It worked!" she said.

Badr was grinning back and Jabari nodded in approval. "I think that's enough for today."

CHAPTER 18
TICKING TIME

"Ugh!"

Kinza was back in her room. She had eaten a few bites for dinner after her lesson with Jabari and came back here. Her "homework" was to continue practicing raising her Aura, but she couldn't seem to get it going again. Never mind the fact that she had a week's worth of real homework she was missing. She'd probably fail this semester for being gone so long. She sighed, thinking about the money down the drain.

She kept the lid on the Aurastone lamp box closed so she would be able to see the faintest light of her Aura if it came up, but she had just been sitting in the dark for the past thirty minutes. Closing her eyes again, she took a deep breath and started to meditate or think good thoughts or whatever.

At first she thought about her parents and how much she missed them, but her mind drifted to Zaid and the fact he still had his mother. Ekaja had seemed like a firm but loving parent. Kinza didn't know where Zaid's father was, but it didn't seem important with the relationship he had with Ekaja. She realized how lonely she felt right now. It was nice that the Apostles were helping her and Khalil didn't think she was a crazy murderer, but the people who were really in Kinza's corner—the ones she could count on no matter what—were far away.

Realizing she got distracted again she growled in frustration and flipped the lid off the Aurastone lamp box illuminating the room. She sat there looking around and tapping her nails. Khalil had still been with a few patients and the Apostles were all busy preparing for the battle that could happen at any time. She felt useless sitting there. Even if she did manage to control her Aura, that wouldn't help her get the angry Anunnaki off her back. What she needed were allies.

She got up and dug through her chest of clothes, pulling out an emerald green scarf and wound it around her head like she had the night before. Zaid wasn't here to chastise her so she didn't feel bad about going outside again. It's not like he cared anyway.

The hallway was empty when she peeked out her door. A few scholars walked past her hall to the right, so she went left. Many of the Apostles had started to recognize her and while they didn't greet her, they would know if she left. She kept her head down and tucked deep into the scarf and made her way to the outer halls. Stopping in a storage room, she grabbed a canvas bag and made her way to the stairwell that led up to the surface.

There was an Apostle in tight blue robes standing by the doorway. This one had an obsidian spear like Tammuz had.

You're going up? he asked. It seemed like the guards here were more interested in keeping people out than in.

Yes, she said, keeping her eyes downcast. *Just trying to collect a few more things before it's too late.* She lifted the canvas bag so she could see. He nodded and she hurried up the steps. This stairwell led to the secret door she had come out before.

She listened for any voices before inching it open and stepping outside. It was near full dark but well before moonrise, a good time for slinking about.

Kinza felt a drive to do *something* while she still could and sitting in her room under the library was getting her nowhere. Ekaja had told her that there were still those within the city who believed the outsider from the prophecy was here to do good instead of bad. These were the kinds of people she needed to meet and Ekaja seemed like a good place to start. Kinza knew she was somewhere near the center of the city and Nazim's group was to the south. If she was careful enough, maybe she could find Ekaja without getting caught. It was extremely risky, but what else was she to do?

She moved through the wide boulevards, keeping to the edges, just outside the line of baobab trees and kept her eyes and ears open. Knowing that the tingling on her neck was a sign she was in danger was almost relieving, despite its ominous warning. At least she would have some indicator when she should hide. She wished she had abilities like Zaid's though, being able to zip through the streets at the speed of sound would make her life a lot easier right now. She had to work with what she had.

Kinza walked for nearly half an hour without seeing a single soul. At one point she heard voices far off but they faded just as quickly. She kept going south, but the problem was the south quarter was huge and she couldn't remember exactly where Nazim's group was so the best she could do was find some people and follow them back. As she thought it, she realized how stupid that sounded, but she had already come this far.

After another twenty minutes she realized she was lost.

This was a bad idea, she thought to herself, looking around nervously. *Maybe I should just go back.*

Voices crept up again from around the corner. They were quiet but distinct, at least three people. She immediately dove into the nearest structure, which happened to be a huge house. This one had people living in it recently, but it looked like they had fled thankfully. Kinza threw herself down by the front window after closing the door. This house had elaborate shutters on the windows that were closed at the moment and only let in slivers of light.

The voice came closer, it was definitely a group of men and by the way they were speaking—glee over the destruction they had wrought—she realized they were Unfettered. She tried to breathe as quietly as she could and it seemed like they were about to pass by when they stopped. She peered out the crack in the shutters. One of the men was looking around, sniffing.

"What is it?" one of the others asked.

"I smell something," the first one said.

"You always smell something," the third laughed.

Quiet! The middle one kept sniffing until his head turned toward the house Kinza was in. Her heart started a painful gallop as he moved closer. The other men drew their swords. Kinza leaped away from the window, hand over her mouth. Was he smelling the soap the Apostles gave her? She backed away, deeper into the house and was careful not to bump into anything as she crept around the corner so she wasn't visible if someone opened the door.

She could hear the voices outside still coming closer before stopping just in front of the door. Her hands didn't tremble despite her racing heart and she was the tiniest bit proud of that. She waited, still as a frightened rabbit about to be caught by a fox, until the voices moved away a minute later. They seemed to be headed further up the street.

She kept waiting, still as a statue, until her heart calmed. Too nervous to go out the front door, she moved through the back, past the kitchen and found a door that led into an alley. She took one step out when a force shoved her back inside—hard. Her back hit the ground and she groaned but saw nothing, only heard rustling. Her heart jumped into her throat as the door shut of its own accord. Kinza scrambled back when a form suddenly came into being.

"Tiamat," Kinza said with a sigh of relief.

What are you doing here you silly girl? the woman said in her mind, eyebrows knit together in concern. She bent down to help Kinza up. *Where is Zaid?*

Oh, um, I don't know, Kinza said. *He left yesterday and I haven't seen him since.*

Hmm, Tiamat said, crossing her arms. *That is not good. What are you doing out here then? If anyone sees you, you could be killed!*

I know, I know. I was actually looking for Ekaja. Tiamat's eyes questioned her so she continued. *Zaid left to go back to Nazim's group yesterday and I don't think he is going to help me anymore and I'm feeling useless and Ekaja said that there were other people in the city that would help me and I guess I'm just trying to find an ally or a friend or something.* The useful thing about speaking telepathically was that she never ran out of breath.

Tiamat relaxed. *Ah, I see.* She sighed. *It is still dangerous for you to be out here, but I can take you to Ekaja.*

Thank you, Kinza said gratefully.

Follow me, Tiamat said heading back to the door. *I cannot make you invisible like me so we will have to hope we are not seen. It's about a ten minute walk from here if we hurry.*

Kinza nodded and followed her out into the alley. The voices were long gone now and thankfully they didn't run into anyone else. Walking behind the other woman, she realized Tiamat was shorter than her, which wasn't a common thing for Kinza. The woman's demeanor had made her seem much taller.

Tiamat led her through the boulevards until they turned onto smaller streets and eventually they entered the more abandoned area of Rhapta. Manicured streets turned to wild foliage and broken fountains. Buildings without shutters or glass in the windows looked at Kinza as they crept past. Tiamat turned to a stack of the many apartment-like homes, taking a hidden outer stairway all the way up to one of the upper floors. It looked like a pile of garbage blocked the remainder of the pathway to the door but Tiamat knocked on a wooden plank. A moment later it slid aside and another woman's face peered out. She took a look at Kinza but Tiamat nodded and they were let inside.

The house looked similar to Ekaja's, only larger. There were several rooms up here and what looked to be a usable rooftop up above. Drapes covered the windows haphazardly, letting in little light. Just a few tiny Aurastone lit some of the inner rooms as they moved deeper into the house. They entered what looked like a bedroom and Kinza was met with nearly ten faces, one of which made a sound and came running over to her, enveloping her in a hug that smelled of jasmine.

I'm glad to see you are well, Ekaja said, pulling back to smile at her. She looked over Kinza's shoulder. *Is my son here as well?*

Um, no, he left, Kinza said, not meeting her eyes. *I thought you would've known because he went back to Nazim's group.*

Ekaja's brow furrowed. *He did?* She shook her head. *Aye! That boy,* she said in exasperation. *After your trial, those of us who still believe in the good of the prophecy left and met up with others who believe the same.* She gestured around the room and several faces looked up from their conversations and smiled. Not one of them looked at her with wariness or hostility, some even going so far as to look at her with hope.

Kinza was surprised at the face that sat at the back of the group.

It's good to see you again, Aisha said. *But I am sorry it is under unfortunate circumstances.*

Aisha! Kinza said. The last time she had seen the assassin was in Moshi, a town just outside of Mount Kilimanjaro. She had helped her and Zaid to hide after they escaped the other assassins. Kinza hadn't been trusting of her then, but that was no longer the case now. *I didn't expect to see you here.*

Come, Ekaja said, pulling Kinza into a room across the hall. *Tiamat said you were looking for me. Tell me what happened with my son.* They sat down in the identical room. Cushions were strewn about the floor and a woman came in and handed Kinza a steaming mug of the spiced tea to her delight. She thanked her and turned back to Ekaja.

Just before the mob came, Kinza said, *Zaid helped me escape and we met up with Khalil. It's a long story but we ended up staying with some people, but last night Zaid and I had a fight. Khalil said he left and that someone saw him head back to Nazim's group, but that's all I know. I don't think Zaid trusts me anymore.* Kinza didn't want to mention she had found the Apostles of Truth despite the fact Ekaja was the one who led her to them. She didn't know if she still harbored the same feelings toward the group that Zaid did due to her son's death. Kinza also didn't want to be pressured into telling anyone where they were located either.

Ekaja groaned. *That boy! Sometimes he can be so thick-headed. It makes me sad that he cannot see the truth when the rest of us can so easily, but give him time. He may be looking for answers of his own.*

Kinza sipped her tea, letting the cup warm her hands. *I know, I just felt like I no longer had any allies. I talked with some people and so far the only ideas anyone has come up with is for me to convince the Elders that I am not a threat. I remembered you said there were people who still wanted to help me so I came here hoping that you would.*

Ekaja gave her a sympathetic smile and patted her knee. *You are correct, there are people here on your side so you are not alone. But,* Kinza didn't like the way this was going, *we cannot convince the Elders—or Rhapta for that matter—for you. The prophecy is about you my dear. You are the only one with the answers.*

Kinza hadn't thought about what to do if Ekaja wouldn't be able to help her. She tried to fight back bitter tears as she said *I didn't want this though, I didn't want any of it.* She wiped at her cheek and sniffed. *I don't know what I am supposed to do, and if I don't do the right thing then I could die. Couldn't you tell the Elders that I'm not a maniac.*

Ekaja had the audacity to chuckle. *No, it has to be you. We all could go to the Elders and claim that you are a savior and not a killer, but the rest of Rhapta would only counter that. The Elders, Hakim in particular, have to know that you are not behind this. Once they make a statement backing you, the rest of Rhapta will follow.*

Aisha walked in and sat down next to them, noting Kinza's tears.

Can't you tell the Elders about what happened on the way here? Kinza asked Aisha. *Tell them about what Jafar said about Tahir and my parents?*

Aisha shook her head. *I'm sorry, I wouldn't be able to hold up that story. You see, I was never actually one of them. I joined them only a few years ago, but had already had connections to this group. Someone asked me to spy on the assassins and that is what I did.* She shrugged. *Regardless, Yusuf was the only one who ever actually received the orders and he trickled them down to the rest of us. So I can't claim that an Elder requested your parent's death—or yours*

—because I was never there and don't know that for sure. I did as much as I could to protect you while I was with them, but I never received much information.

Kinza drank her tea quietly but the intermittent panic she had been feeling over the past few days started creeping back. The task before her was daunting and seemed that there was no way around it. She felt trapped, like a wild animal backed into a corner. She wished she had nothing to do with these people. Zaid had left and Khalil was busy healing those who needed it. Both the Apostles and Ekaja's group say they are on her side, but were providing little help when it came down to the life or death situation that was before her.

The drive she had felt earlier was entirely gone. Anxiety had her mind racing, trying to find a way *out*. She had thought before that leaving would be a bad idea, that people would only follow her back home. But what if she didn't go home? What if she kept moving? If she left now, before the battle started, while no one knew where she was, she could sneak out of the city and back into the forest. If she could make it back to the outskirts where she and Zaid had entered she was sure she could find her way back to the right section of the barrier and then she would be free from there.

The more she thought about it, the better it sounded. That way she wouldn't have to convince anyone of her motives. If she was just gone wouldn't that be sign enough that she didn't want anything to do with them?

Kinza finished her tea and looked up, trying to act calmer than she felt. *I think I need to get going,* she said.

Are you staying far? Ekaja asked. *Just stay here with us, we can keep you safe for now.*

No, I told Khalil I would be back and I don't want to worry him. I don't think it's far, but you don't have a map by chance do you? Kinza asked.

Ah, yes! Aisha said. *Just a moment.* She disappeared into one of the front rooms and returned later. It was a rough sketch of the city, but had been clearly labeled. *We are here,* Aisha said, pointing to a spot at the edge of the abandoned south quarter, close to the city center. Kinza could make out the outskirts to the east and from there would be the forest.

Perfect, she thought to herself. And then to the women, *This is great, thank you. I really appreciate that you are on my side.*

We believe in the prophecy and the Creator's grand design, Ekaja said, pulling her in for a hug.

Be careful, Aisha warned. *There are still many Unfettered out there and now everyone else is looking for you too. The only good thing is not everyone knows what you look like so keep that scarf up.* Aisha placed a warm hand on her shoulder.

Thank you. I'm really glad to have met you both. The three of them stood and Kinza waved to the group in the other room on her way out, many of them smiling and waving back. She was sorry that the prophecy wouldn't turn out in their favor, but Kinza wasn't a savior.

She stepped out into the night air and took a deep breath. It was time to get out of Rhapta.

CHAPTER 19

ESCAPE

Kinza looked at the map Aisha gave her. It looked like it was of everything inside the psionic barrier that surrounded the city with a few main reference points. If she was going to leave, she should go now while no one knew where she was.

The outskirts were to the east and beyond that was the exiting point back into the forest around Rhapta. She only had the canvas bag with her, but it was probably a good idea to bring a few supplies with her. It was nice that she wouldn't need to eat as often, but she didn't know how long it would be until she could get food again.

Turning her feet back north, she headed toward the city center. The wealthier Rhaptans lived in the inner plazas that ringed the Grand Hall and central plaza. If she could get into one of those homes, there was bound to be food and other supplies she could bring with her. She did feel a little guilty for stealing from someone, but it was the least this city could do after all they had done to her.

There was a pep in her step again as she crept down the

boulevards, back the way she came. It gave her a sense of purpose to have a plan and the idea of being back in human society was thrilling. As much as she liked the beauty of Rhapta, she missed more familiar things. If only she had her phone to listen to music or be able to head to the gas station for a bag of Hot Cheetos. She wanted to feel like she wasn't in a nightmare anymore.

She was proud at how quickly she made it back, and without running into anyone either. The houses here were much bigger, looking more like massive townhomes packed together around manicured plaza with elaborate fountains and statues. No vines overgrew this area of the city and all the windows and shutters were intact. There was still the destruction of war here with people's belongings scattered across the white streets that gleamed in the moonlight.

She entered the first plaza that looked empty and chose the first house at the end of the row. It was big enough to be three times the size of her and Gram's house back home. She peered in a window, one with the shutters open, and didn't see any movement inside. The front door was made of unpainted wood and it swung open quietly when she turned the handle.

Kinza paused in the doorway, waiting to see if someone would jump out at her. When nothing but silence continued, she hurried inside and shut the door behind her. Waiting until her eyes adjusted to the darkness, she fumbled her way to the back of the house and found the kitchen easily. Baskets and crates had been upended and a long, low table had been smashed to pieces, but she picked through the debris. There were a couple of stray oranges and *guakal* hiding under the broken boards, and she found some kind of flatbread that only had a couple pieces of mold that she picked off. It was better than nothing.

There was a large bookshelf on the other side of the room

that looked to be used as kitchen storage. In one jar she found a small paring knife that she stuffed in her bag and in another she found the remnants of a bag of the spicy tea she was growing fond of. She threw that in the bag as well.

Upstairs were a few bedrooms, one of which had clothes that looked close enough to Kinza's size. She grabbed an extra shirt, pants, and scarf just in case. She would probably need to find new clothes so as not to stand out in Tanzania, but she would worry about that later.

As she made her way downstairs, she heard a sound coming from the plaza. Freezing in place, she strained her ears to listen. When the sound didn't come again she tiptoed toward the front window and peered out, looking for what had made the sound.

A hand clamped over her mouth from behind. *Shh, I won't hurt you,* a voice said from behind her.

Kinza tried to inhale to scream but couldn't get any air in. Out of reflex, she shoved her elbow back to connect with soft tissue. The person groaned but held on tight.

Mitra, it's me. Be quiet or you'll get us killed.

Mitra? Kinza stopped struggling and craned her neck around to get a glimpse of her assailant. It was the man from the other night–Mikah. She relaxed measurably. If he called her Mitra, then he still didn't know who she was. That didn't mean she was safe, but better than if he did know her.

He dropped his hand from her mouth and held a finger to his lips. She nodded and looked out the window. Just then she could see figures moving through the plaza, one of which looked no more than a shadow flitting from corner to corner, avoiding the moonlight. Mikah gently tugged her back away from the window and she realized he had an arm wrapped around her waist. She took a few steps back with him, but removed his arm. Despite the fact that he was helping her, she didn't want him getting any ideas.

They went back into the kitchen and waited in silence for several minutes, standing in the near-dark. There were tiny slivers of light coming in from a boarded up window so she could make out the man's face. Even in the darkness he looked...clean. Neatly cropped hair, his loose red shirt didn't have a single wrinkle or fleck of dust, and he stood with an immaculate posture.

She caught his eyes glancing down at her canvas bag and she tucked it behind her back. He only raised an eyebrow. Before the silence could get awkward, Mikah spoke. *Fancy meeting you here,* he said with a smile. Perfectly straight teeth glinted in the light. *It's nice to see you again, Mitra, but I didn't expect to find you again so soon.*

Ah well, Rhapta is only so big, she said, taking a step back. She wanted space.

And you are still out alone. Where is your family? he asked. It almost sounded like he was admonishing her.

They are...back home, she said, hoping it sounded truthful. *I'm just gathering supplies.* She lifted her canvas bag so he could see.

Uh-huh, he said, eyeing the bag, before looking around at the expensive house they were in.

Don't judge me for doing what I have to, she said. Even if the pretense was a lie, she didn't want anyone thinking she was just a common thief. If she had truly been a Rhaptan in the middle of a war, she would have done the same to take care of her family. There was no shame in that. Well, maybe a little, but not enough for him to be looking at her like that.

Not judging, he said, putting his hands up in mock surrender. *You have to do what you have to do.* He shrugged. *Is your family well then?* He started wandering around the kitchen, hands behind his back.

Yes, she said, not meeting his eyes. He had made a circle around the kitchen and came to a stop a few feet from her.

Then why do you look so sad? The impending battle notwithstanding. He cocked his head to peer at her with an open expression. The question was so direct, and she hadn't been expecting it, so she had to fight to keep from dissolving into another crying mess. Thankfully, her eyes stayed dry for the moment.

Everything is hard now, she said. It was as close to an admission of bone-deep exhaustion as she would get. She leaned back against a wall, sliding slowly to the ground. The bag of stolen items pooled near her feet. *There is nothing left for me here,* she said so quietly that she was sure he didn't catch it.

Mikah just nodded as if that made complete sense and sat down across from her against the opposite wall. *I think a lot of people feel like that right now.*

Kinza snorted. She didn't think there was a single person on the planet in a similar position.

Would you go live as a human then? he asked, eyeing the bag again.

He asked it so nonchalantly but she knew he was prying to see if she was one of those who would turn to the blood rite. His line of thinking was still better than if he knew who she actually was.

I was thinking about it, she said. She didn't mention that she had lived as a human her entire life and didn't know there were alternatives until recently. It actually made her lucky, the fact that she *could* go out and not have to worry about losing her memories or abilities. Not that she would have minded losing some of them—she was sure she could do without the explosions and fire, but the rest could come in handy.

Would she keep her healing ability forever then too? She realized that no matter the outcome, she could never see Mitra again. Grams knew what she was, but Kinza would start aging much slower and Mitra would know if a single eyelash was acting differently on Kinza's face. She could never explain what she was without Mitra thinking she was a lunatic or putting her in danger.

Mikah had clasped his hands in his lap. Even sitting on a dirty floor in the dark, he still looked like he was ready to announce the morning news. *What of your family?* he asked quietly.

I'd have to leave them, she said. In truth, Kinza had probably seen Grams for the last time, regardless of how this turned out. She could no longer keep the tears back and they silently welled up in her eyes.

So you wouldn't mind being alone? Mikah asked, brows knitting together. *Wouldn't you feel guilty?*

Kinza wanted to strangle him for that question. *Well yes, but—ugh!* If she said any more she was going to cry in earnest, so instead, she put her chin on her hands on her knees and stared at the floor like it would dig a hole back to Chicago. Of course she minded being alone! Truly thinking about what her life would be like if she ran made the tears continue to fall. She wouldn't be able to have anyone in her life ever again. It's not like she could use the portals; the *venari* would find her in a heartbeat. Humans couldn't get to know her because before long they would figure out something was off about her. She would be alone for the rest of her life with no one to help her. If she really thought about it, she would be lucky if she survived alone in the world while running from the Anunnaki.

Mikah looked thoughtful for a moment. *I have both good and bad qualities, some more than others. My father has always been...harsh. He would be relentless in telling me that I needed to achieve something, and to some degree I agree with him. My mother never stepped in when he yelled at me or told me I was a disappointment. Despite all of that, they are my parents. I think if I was in the same position, and I chose to leave, the guilt would eat away at me. Maybe not at first, but eventually the fact that I had abandoned them would catch up to me.* He barked a laugh. *Well, never mind, I supposed we would all just forget about our families entirely soon after leaving, right?* he said with a half smile.

Kinza wondered if maybe he did know who she was and was toying with her. *She* wouldn't get to forget. It was odd, thinking of the forgetting as a luxury, but she would have to live with the fact she abandoned everyone; Grams, Mitra, Khalil, the Apostles and Ekaja's people, even Zaid. She wouldn't be able to assimilate into human life or culture again; her life would be separate from everyone's if she left.

I know that's not really a helpful answer, Mikah said, resting his forearms on his knees. *But I also don't blame you for wanting to leave Rhapta when it's about to be filled with even more chaos and destruction. It feels a bit like being in a pen with ten thousand angry bulls and nowhere to go.*

Yeah, it does, she said. She had realized how stupid her idea to leave was and it made her bitter. The canvas bag filled with stolen items looked like a child's attempt to run away when they couldn't get what they wanted. How did she think she was actually going to make this work? She had no money and she wouldn't be able to stay in one place long enough to get a job in fear of the Anunnaki coming after her. So she would have to resort to stealing and not getting caught. How would she travel with no money? There was certainly no way to get on a plane and she didn't have any secret hacker friends like in the movies, the ones that would give you a fake name and I.D. as easily as if they had popped it out of a vending machine.

Gram's would be disappointed in her for not thinking

before she made such a rash decision. She was so intent on getting out of the city that she didn't stop to think that it might be just as dangerous out there as it was in here. That only put her back at square one, though. She was stuck in Rhapta with people wanting her dead and no way to fix it. A bitter emptiness fell over her like a blanket and it seemed there was no way out of this.

Kinza cleared her through and stood, brushing off the dust on her pants. *I need to get going,* she said.

Mikah stood and walked over to her. *Well,* he said in a slightly cheerier tone. *I'm assuming I don't need to escort you anywhere and you are not going to come with me?*

Kinza gave a small smile and a shake of her head. *No, I'll be okay.*

That's what I thought you'd say. Well then, I wish you the best and hopefully we'll meet again on the other side of the war. He hesitated before leaning to wipe a single tear left on her cheek with his thumb. Giving her a small smile, he bowed and slipped out the back door.

Kinza stood there for a few minutes, gathering herself before she, too, left, leaving her bag of stolen goods still sitting on the floor.

CHAPTER 20

A BETRAYAL SO COLD

Z aid placed another crate on the back of the makeshift cart, grunting with the effort.

What is even in here? he thought.

After the evening meal, Zaid had requested Tahir for something to do, something he could help with. He couldn't stand around doing nothing while his people inside the city were afraid and those that were here were still penned. He wondered if his mother was all right. Before Mikah had sent him to the camp with the warriors, he had asked Nazim about after his mother. The older man had said that she and a few others had left and didn't know where.

Now he didn't know where she was and the longer the city was held by the Unfettered, the higher the chance that she was hurt. Zaid had no intention of losing his last surviving family member, so he did what he could and hauled the crates faster.

Tahir had pointed him in the direction of a wiry young man, a few years older than Zaid, who was working on loading the few goods they had taken out of the city back onto carts they had put together with materials they had. He was surprised so much had made it out during the attack. Just before Zaid had made his way over to the edge of the camp, Tahir had told him that he was making an announcement shortly; the counterattack would happen tonight.

Shortly after the declaration the camp had thrummed with activity and nervous energy. Finally they had some sort of direction, something to look forward to. There were just as many people crying for their loved ones not to go into battle as there were those craving to be at the forefront. All warriors and other abled bodied men—and a few women—were preparing to head back in. Zaid assumed he would be going as well, but seeing as he had never been trained to operate in formation, he would be something of a backup. For now he helped with the hard labor, getting things packed up because, hopefully, they would be able to go home soon.

He didn't want to think about what would happen if the warriors lost. It was a very small chance seeing as the Unfettered's numbers were so small, but one always had to be careful. There was no precedent for this, so it was hard to tell. Anunnaki abilities made things even harder to predict. There was a master log in the city that the Elders and a few scholar's kept of all registered abilities, but it wasn't here. The people on the outskirts rarely registered their abilities anyways and the Elders never bothered to take a census of them. It was very possible that some of the Unfettered had destructive abilities and there was no way to train for what you didn't know existed.

The last time Anunnaki had truly gone to war was before biblical times. Their histories date the hiding of the city somewhere about one to two thousand years before the birth of Christ. Even during those times, Anunnaki had only ever *defended* their city from outsiders; humans. Some texts say that the barrier around the city was much larger, ranging miles and miles, but that was difficult to verify. One thing was for sure, the Anunnaki had never gone to war against *themselves*. It was blasphemous to think about. According to the texts from the original Rhaptan kings, their purpose was to help guide humanity as an older sibling would. If we were fighting amongst ourselves, how could we expect to help humanity?

Zaid shook his head, no use dwelling on the past and he couldn't change the fact the attack had already happened. But if he wasn't thinking about the upcoming battle, his mind would just wander to Kinza. He tried to keep the concept of her mentally at arm's length, but then he would remember how an errant curl had fallen over her forehead when she had been yelling at him. Trying to push the memories of her back down only brought them up stronger. Waking up next to her in that house in Moshi. He had been so relieved she was all right, it had taken him ten minutes to even remember that he had almost died as well.

Zaid looked for another box to haul, but the pile was empty. He looked around for the wiry man, maybe he would have new orders for him, but he didn't see him. The camp was a flurry of activity by now. People ran back and forth, delivering messages and helping amidst the chaos.

This storage area was on the far side of the camp, right at the edge. Rows of tents were erected back here to hold some of the Elder's personal effects; each tent was marked by a design of beads and feathers tied out front to indicate whose tent was whose. About halfway down, there was a tent that even had a guard, and it was the only one.

Who would need their belongings guarded? he thought to himself. *Surely that man was needed elsewhere right now.* The man shifted to the side and Zaid caught a glimpse of the beading. He was surprised to see it was Tahir's. Curiosity peaking,

Zaid took a step toward the tent before remembering the guard. It's not like he would let Zaid in. He sighed and turned to go look for more work when a messenger ran up to the guard. They spoke animatedly for a moment before the messenger left, taking the guard with him.

Zaid could not have asked for better timing. Without wasting time he zipped over to the tent and when no one yelled at him for being there, he slipped and nearly fell over.

There was a person.

A person tied to a chest.

A person tied to a chest who looked suspiciously like his brother's old mentor; the one who lured him into the Apostles.

Hunar, Zaid said, scowling. He figured Tahir would have some sort of secret, but this? He stepped further in the tent. The man was tied to a chest and looked half drugged. *Did Tahir finally have enough of you and the rest of the Apostles framing him for everything under the sun?*

Hunar's head lolled to the side and looked up at him. He garbled a half sort of chuckle. *You would think that,* he said and sighed. *It's nice to see you too, Zaid. Care to release me?*

Zaid snorted and turned to go. If Tahir wanted to keep Hunar tied up here for the rest of his life then good for him; Zaid would look the other way.

Wait! Please, Hunar said. *I know you think I am the reason that Amir died, but that isn't—*

Don't! Don't you ever say his name! Zaid snarled as he whirled back around. *Amir didn't start acting weird until he met you. He spent more time away from his family after he became your apprentice. He recited the crap you preached to him and he became ubir after you encouraged him to. You see the pattern here?*

I did not encourage him to become ubir, Hunar said quietly, coughing a little. Zaid wondered what sort of drug they had been giving him to make him stay quiet. By the harrowed look on his face Zaid assumed it was mostly due to giving up. Good.

And I assume you didn't tell him to question every single thing Tahir did as well? As soon as they got back to Rhapta, Zaid planned on telling Tahir where the Apostles of Truth were. He honestly didn't know why he hadn't done it sooner.

No, Hunar said, sounding irritated, *I did tell him to question Tahir. And for good reason. I will admit I think he took it too aggressively because of me and Tahir found out about him and led him to the Unfettered, who in turn convinced him to do the blood rite. But I tried to keep him from that, and I thought I had. Amir was a good kid, Zaid, but he was wholly unprepared to deal with Tahir.*

Zaid shook his head. *You are so fixated on Tahir that you are willing to drag other people down with you. I hope you rot in here, Hunar.* Zaid truly turned to leave now, but Hunar shouted on his way out.

Just watch him, Zaid! Truly watch him and you'll see what he has done!

Zaid let the flap on the tent fall closed and he stalked across the grass, headed toward the main collection of tents. He wouldn't tell Tahir he had seen Hunar, but he wouldn't tell anyone else either. It was time someone had dealt with Hunar before he got someone else killed. It had taken all of Zaid's strength not to deal with him himself.

Tahir had told him to meet him at his tent around sunset. It was a little early but Zaid had run out of things to do and he was still fuming from the conversation with Hunar. He needed something to take his mind off of everything now that images of both Kinza and Amir swirled in his head. If ever there was a time that he missed Amir's calming hands, it was now.

People ran back and forth in the main area of the camp, everyone engrossed in their work. Zaid stalked up to Tahir's tent and the usual guard wasn't there. He stopped when he heard Tahir talking inside, so he stepped back to wait patiently until he was done. Zaid wondered where the guard had gone, there was always one outside of Tahir's tent.

He watched the buzzing activity of the camp at this late hour and wondered at the last time Rhaptans had ever worked together so eagerly. It was one thing to keep the well-oiled machine of a city running for millennia, but as soon as they were threatened, people came together like the person standing next to them was their mother, brother, or cousin. It was heartwarming in a bittersweet way.

People used their abilities however they could to help those around them, when not more than a week ago the city was deep in its usual gossip and petty rivalries. It was one of the few things Zaid didn't like about his people, that they could be so childish when they should have been the wise leaders for the rest of the planet. The wealthy and powerful of the inner plazas normally paraded around showing their advantages to those less fortunate. Even in his mother's neighborhood, Zaid had seen wives and mothers silently battling whose child was better than whose. He supposed when you had little access to the rest of the world, you turned on those closest to you for a bit of competition. The problem was that they had taken it too far for too long.

In a way, the attack on the city was probably good for its inhabitants, despite the death and destruction. *Good job Kinza,* he thought sourly. *You only managed to bring us together.*

After several minutes of waiting, the voices inside the tent became a little louder, as if in argument. Curious, Zaid focused closer on them in hopes he could pick out what they were saying. He trusted Tahir, but the man had proved to have a few large secrets.

And what if she gets to the Elder's first? came a voice that sounded a lot like Elder Harran's. Zaid had not met the representative of the north quarter, but knew he had a relentless reputation and zero tolerance for prophecies, no matter how many times they were proven.

It won't matter either way. Hakim had his vision so they will know she is lying; that's if she isn't killed in battle either, Tahir said. Zaid realized they were talking about Kinza and a pang ran through him.

I don't like this, Harran said. *This is all resting on the fact that Hakim had a vision. What if the others gain a shred of intelligence and ask to hear it from him directly?*

You know he is too old and far gone to be hosting an audience.

That's my point. Almost no one except you had heard a vision from him in years. Eventually people are going to question whether the visions are actually from Hakim, or your own design.

What? Why would people think Hakim's visions are Tahir's making? That made no sense. Zaid focused harder on the conversation.

It won't come to that.

How do you know that, Tahir? I want to know that this is going to work and that little girl isn't going to be sitting on a throne in a day's time!

Quiet! There is nothing she could do to change the mind of the people, I've made sure of it.

And what of the Unfettered? Are we actually going to be able to surprise them or have you already told them we are coming?

I've told them nothing, I want this to be as real as possible. It truly didn't take much, they were already intent on anarchy. Now this is just fun for them.

I really don't like this, Tahir. There are too many loose ends.

Zaid heard Tahir sigh. *Like what, Harran? Where have I missed?*

That assassin. Not only did they completely botch their assign-ment, one of them was stupid enough to reveal where he got is orders and the woman is now missing. What if she goes around telling people where she got her orders? Just one step and it's back to you and this whole thing falls through.

She'd never be able to prove it...

Zaid pulled away, no longer able to listen. His blood had turned to ice and he fought to keep from throwing up. There had been many times when he was younger and had made decisions that ended up making him feel more like a child; more naive. That was nothing compared to what he felt right now.

His world was collapsing inward and the rug was swept from under his feet. He looked around and the people went about their evening, completely unaware that the person who led the attack on their city was nestled in the middle of their camp.

Zaid could feel a storm of rage and sadness and betrayal build at the edges of his mind. The ice that had been there a moment ago slowly started to boil. He couldn't see past the rage that wracked his body and through a haze of anger, shoved his way into the tent.

Both Harran and Tahir were seated inside and jumped to their feet at Zaid's entrance.

Why? he asked, looking only at Tahir.

Who is this boy, Tahir? Does he not know respect—

WHY?! Zaid screamed, taking a step forward.

Tahir's face changed then. One moment it was in shock before it practically melted and was replaced by something else. The creature underneath was cold and calculating, and looked at Zaid with merciless pity. There was no love or compassion in his eyes, only power and greed. How had he never seen it? He felt like such a fool; the world's largest fool.

Oh Zaid, my boy, curiosity is not a good trait on you, he said, but stayed where he was. Zaid realized then that the guard that usually stood outside was just inside the doorway. He didn't have a moment to react when a hand was placed on his arm and he was dragged down into a sea of unconsciousness. That last thing he saw was Tahir's disappointed face looking down at him.

CHAPTER 21

THE BATTLE BEGINS

The cold from the marble floors seeped into Kinza's feet as she walked through the Hall. Shadows twisted at every corner, but these each had twin flames for eyes. They prowled closer so she broke into a run. At the end of the hall was a set of massive doors covered in ice. She needed to get inside but couldn't remember why. The shadows were coming closer, lurking at the edge of her vision. She clawed at the ice on the door, frantically trying to get inside, but the ice was too thick. The tingling at the back of her neck started, warning her of danger. She screamed for help but no one was there, she was all alone with the shadows behind her, reaching out their clawed fingers as she scrabbled against the ice...

Kinza gasped awake in bed. There was nothing but darkness at first, but then her eyes adjusted and she saw the light coming from under her door.

Just a dream then.

She was about to lay back down when she realized the tingling on her neck wasn't just in her dream. A second later she heard shouting outside her room and pounding on the doors. What was going on? It couldn't be morning yet.

Throwing back the blankets, she flew across the room and ripped the door open. As she did a boom as loud as a grenade sounded above her head and dust rippled through the hall. Instinctively she covered her head, but it stopped a moment later.

Apostles were running back and forth in various states of dress, some carrying books and baskets, others carried spears and swords. Still wearing her pajamas, she jogged down the hall trying to stop someone to find out what was happening. As she neared the end, she saw Nim tying his indigo robes and barking orders at a cowering scholar.

"Nim!" she shouted, not bothering to use telepathy. She wanted to make sure he heard her, and he turned toward her at the sound. "What is going on?" she asked, running up to him.

"Get dressed!" he yelled at her and started hurrying away. She ran up and grabbed his arm, pulling him back.

"Nim! Tell me what is happening!" she yelled.

He whirled back and placed hands on her shoulder. "The attack," he bit out. "It's happening now. The warriors have returned and the battle wages above our heads. Time has run out, Kinza."

Panic built in her chest as another boom rocked the halls, sending more dust floating down from the ceiling. "Where is Sa'id? Nim, what do I do?" This couldn't be happening yet, she wasn't ready.

"Sa'id is already above helping in the fight. It's a mess, Kinza. I can't tell you what to do, but the Elders are in the Grand Hall. Getting to them won't stop the battle, but convincing them you are not a threat might save your life. If I die, it's was an honor to have met you." Without another word he turned and lumbered down the hall, grabbing an unsuspecting scholar and hauling him along as well.

Kinza sprinted back into her room and ripped the lid off the

Aurastone box lamp, letting the light flood in. Her heart was pounding as she dressed herself. She found another set of clothes in a similar style to the ones she had been wearing, but instead this set had a loose, long-sleeved cropped shirt to go along with the pants, and both were black. They were also a slightly heavier material than the silks she was growing used to. Still not appropriate for battle but she didn't have time to go search for something better. She yanked them on and found a pair of boots in another box. She didn't bother looking in the mirror as she pulled half her hair back into a bun and ran out the door.

Many of the Apostles looked frightened as she jogged down the hallways. Without thinking she headed toward the main staircase that led up into the library, but as soon as she got close she saw several Apostles backing away and running in the opposite direction.

The library collapsed! someone called to her. It must be blocking the doorway. She headed to the other door that she had used to sneak out the night before. After she had gotten back last night she had gone straight to sleep so she couldn't wallow in her own despair for too long. She had decided not to leave Rhapta for now, but staying was starting to feel like a bad decision too. How was she supposed to get out of this? Once the battle was over, someone was going to come looking for her, and regardless of who, there was a good chance she was going to die.

She made it to the door and hurried up the stairwell and paused before the door. She could hear the sounds of battle but they were muffled, possibly far off. Gingerly, she pushed the door open and slipped out. The fighting was much closer than she had thought. Groups of what looked to be Unfettered were locked into battle with formations of warriors in their red paint. The door was in an alley, but it was only a few steps to the street and the fighting. She would have to make a run for it and then figure out where to go.

Stepping out into the street, she was nearly impaled when four sharpened daggers of wood came flying at her head. She ducked and they lodged in the wall behind her. Upon closer inspection they weren't wood at all, but looked like large porcupine spikes. She saw why when an Unfettered woman sent out another round in a spiral around her in retaliation to the three warriors before her. Kinza screamed as one grazed her bicep, tearing out a tiny chunk of skin. She would heal just fine, but her abilities thought otherwise and she immediately burst into flames.

The panic that had been building was at full throttle now. Warriors and Unfettered alike stumbled away from her while trying to hold their positions in battle. She didn't know what to do. An Unfettered came running down the street with a warrior with the legs of a goat in pursuit. The Unfettered didn't see her at first and came too close and his clothes caught fire. Within moments he was screaming on the ground.

Kinza gasped and ran through the street, trying to avoid getting too near to others while she searched for someone to help her. The last time this happened, Zaid was there to calm her down. But he wasn't here anymore and wasn't going to be there for her ever again. She didn't get far before she entered a small plaza. There were more people here fighting but Kinza didn't pay attention to them as she ran head first toward the fountain and threw herself in.

Her idea proved successful as she pulled her head above water, gasping for breath but without the flames any longer. She stumbled out of the fountain dripping water and curls falling onto her forehead. She looked around to see where she was. Standing still for too long seemed like a bad idea, but she needed to think.

What to do? What to do? Anxiety bubbled through her and she could hardly calm her mind enough to get a rational thought in. Nim had said the Elders were in the Grand Hall. That seemed like a good place to start and hopefully she would come up with a plan to convince them of her innocence on the way there.

Jumping on the fountain ledge gave her a slightly better vantage. She was only a street or so away from the central plaza and she could see the top of the Grand Hall peeking over the row of houses in this adjacent plaza. A heavy gust of wind barreled through the street, whipping her wet clothes and hair, and she threw her hands up as if to ward it off, but it only lasted a second.

Must've been someone's ability. She didn't want to be there to see if they could make a tornado out of that so she jumped off the ledge and ran through the streets. She had to continuously throw herself left and right to avoid oncoming swords, spears, and elements. All of Jabari's lesson was gone from her mind and it took all her effort not to succumb entirely to the panic. The only thing that kept her abilities at bay was knowing that if she did let her explosions out now, someone innocent would surely die.

She left the little plaza behind to enter onto the main boulevard that bisected the city from south to north and turned right. Hundreds more warriors were here and fought against the Unfettered. Kinza could see the occasional person here or there fleeing the battle. She did rather well weaving in and out of individual fights as she made her way to the massive plaza in the center of the city. She had only glimpsed it before but it struck her how real her nightmares had been.

To the far left and right of the plaza were parallel pools of water that now had Unfettered, warriors, and those she couldn't identify battling in the shallow liquid. It was too dark to see, but she thought the water looked black.

On the side closest to her was a tall statue that faced the Grand Hall on the other side of the plaza; it truly was massive, looking like a squat plus sign with the arms perpendicular to the plaza longer than the one that faced her. In the dead center of the plaza was the largest Aurastone Kinza had ever seen, looking like a giant replica of the hundreds that lit the streets around Rhapta.

Right now there were more Unfettered with their backs to it fighting off a troop of warriors. One of the warriors shot out bolts of lightning but it stopped when it connected with some kind of shield that surrounded the Unfettered. The Unfettered looked like they were outnumbered by far based on the sheer numbers of warriors in their red paint and unified formations. But there were just as many people fighting who Kinza couldn't tell which side they were on, and it looked like both the Unfettered and the warriors were doing the same.

She had seen battles on tv and in movies, but they always had distinct sides, each waving a banner and brandishing their colors. This, on the other hand, was absolute chaos. People couldn't tell who was who, no one wore matching colors— other than the warrior's red paint—and the only way to tell friend from foe was if they attacked you or not. The only light came from the few Aurastone lamps that still stood in the plaza and Kinza could make out a few of the black bands on the arms of the Unfettered, but many of them did not wear them. Whether it was because they had lost them or they were trying to stir up more confusion, she didn't know.

She started running straight through the plaza, aiming to weave around the statue before her, but suddenly a line of warriors was coming at her with swords raised. Just as in her nightmare, they all towered over her and wielded the obsidian swords and spears. Rage and bloodlust painted their faces, intent on cutting her down; one of them had the eyes of a snake. At the vivid reenactment of her nightmare, Kinza screamed, throwing her hands up.

"Stop! Stop!" she yelled. "I'm not Unfettered, please don't!" Her stomach was in her throat but they stopped inches from her.

One of them snarled and another shouted at her over the noise of battle. "Get inside!" he said before shoving her back toward the buildings that lined the plaza. They didn't wait to see if she went before running off to take down another pack of Unfettered.

Kinza was shaking as she started back into the plaza, she couldn't stop now, no matter how terrifying those warriors had been. From where she stood she could see the front of the library on the right side of the plaza and two of its walls had collapsed. She couldn't worry about the Apostles now and instead headed toward the Grand Hall.

She made it past the statue and ran toward the giant Aura-stone. Even from where she was, she could feel a faint thrumming coming off of it, but there was no time to inspect. She kept her eyes up as much as possible, trying to avoid the bodies that littered the ground, but several times her body retched at the stench. Most of them looked to be Unfettered, but there were some warriors too. She didn't know what she would do if it was someone she knew.

Zaid….No, she couldn't think about him now, she needed to keep moving.

She was in an open space between the statue and the Aura-stone. Up closer to the building the battle was more condensed and there was little chance of her getting through without getting close enough for someone to swing a sword at her. It was best she had something to defend herself with. Looking around, she spotted an obsidian sword on the ground. Not looking at the body next to it, she gingerly picked it up. It was much heavier than she had expected and she didn't know if she actually had the guts to stab someone, but it made her feel slightly better to hold something.

She was almost to the Aurastone when she reeled back, eyes going up. Before her lurched the largest man she had ever seen, so large that he nearly blocked out her view of the Aurastone behind him. His size had to be some sort of ability because his skin was also covered in what looked like a layer of rock and stone. The stone man bellowed at her as if he was more animal than man, wielding a massive greatsword.

All thoughts of swinging the sword drained from her head as fear shot through her. Her sword clattered to the ground as she took a step back. The stone man only took one yard-long step closer, raising his sword to strike her down.

Kinza didn't even have time to realize she was going to die when the stone man brought the sword down over her head. Right then, something slammed into her from the side, taking her to the ground in a painful crack. The stone man's sword struck the ground, sending fissures out into the limestone plaza.

The breath had been knocked out of her but she was hauled to her feet before she had a chance to regain it.

"Run!" The voice came from the person who had knocked her down.

She turned to find Sa'id in his scholar's robes, carrying an obsidian short sword, his graying hair glinted in the Auralight. Two other scholars flanked him and faced off the stone man. Kinza was still too stunned to speak, just inhaling air and gaping at him. At the back of her mind she thought she probably looked like a deer in the headlights, too frightened to move.

"Kinza, run!" Sa'id yelled again, waving his sword at her to get her to go.

She didn't think and just ran. Several buildings around the plaza had started on fire, casting the bloody battle in a sinister glow. Her breath came back and she sucked in huge gulps as she got closer to the Grand Hall. There were even more people here now and getting up the steps looked near-impossible. She would have to find another way.

There were less people on the right side of the building so she ran that way. Thankfully she didn't have any other major run-ins, but it took forever to get around the long right arm of the building. Around the side she found a set of large wooden doors that had been half ripped off their hinges. It was almost quiet over here though and she didn't see anyone close by so she jogged up the steps and slipped inside.

The tingling at her neck was a near-constant warning now. "I know, I know," she mumbled to her abilities. "I can see the danger, thank you."

The inside of the hall was unlit other than the bit of light that trickled in through the doorway from the Aurastone lamps outside. The ceiling stretched far above her head and she recognized the marble floors underneath her feet. There was no one here, but she could hear sounds from the other side of the building.

Kinza wasn't sure what she was really doing as she crept past the long row of doors on either side of the hall. Her only objective now was to find the Elders and she would figure out what to do after that. Eventually the long hallway ended and she found herself in a perpendicular hall that bisected the building. In fact, if she looked far down to her left, she could make out the front entrance and the battle that was raging there on the steps. A few Unfettered had made it inside, but they were only fighting the warriors there by the steps.

Looking around she realized that she was probably in the dead center of the building at a crossroads. If she went right, she would go toward the back of the building, but she heard noise from the opposite hall and decided to go that direction instead.

This way was identical from the way she had come. The hall was wide enough to practically fit Grams' whole house in it, but she stayed to the edge to keep from being seen. As she got halfway down, she saw the source of the noise. On the right side of the hall, two warriors were fending off nearly fifteen Unfettered. It looked like the warriors were guarding a doorway behind them and Kinza could guess who was inside. The warriors looked haggard and exhausted and step by step they were losing to the Unfettered that hammered away at them. Cries for help echoed out of the room as the warriors were in their final moments.

Finally, Kinza knew what she had to do.

CHAPTER 22
AN OCEAN OF STARS

Zaid woke with his face squished into the ground.

It took him a moment to remember how he got there, but then he heard the sounds of camp and groaned. He tried to push himself up but his hands were bound behind his back, and with *laqueus* based on the lack of heartbeats.

Told you so, chuckled a voice near his head.

Zaid blinked and craned his neck around to look at the man sitting next to him. The short face of Hunar hovered near him looking rather pleased with himself. *Sorry, but I've wanted to say that for a long time now.* He exhaled a contented sigh. *Feels good.*

Zaid groaned again and rolled over before sitting up. He didn't have any right to snap back at Hunar; he had been right the whole time. Zaid felt broken, and shameful, and so, so defeated. Tahir had been a spider waving a massive web around Rhapta for decades, and Zaid had thought him a hero. Zaid had *helped* him. What did that make him then? An accomplice?

Oh don't look so glum, Tahir bamboozled an entire city. Even I am here because I couldn't escape his reach, Hunar said.

Bamboozled? Zaid said, finally peering at him from the corner of his eye. Hunar shrugged. He couldn't even look at Hunar without feeling a sense of regret. And Amir—oh, Amir—had been one of the few who had seen through Tahir and had tried to warn them but they had all thought him crazy. Now he was dead. Old anger melted in with the shame. So many people had been hurt because of one man.

The sound of drums echoed throughout the camp, but it was still dark outside and the only light came from the moon shining down on the tops of the tents. It looked like Zaid had been thrown in the same storage tent as Hunar.

What is going on? Zaid asked. Why were they beating the drums?

Battle started, Hunar grunted.

What?! Zaid said sitting up higher. *When? How long ago?* How long had the warriors been in the city? At that thought, Zaid's blood ran cold.

Kinza!

No, no, no, no.

He had abandoned her and now she was going to die too.

Mmm, probably half an hour ago, Hunar said. *What are you doing?*

Zaid had struggled to his feet and was trying to look in the stacks of crates that lined the edges of the tent. With his hands bound he tried kicking off the lids but only managed to knock a crate of *guakal* wine to the ground, several bottles smashed open.

We have to get into the city, now! Help me find some obsidian. I need to cut these ropes. He kicked around in the crates. There must not have been a guard outside because he was making a racket.

And do what? Hunar said from his spot on the floor. *You*

think you can stop Tahir now?

I'm going to try. And Kinza is there. He kicked at another chest that seemed to be locked.

Kinza Solace? The outsider? Do you even know what she looks like?

Zaid snorted. *Of course, I brought her here.*

You—oh. Ohhhh, Hunar said with a sense of realization. A slow smile spread across his face. *Oh, this just got very interesting.*

Zaid eyed him from the middle of the mess he was making. There didn't seem to be any obsidian here which was a problem because you couldn't cut *laqueus* with anything else. The sound of the war drums beat in time with the anxiety buzzing in his veins.

Hunar let out a chuckle. *Little Zaid is in love with the outsider from the prophecy.* The chuckle turned into an outright belly-laugh.

I'm not—Arg! Just help me! I can't find any obsidian here, he said looking around.

Hunar had stopped laughing and was slowly returning to seriousness. *Well, there's the knife pen in my robes.*

What?! Have you had that there the whole time? Why didn't you try to escape? Zaid asked.

And do what? If you hadn't noticed, all five foot five inches of me are not exactly primed for a fight. I'm a scholar, not a warrior—or a venari. No, it's in the other pocket.

Zaid had to turn around and sit down to reach into Hunar's pockets. It was an awkward position, but he managed to pull out a stylus that looked like a fountain pen. With a little adjusting, the top half screwed off to reveal a thin obsidian blade underneath. Zaid grinned. *Hunar, you sly fox.*

It took a matter of seconds for Zaid to cut his own bonds before cutting Hunar's and then they were out of the tent and into the night. Fires had been lit on the other side of camp to illuminate the massive stream of warriors emptying out into the forest nearby to enter into the tunnel that was hidden there. At the back of the line of warriors, civilians and those with abilities that could help to fight or heal those that were fighting trailed behind. Children and the elderly stayed in their tents, some of them watching with sorrowful eyes as their family members went to battle.

We need to get in that group of people at the back, Zaid said as he stalked across the grass. Hunar hurried behind him, pulling out a pair of spectacles and setting them on his nose. After that he seemed to move faster.

And how are we going to do that without being seen?

Ahh, I was just going to jump in and hope for the best. I doubt Tahir would tell the other Elders about what happened, so only he and Harran and their guards would stop me. Zaid paused for a moment before turning back to Hunar. *Who else is involved in Tahir's lies?*

We—the Apostles I mean—believe that Elder Minesh and his pupil are with him. I doubt Elder Sumai can keep a secret, but I wouldn't doubt that he would do what Tahir told him to. There might be others, but I'm not sure.

Zaid nodded and moved toward the stream of people leaving the camp. A few warriors were corralling people through, the tunnel was only big enough for a few people to stand next to each other, so it was slow going. Keeping his head down and hoping Hunar followed his lead, Zaid melded in with a group of extras at the end of the line and shuffled along within them. As long as he stayed in the middle of the group and kept his head down, he was sure they wouldn't see him.

The line was moving slowly though, and Zaid's anxiety was building by the second. The longer it took him to get there, the higher the chance that Kinza would be killed. Hopefully she had stayed down under the library with the Apostles instead of going up to the surface.

Where are the Elders? Zaid asked Hunar who just shrugged.

A man next to Zaid had heard him and leaned closer. *The Elders all went ahead with a contingent of warriors. Even Hakim.*

They did? Zaid said. *What do they think they are going to do? Fight?*

The other man shrugged and the woman next to him said, *I bet they are trying to be a show of strength.. You know, get out there and reunite with the other Elders. Showing Kinza Solace and her Unfettered that they are a unified force might be enough to scare her off.*

Zaid nodded but didn't say anything. He really needed to get back to the city. Within ten minutes he and Hunar were in the tunnel. The occasional Aurastone torch was set into the wall, but it was still pretty dark. People had spread out more so as not to step on each other, but it only slowed the march down.

Hunar jabbed him in the ribs.

What? Zaid said.

Right as they were in a dark patch of tunnel, Hunar said, *Follow me,* as quietly as possible and dragged Zaid hard to the left. Where he had thought was the wall of the tunnel, was actually another narrower tunnel leading in a different direction. There were several branches like this, but the main host knew to stay on the lighted path. The tunnels underneath Rhapta were a network of confusing lines that crossed back and forth, some overlapping several times. As a child he was always warned to stay out of here if he ever found one. When he was nine a classmate had gone missing after he was seen entering the mouth of one of the tunnels. His body was never found.

I know a faster way back to the city, Hunar said. *You can probably get there even faster if you run.*

You do? These tunnels are chaotic, Hunar. And I don't think I could carry you and run fast enough, Zaid said.

Don't worry, I will follow behind. You go on ahead. Take this tunnel straight for a quarter mile, then take the third fork for another quarter mile, and then finally take the far left fork and it should come out in the eastern quarter. The tunnel the Elders are taking comes out in the north. You'll be far from Tahir and can get to your girlfriend faster that way.

She's not my—never mind. What if you get lost?

Well if you don't die in battle, come get me! he said like it was obvious. *Now go!*

Zaid wasted no time and started running down the side tunnel. He quickly had to slow as it was pitch black and couldn't even see his hand in front of him, but he was still going faster than the procession had been. He followed Hunar's directions; quarter-mile, third fork, and then finally far left fork. Several cobwebs wrapped around his head that he had to wipe away. Clearly no one had been here in a long time. When he got to the end of the final tunnel, it ended in a wall. For a moment Zaid started to panic, but fresh air wafted above his head and he looked up to find a sewer grate above his head. Feeling along the wall, he found a few indents for handholds and pulled himself up. The grate was heavy, but surprisingly not rusted shut. It took a little effort, but he lifted it up and wiggled out and onto the dark street.

Hunar was right about where the tunnel came out. The neighborhood he was in was close to his mother's home. It would only take him a few minutes to get across the remainder of the eastern quarter and into the central plaza. He took off into the night, aiming for the vast sea of heartbeats in the center of the city.

There was only a little fighting this far out and he dodged it easily, but the closer he got, the more he had to slow to avoid running into flying projectiles and bodies locked in battle. When he got to the edge of the central plaza he stood and looked out in horror. The city was ravaged by fire and blood, both Unfettered warriors and civilians fought in chaos and he hardly knew who was who.

Tahir had done this. He had destroyed their home and Zaid could never forgive a monster like that.

To the left he saw the library, two of its walls caved in. Alarm panged through him at the thought of Kinza crushed under the rubble. He started to run again but suddenly found his feet rooted to the ground, unable to move. Zaid tried to thrash his legs but it was as if they were magnetized to the Earth's core.

Of all people, he mentally groaned. He looked around and found him walking closer. The warrior who had stopped him back at Nazim's camp had a blade out and stalked closer. *Let me go! I'm on your side, idiot!*

You brought her here! the man shouted. *You defended her. As far as I'm concerned, you are the enemy just as much as she is.*

Zaid was looking around for a weapon or something within reach, but the warrior was too close and moved to strike. A small rock came hurtling out of nowhere and struck the warrior right on the wrist of the sword hand. The warrior cried out as he dropped his sword and a shadow came barreling straight into the warrior's midsection taking him to the ground. The shadow—Zaid could see it was a man now—gave him one crisp punch in the jaw and he went out like a light.

The man stood, taking the warrior's sword and threw it to Zaid who was free to move now. He saw that it was Tejas, the only other boy his age when he was first brought into *venari* training. They had been rivals at first, but they had slowly realized it was the rest of Rhapta against them and it was better when they were at least civil with each other. He wouldn't exactly call Tejas a friend, but he wasn't a stranger either. Even though *venari* rarely saw each other anymore once they were out of training and working, they still had the bond of ostracization from the Rhaptan community.

The aim with the rock was a near-impossible shot, but Tejas was lucky. That was actually his ability; luck. It made for some interesting sparring sessions back in the day but Zaid was thankful he hadn't been killed in battle. It had been almost three years since he had seen him last.

Tejas gave him a curt nod that Zaid returned, and ran off. Zaid immediately went toward the library before someone else got crafty and decided to slow him down. He ran up the steps that were devoid of Unfettered. He had expected only to find the dead inside but there was actually a small contingency of healers spread out around the fallen bookcases and broken tables. The injured were being carted in and the various healers were running around trying to help as much as they could. A few warriors stood guard at the door to fend off and brave Unfettered.

Zaid pushed his way past people, looking at both the injured and keeping an eye out for Khalil. He found the man toward the back with the worst of the injured. A sky blue Aura glowed faintly from the person Khalil was focused on, but it didn't look good. The woman was still as the grave and Zaid almost missed the shallow rise and fall of her chest.

Khalil! Zaid shouted, coming closer. To his relief, Zaid didn't see anyone he recognized among the wounded.

Without looking up, Khalil said, *Glad to see you are still kicking, my friend.* Even when Zaid had practically disappeared without telling him where he was going, Khalil never held any grudges against him.

You as well. Where is Kinza? he asked.

Oh, so now you care? Khalil said, focusing on the blue Aura.

Zaid retracted his prior statement. *I was looking for answers, Khalil. I needed to know the truth.*

And did you find them? Khalil exhaled a pained sigh and pulled his hands back. The woman's chest had stopped moving.

It's Tahir. It's him.

Khalil finally looked up at him and nodded before turning to the patient on the table next to him. Within moments a bright orange Aura started glowing, this one stronger. *I don't know where Kinza is, I haven't seen her since yesterday morning, but the Apostles told her she needed to convince the Elders she wasn't a threat. There was no plan Zaid, the Apostles were ready for this.*

I told you to watch her!

Khalil glanced up briefly in annoyance. *She's an adult, and besides, what was I going to do? Stop her?*

You could have done something; follow her! Zaid threw up his hands. *Now she's alone.*

Then you shouldn't have left her, Zaid.

That stung. He knew Khalil was right, and it wasn't his responsibility. It hadn't been Zaid's responsibility either until he realized the thought of her hurt or dead made him want to throw up. He was the one who didn't believe her and he was the one who had left. He didn't have the right to feel sorry for himself.

I would try the Grand Hall, Khalil said. *I think the Elders* —Khalil stopped and looked up, as everyone else in the room did.

Zaid turned to see what everyone was looking at, pushing his way back toward the street, and was met by a white light so bright it looked like an ocean of stars had fallen all across Rhapta.

CHAPTER 23

THE LIGHT OF KINGS

Kinza was calm for the first time in days. Looking at the Unfettered beating down the warriors and listening to the cries from the Elders behind the door had her mind narrowing to a crystalline focus.

To her left was the outer wall of the building that faced the plaza and she kept to the side as she hurried forward. The heat in her abdomen was sharp and hot, her Aura begging to be released. Up ahead, one of the warriors had fallen back and it looked like he was wounded. The Unfettered only pressed harder against the remaining warrior who was whipping his sword back and forth with deadly accuracy, but it wasn't enough. One of the Unfettered laughed and the floor under the warrior rippled, sending him to the ground.

She could do one better.

"Hey!" she shouted at them. The group whirled to see her. It only took a moment for them to see she was alone before the majority of the group came running down the hall toward her with swords and spears raised.

Good. *Get inside!* she mentally shouted to the warrior that had fallen. He must have taken the hint because the door slammed shut. One or two of the Unfettered started hammering at it, and the door started crumbling under the hands of another, but it wouldn't matter.

Kinza stopped a good distance from the door and waited the last half a second before the Unfettered reached her. For the first time she didn't fight the boiling heat or the tingling in her body. She only screwed her eyes shut as a white light burst out of her followed closely by a wave of energy that had her stumbling.

She was slightly disappointed as she opened her eyes because that was the smallest explosion she had ever done, but she hadn't been trying to blow them up. Instead she had been standing by the outer wall and had blown a small hole in the bottom.

The Unfettered watched as the remains of the massive walls cracked and collapsed inward. Car-sized boulders came crashing down on the group and Kinza threw herself to the side to avoid being crushed to death. The floor shook and she could hear screams coming from somewhere in the dark.

When the shaking finally stopped she coughed and opened her eyes. Dust and debris billowed around the room in the breeze that had been let in. She heard a faint cheering from the plaza. The Unfettered must have thought their brethren had toppled the wall. Kinza stood and waved dust out of her face, but it was clearing fast. It was much brighter in the hall now, the light from the fires and a few Aurastones shining in from the plaza.

She moved over broken bits of wall, trying to get to the door. A shape moved in the dust far too fast for her liking and she realized too late that a few of the Unfettered had survived. Before she had a chance to back away, vines shot out from behind the Unfettered and wrapped around his ankles and yanked. He was dragged down as a man in loose white robes came out and rapped him on the head with the end of a spear and he fell unconscious.

Kinza coughed again and said, "Thank you."

"Come inside quick!" the man in the white robes said, ushering her in. She followed him inside and realized the vines had come in from the window, controlled by the injured warrior on the floor. She nodded to him in thanks as well.

The room was much larger than she had originally thought. Instead of some kind of meeting room, it was a long hall with a set of raised tiers on the far side with many chairs set upon them. On either side of the tiers were doors that led deeper into the building. The left side of the room held tall windows set high in the wall, letting the rising moonlight filter through. It looked more like a throne or court room to Kinza than anything else. Except there were many thrones instead of one.

Huddled toward the back of the room were close to forty men and a few women dressed in white robes identical to the man with the spear. The only other people were the two warriors, one of which was wounded on the ground.

These must be the Elders, Kinza thought to herself. Several of them ran over to her, while others stayed back.

"Thank you, child," a man with light brown skin said to her.

"Was that explosion your ability?" an old wrinkled woman asked.

"You are from the outskirts then?" the man with the spear asked since she had spoken out loud.

Now was her chance to convince them. They would either believe her or they wouldn't, but she had to try something.

"No, I am not from the outskirts," Kinza said loud enough that they all could hear. She took a deep breath and continued.

"My name is Kinza Solace and I desperately need to speak with you."

Several of the Elders gasped and the ones standing closest to her backed away. The man with the spear came to attention and had it pointed at her in defiance. She held her hands up pleading.

"Please! I need you to listen to me," she spoke quickly before they decided to stab her. "I know you've been told that I am your enemy or the leader of the Unfettered or whatever, but that's not true!"

"Liar!" one of them called. He pointed to the remaining warrior and said, "Arrest her, warrior!" The warrior looked too weary to stand but slowly made his way toward her.

"Wait!" she cried, taking a step back. "Please listen! I'm being framed. I didn't start this. I didn't want—"

Both doors at the back of the hall burst open and a small stream of warriors filed in followed by several more men in white robes and a few who weren't. One of the men in white robes strode ahead of the others and the warriors seemed to follow his direction. He looked no older than fifty, but there was something in his cold eyes that said he was much older.

These are lies! the man boomed inside their heads. *This woman seeks to trick us. She wants us to welcome in her chaos and destruction. We must resist it!*

She didn't have to guess much to know who he was. *You must be Tahir,* she said as his warriors circled around behind her, blocking her from the exit.

See! another Elder cried. This one was short and round and had a nasally voice inside her mind. *How would a human know who we are?*

I'm not human, as many of you just saw, she said, gesturing to the hall behind her. *But I am from the United States, not Rhapta. I was taken here against my will. I have nothing to do with the Unfet-*

tered. Please, you have to believe me! she shouted, stepping forward. Spears blocked her path and many of the Elders grumbled and shook their heads. She could see a cluster of them whisper and look toward the back as a warrior came in carrying the oldest man she had ever seen wrapped in furs. Many of the Elders reached their hands out to him and he was brought in the cluster of them at the back, blocking Kinza's view of him.

Even if you were human and had known nothing of us, can you not admit that your very existence causes chaos within the city? You must know of the prophecy that was foretold nearly two hundred years ago. It said that an outsider would come and rain either prosperity or destruction down upon the Anunnaki. From where I stand, your existence will be the death of our race. Should we allow all Anunnaki to die so you can live? Tahir looked around the room with both sadness and determination, many of the Elders nodding in agreement.

It was then that Kinza realized this was a madman. He might've truly cared for the city in some small dark way, but he would rather let it burn than let her live.

The only reason there is a battle out there, she said, flinging an arm toward the plaza, *is because you framed me! You did this! You killed my parents! You had me kidnapped and framed! You!*

Tahir turned and addressed the crowd of Elders. Kinza saw that more of them than she had realized were actually glaring at Tahir or eyeing her with worried expressions. Was there a chance that some of them would see the truth?

As long as she lives there will be doubt amongst our people. We will never return to peace and we do not have the luxury of a large population to wait and find out.

Because you are killing everyone! she screamed. The warriors shoved her back.

Do not forget, Tahir said to the other Elders, *that even our own Grand Elder Hakim had a vision stating that she was the leader of the Unfettered. Will you doubt him?* Many of them turned to look at the old man in the furs. Kinza caught a glimpse of him, they had placed him at the foremost chair that sat on the ground at the back of the room. His eyes were closed and he could've been dead for all Kinza knew.

Shouts came from down the hall and suddenly the warriors' attention was no longer on her because a swarm of Unfettered burst into the rooms and chaos erupted again. Screams came from some of the Elders as they pushed to the back of the room. The Unfettered were merciless in their attack. Kinza saw terrifying abilities up close as she tried to avoid them. She was stuck in the middle of the room with the Elders and a few warriors behind her and most of the warriors, Unfettered, and Elders who could fight in front of her.

Fire and wind and lightning struck and the floor cracked in places. Ice speared through several of the Unfettered and she saw one warrior scream as his hands turned black with fast-spreading necrosis. The warriors had the upper hand though with greater numbers and the wealth of experience of the Elders behind them. A very short Elder woman used a force Kinza couldn't see to lift and throw one of the Unfettered out the window.

She was distracted by the Elder woman when a spear came hurtling at her through the air. In half a breath she had teleported to the other side of the room, and heard a couple Elders cry out in surprise. Kinza saw that they had huddled around the old man—Hakim—to protect him, but not one of them nor the warriors lifted a finger to help her, she was on her own. Not another moment went by when a fist connected with her jaw. She saw stars that quickly turned to an inferno.

Oh no, not here, not now!

The fight was dwindling as the remaining Unfettered were

beaten back and Kinza's flames rose higher. Without the distraction of the Unfettered, many of the Elders' eyes turned to her in fear. A fleeing Unfettered tried to drag her down on the way out but he only caught fire as well. He stumbled in the doorway as the flames consumed him, but one of the warriors put him out of his misery.

The door was blocked so she couldn't leave, but she wouldn't be able to calm herself down. The Elders were all turned toward her now. *Please, let me out!* she cried. *I don't want to hurt anyone!*

One Elder was brave enough to come forward, but his movements surprised Kinza and she whirled. He jerked back but not before the sleeve of his robes caught fire. Several Elders and warriors rushed to help him as Kinza backed away in fear.

Ice suddenly crept across the floor and crackled up her body, smothering the fire. She didn't resist as Tahir walked closer with a dark look. The ice spread from the floor underneath his robes and kept coming until her eyelashes frosted over and frost spread across her cheek. She was so cold she started shivering and her breath came out in puffs, but she still didn't resist. At least the fire was out. It was better that she was cold than someone else hurt.

As long as she lives, we are not safe, Tahir said quietly. He didn't need to speak up as the room had gone almost silent. The Elder's robes were no longer on fire and they all looked at her with mixed expressions. Some with fear or hatred, some with confusion, and some with sorrow. Kinza realized then that Tahir was right. He had won and even if there was a chance that the Elders might believe her, it still wasn't worth the risk. Outside the hall she could hear the screams of people in battle out on the plaza. She may not have done this, but it revolved around her now and she had been *so selfish* these last few days.

All she had thought about was how she was going to get out because she was worried about herself. Tahir was right that their population was small and humanity was vast. Even if the Elders accepted her, there was a good chance that the people of Rhapta never would. They had been led to believe that she was the cause of their pain and that pain ran deep. If she decided to run away, she would have to live the rest of her life with the guilt that people had died because of a prophecy about her.

She didn't want to live like that. Better to die knowing that her death might mean that others can live versus living and knowing people would keep dying because she still existed.

Kinza looked around the room and finally her eyes came to rest upon Tahir who looked down at her with those eyes as cold as a winter storm. He held an obsidian sword at his side.

Okay, she said quietly. She nodded and said it again a little louder, *Okay.* Time slowed as Tahir stepped forward and Kinza lowered to her knees, the ice cracking underneath her. She decided that she wanted her last thoughts to be happy ones, of things she had and of things that she *might've* had. So she closed her eyes and waited for the blow.

Kinza thought about Grams first, about the woman who had raised her as best she could and she knew Grams would've been proud of her now. She thought about her parents and the brief, but loving time they had together and she was happy she had them in her life for a little while instead of not at all. She thought about how good a friend Mitra was and hoped that she would live a happy life. She thought about Rhapta and how beautiful it would be when it was rebuilt; oh, she knew it would be rebuilt. She thought about the families that would be relieved once the battle was over and she hoped they would grow and live long, exciting lives here. She even thought about Zaid.

Kinza knew that Zaid had left and probably wanted nothing to do with her, but instead of thinking about that, she focused on the moments she did have with him and their possible futures had she been someone else. She remembered their deep conversation on Haris's balcony, and walking through Moshi together. She thought about the car ride up to Mount Kilimanjaro in the morning sun and the radio blaring; he had actually laughed that time. She knew his life had been hard and she hoped that from here on out he would be happy.

Kinza realized that the blow had never come and she was no longer cold. She opened her eyes and looked out from the inside of a star. Everyone in the room stood in awe or horror or joy—she couldn't tell which—at the white Aura that pulsed out of her, turning the room from night to day. Like the Aurastones had, Kinza felt an undulating energy come from the Aura. It felt like she was energized, and awake, and alive! She saw the cuts and scrapes on the nearest Elders and warriors start to knit together faster and those who had been sitting got to their feet.

Kinza didn't need them to tell her that the same energy she felt was felt all across Rhapta as every single Aurastone in the city lit up like a fallen star. The massive Aurastone in the central plaza was by far the brightest and sent waves of the same energy back to her like merging currents.

The glow slowly faded back down to nothing and Kinza realized how quiet it was. The fighting in the plaza—in all of Rhapta—had stopped as everyone stood and looked at the light that bathed them with life and energy. When the glow finally dissipated, everyone was still staring at her in silence.

From across the room, Hakim opened his eyes, and spoke to her. *Kinza,* he said, as if he knew her. Elders looked at him in surprise, as did Kinza because she thought he was near death. One of the younger Elders held him around the shoulders and

Kinza realized they had the same nose. A tiny young woman in pale gray robes crouched at his feet.

You look just like him, Hakim said.

Who? she asked.

Prince Malik, your many-times great grandfather. Shock ran through the room at his words and eyes that had glared at her before truly *looked* at her now, as if seeing her for the first time. *Your Aura is just like his,* he said. Hakim turned to Tahir, still looking too ancient to be alive, and spoke gently, as if a parent to a child. *She is here to heal us, Tahir. Not to destroy us. Everything will be all right.*

Instead of backing down at Hakim's revelation, Tahir's face twisted in rage. Elders cried out for him to wait but he lifted the obsidian sword and brought it down over her head in a final act of hatred.

A fist came out of nowhere, catching Tahir's sword hand in their own. Kinza looked up in surprise to see who it was.

Mikah stood over her, keeping Tahir from bringing the sword down. His normally charming expression was practically made of stone. How long had he been here? Did he know who she was?

The two men stood locked for a moment; Mikah's eyes were as cold as Tahir's ice. An unspoken understanding came over them and Tahir jerked away.

Before anyone came out of their own shock, Tahir strode across the room and out the door in a swirl of white robes, several of the Elders following at his heels. The door closed behind them and was soon frozen over in a sheet of ice.

CHAPTER 24
POSSIBLE FUTURES

Zaid watched the light with the rest of his people. Unlike the rest of them, he knew who fueled it.

He felt the waves of living energy that rippled across the city and through his bones. He felt the exhaustion drain away and saw the change in the other Anunnaki. The battle had come to a standstill, friend and foe stopped to look around at the pulsing light of the Aurastones. Those nearest the massive Aurastone in the center of the city moved to place their hands on it, closing their eyes as if in prayer.

Eventually it got so bright that he had to shield his eyes and could barely make out the figures in the plaza. It only lasted a minute or so, but the light did fade and the creeping rays of the coming dawn looked bleak in comparison.

Behind him, those who were gravely wounded eased their crying as their injuries started knitting back together faster. Even Khalil looked around in amazement as many of his patients moved to sit up. Unfortunately, the dead stayed in their eternal slumber.

A breeze wound through the plaza, carrying away the

stench of war, so Zaid made his way toward the Grand Hall. The warriors had the clear advantage over the battle and regardless of the light they would have won. Very few of the Unfettered remained standing, and the few that did started to flee. Some got away but most were captured quickly, putting up little resistance after seeing the light moments before. Warriors and civilians cheered at the victory but Zaid knew that they would only be shedding tears in the coming days when the weight of the dead returned to them.

As if proving his foretelling, Zaid stopped near the large Aurastone when he saw a familiar head of graying hair on the ground. In the dawn light, Sa'id's lifeless eyes stared at the sky, so Zaid closed them for the last time before continuing on. He felt the acute pain that he would never get to apologize for the things he had said.

He kept walking and would only see the occasional familiar face, the baker that lived around the corner from his mother, Parwez, the boy Zaid had sparred with when his abilities had emerged, and Walid, the overseer for the quarries. Zaid was sure there were many more faces that would never speak again but right now there was only one face he wanted to see.

He made it to the steps and climbed them into the Grand Hall. He followed the general path of destruction to the left wing of the building and almost laughed. The outer wall of the hall had completely collapsed and a pile of rubble sat before the open door of one of the receiving rooms for the Elders. The door was edged in ice fragments and looked like it had been busted open. That kind of damage could have only been one person, so he hopped over the rocks and found a crowd of people inside.

From his spot inside the doorway, Zaid could see most of the Elders were here and alive, if scared. Many of them crowded around a form at the back of the room and he could see it was Hakim, whose eyes were closed. Zaid could still hear his heart beating faintly, but it was as slow as those who would be gone from this world soon.

There were several warriors as well, but Zaid was looking for one person in particular. He sagged with relief when he saw her and took a step to go to her when he saw who else was standing there. Mikah stood looking down at her with concern, asking something he couldn't hear. Kinza nodded and didn't move away from him despite how close he was standing. She looked confused and worried and a little in shock but she gave a small smile in response to something Mikah said.

You're too late, a tiny voice said in the back of his mind and Zaid was resigned to believe it, no matter how much he wished otherwise. He had abandoned her and had no right to expect her to come running when he showed back up. That didn't mean it didn't hurt seeing her standing there with one of the most repulsive people he knew.

I'm really not surprised you are alive, a dry voice said to his right. Zaid turned to find Elder Ishar standing by the doorway as well, surveying the room.

I'm glad someone has faith in me, Zaid said. *What happened?*

Well, our enemy turned out to be our friend, and our friend turned out to be our enemy. Ishar actually looked mildly impressed which was saying something. *She revealed the Aura of long dead kings and Hakim said she looked like Prince Malik. Also Tahir seems to be the cause of this mess and I am ashamed to say I would not have believed it had I not just watched him defy Hakim and try to kill her,* he said nodding toward Kinza.

Ah. There wasn't a whole lot he could say about that. Looking around, he noticed a few faces missing. *Where is Tahir?*

After Mikah stopped him from killing her, he stormed off with a handful of other Elders. He sealed the door long enough to get away.

There are some warriors looking for them, but they haven't returned. Ishar moved to help some of the weaker Elders.

Mikah went against Tahir? He shouldn't be surprised after the week he's had, but it seemed more likely for the moon to disappear.

Zaid wondered then at the future. What would Rhapta look like in the coming weeks, months, years? The outsider from the prophecy—and the heir to the Rhaptan throne—had returned and the council of Elders was in shambles. He wondered where Tahir had gone, but where could he even go? Zaid knew that Tahir had the knowledge to give the *venari* the extended tattoos, so it wouldn't be unlikely for him and the other Elders to flee.

Zaid sighed. He would probably have to hunt down his old mentor.

That was the last of his worries right now. The city was broken and needed to be rebuilt. He didn't even know if his mother was alive and would need to find her among the chaos. Despite the fact that battle against the Unfettered had been won, Tahir was still out there, and the psionic barrier that held the city was still weakening—probably more so now with the number of deaths.

There would be work to do.

Kinza's dark eyes swept across the room and finally landed on him. He couldn't read her expression but it looked something like sadness and relief and the tiniest bit of betrayal. Maybe there would be a chance for them to be friends in the future but right now he couldn't see a path that led there.

He strode across the room, making a beeline for her when the most out of place sound came from his pocket. It was so loud and obnoxious that the entire room stopped to stare at him. Confused, he dug around in his pants pocket and pulled out his cell phone he used when he travelled in the human cities. Somehow it was still in his pocket and working.

His confusion doubled to see that it was ringing and on the screen was Haris's name. The oddest part was the fact that it was ringing at all. There wasn't any cell service in Rhapta and he never actually got any calls from anyone when he was out in the world. He really only used it to search the internet.

Zaid clicked to accept the call and held it up to his ear. His eyebrows pinched together at the voice on the other end of the line as he walked over to Kinza, still listening to the caller speak. When the caller was done speaking he held the phone out to Kinza. She looked at him and he hoped that even in that brief second she could see how sorry he was for everything he had done and hoped that maybe one day she could forgive him.

"Who is it?" she asked. Her expression was a mirror to his own as she took the phone.

"Your grandma."

EPILOGUE

Kinza sat on the steps of the Grand Hall, looking out at the early morning sun coming down on the central plaza.

She might have called it beautiful if it weren't for the carnage the light had illuminated. People were already starting to repair what was broken just hours before. Frightened citizens emerged from their homes and shelters, and warriors and scholars worked together to gather the bodies of the fallen. Most kept a good distance from her, besides the two warriors that stood protectively in the shadow of the Hall behind her. The protection was a sign of peace—at least temporarily—from the Elders so no one would harm her while she was still in Rhapta.

She fiddled with the phone in her hands, turning it over and over. The last thing in the entire world that she would have expected to receive was a call from Grams. Kinza was surprisingly dry-eyed, having been drained of every emotion from the last few days. Somehow she felt both better and worse having talked to her grandmother. It was the final nail in the coffin that confirmed none of this was a nightmare and would go away. This was all real and she would need to face it.

A shadow blocked the sun momentarily before sitting down next to her.

"Is she all right?" Zaid asked, squinting into the sunlight.

"Yeah. She just spent the last forty-five minutes apologizing to me," Kinza said. She held the phone out to him.

"That's good, but I'm dying to know how she managed to call me; and from Haris's phone," he said, taking it.

Kinza chuckled. "Apparently she still had contacts in the Ummanu network and Haris was the closest to her. She drove up to his place and they managed to track another *venari* down, Laiq?" It had sounded like Grams had almost as rough a time as she had over the past week.

"Ah," Zaid said, as if everything made sense now.

"You know him?"

"Yes, Laiq's ability has a lot to do with human technology. Radio waves, electronics, coding, signals...it was why he was tapped to be *venari* in the first place. He must have been able to boost the signal to reach my phone." A group of people walked by, hauling debris away. They cast quick glances in their direction and Kinza knew that for once, people were looking at her instead of Zaid. "Come to think of it," he said, "there are many *venari* that will return to the city in shock."

"I didn't even think of that," she said. She tried to imagine leaving Chicago for a few days only to return to find it demolished. "What about Tahir?" she asked instead.

Zaid let out a tired sigh. "No word yet, but a few warriors are looking for him. He and a few other Elders know how to manipulate the tattoos to make them like those of the *venari*, so it's not unlikely that they escaped into the world. The effects won't last forever though. Honestly, that is probably what he used to get the Unfettered to work for him. Offer them a way out and they would do anything."

"Will we ever know for sure?" she asked. They were dancing around the topic of how he left her and she was trying to avoid the awkwardness.

"Yes," he said with a nod. "Mikah is looking into the minds of the captured Unfettered now. He'll probably find out within the next few hours here exactly what happened."

Kinza thought about the charming man, Mikah, that she had met under the moonlight. He had been vastly different from the person who had saved her from Tahir but she was thankful for him nonetheless. After Tahir had escaped, some of Mikah's anger had drained away. He had arched an eyebrow at her and said, "Mitra, huh?"

She had spent the next twenty minutes babbling excuses about how she needed to hide and didn't want to get caught. Instead of accusing her of lying, he gave her an admiring look and told her he was impressed that she fooled him. Kinza thought he would go back to his usual charming ways—and he did—but she kept catching him looking at her with a spark in his eye when he thought she wasn't looking.

She would decide how she felt about that later.

Zaid stayed quiet next to her, watching the people in the plaza. She remembered there was something she still hadn't told him. Glancing over at him, she said in Rhaptan, "I forgot to tell you something."

Zaid's head swiveled toward her so fast she thought he would hurt himself. "Did you just—"

"Yes," she replied in Rhaptan with a smile.

"Wow," he said, looking impressed as he turned back to the plaza. "I guess I shouldn't be surprised."

They sat there together and the silence between them

stretched on again until she could no longer fend off the awkwardness. "I tried to find—"

"Let me go first," Zaid said, interjecting. He was the one now fiddling with the phone. "I—I'm sorry, Kinza," he said, finally turning to her. His dark eyes looked a warmer brown in the sun and pleaded with hers. "I was the one who took you from your home in the first place and then I brought you here and all but left you to fend for yourself. I got confused by all of *this*," he said gesturing around, "and I didn't know what to think so I went looking for answers. Before we got here, I thought that we might've been...friends and I know I've royally screwed that up. I don't expect you to forgive me, but I just want you to know that I'm sorry." He let out a breath like releasing a weight he had been carrying.

"Wow," Kinza said, after a moment of silence, both impressed and in disbelief. "An apology from Zaid himself. Hmm. I'll have to add this to the history books." A small, playful smile danced over her lips.

He gave her half a smile in return but his eyes looked at her warily, as if waiting for her anger to come down on him.

"I propose we start over," she declared instead.

"What?"

"I think we should start from the beginning," she said, turning to him and holding out her hand. "Hi, I'm Kinza. Nice to meet you." When he only eyed her quizzically, she gave him a look that demanded he play along.

His half-smile turned into a full grin. "Hi, Kinza," he said, taking her hand and shaking it gently. "I'm Zaid. It's a pleasure to meet you, Your Highness."

Kinza groaned, having totally forgotten about Hakim's revelation, and Zaid chuckled. She had a thousand questions about that and didn't know where to start. The thought of being the heir to a long-dead prince's throne made her queasy enough to drop her head to her knees.

"Can we deal with that tomorrow?" she mumbled into her legs.

"I think you'll get a few hours of peace before you'll need to do something about it," Zaid said, eyeing the group of Elders that stood talking on the other side of the steps.

Kinza lifted her head and saw they were deep in conversation and kept gesturing over at her. "Fine," she said. "As long as you're there when they start demanding things of me."

"I'll be here," he said, as seriously as ever, and Kinza felt the tiniest bit of peace wash over her.

They sat there, in the morning sun, watching the city start to rebuild and heal itself. There would be mountains of work to do and she had no idea what her future held, but for right now she was content to sit there with Zaid next to her.

She would put on the crown later.

GLOSSARY OF TERMS

abilities *(ah bill it ees) n.* Powers that each Anunnaki has. The abilities vary per person and are supernatural in nature.

Anunnaki *(ahn new nock ee) n.* A species thought to have originated from Rhapta to guide humanity. They live longer than humans, can speak to each other telepathically and have abilities. They reside only in Rhapta. If an Anunnaki leaves the city limits, their abilities fade and they slowly become human and forget Rhapta. Some live outside the city limits, but still within the psychic barrier. Their abilities are weakened and have developed a need for verbal speech.

Elder *(ell der) n.* One of the fifty leaders of Rhapta. One out of every fifty is a Grand Elder who leads in ceremony and prophecy.

guakal *(gwa kall) n.* A fist-sized, rigid-shelled, lime green fruit with miniature red spikes on its exterior; native to Rhapta.

laqueus *(la kwees) n.* A rope, silvery-gray in color, made by Anunnaki used to bind or dampen abilities. Mildly annoying to Anunnaki, physically painful to humans.

magalkan'a *(muh gal kahn uh) n.* Commonly known as Aurastone, believed to be the origin of Anunnaki abilities. Shades range from white to azure.

mark *(mar k) n.* The tribal tattoo that every Anunnaki is born with. Only *venari* and ubir have different tattoos. *Venari's* are larger and need to be reapplied monthly; it allows them to enter the human world while retaining their abilities for a short time. Ubir tattoos are similar but red and swollen, as if infected.

reykalkan'o *(ray kal kon oh) n.* Commonly known as Deathstone. It is cracked Aurastone. Created either by blood magic, or taking it from Rhapta. It's presence is extremely painful to Anunnaki, creating a high-pitched ringing. If the Anunnaki cannot hear it, it's unlikely to be harmful.

Rhapta *(rap tuh) n.* An ancient city located near Mt. Kilimanjaro. It is hidden behind a psychic barrier and unknown to humanity. Currently at half capacity due to its dwindling population.

ubir *(oo beer) n.* Anunnaki that have defected from Rhapta and turned to blood magic to exist outside of the city while retaining their abilities. They quickly become rapid and need to sacrifice humans to retain their abilities. Their Aura is chaotic and painful.

Ummanu *(oo mon oo) n.* Humans who are aware of Anunnaki existence and have allied with them. Most watch over the portals around the world.

venari *(venn are ee) n.* Anunnaki bounty hunters tasked with locating and returning ubir from human society. They are shunned within Rhapta due to their "dirty" work and closeness with human society.

AUTHOR'S NOTE

Dear Beloved Reader,

I'm so grateful and appreciative that you decided to continue the journey with Kinza and Zaid in Erratic Magic! Their story is truly just beginning, and I hope you are enjoying it. If you are, I would be so thankful if you would consider leaving a review. Reviews help other readers find my work, and each review means the world to me.

I know you're probably anxious to see what happens next in the story with Mikah thrown in the mix! Is there a love triangle in the works? Don't worry; book 3, Infinite Magic, will complete the trilogy and is available now.

In addition, I've published a new novella that is only available to those who sign up for my mailing list! Portal Magic: A Rhaptaverse Novella is a glimpse into my upcoming Rhaptaverse series which will show the new batch of venari as they go out into the human world to save humanity from the ubir. You absolutely don't want to miss it! Click here (https://swiy.co/PortalMagic) to download your copy today.

Visit my website (LilySkyy.com) and interact with me on social media. There's awesome merch available for each of my series. Also, make sure to sign up for my mailing list to be the first to know about new releases and special happenings such as previews and give-a-ways!

I love getting feedback from my readers, and if you'd like to stay in touch (or discuss my books), join me over at the Lily Skyy Readers' Group. I'd also love to connect with you on Instagram, TikTok, and Twitter! Feel free to reach out to me directly via email at social@lilyskyy.com. You may access all of my social media profiles by visiting: https://smartpa.ge/lilyskyy.

Again, I thank you for reading, and I can't wait to join you on the next adventure!

Sincerely,

Lily Skyy